IRISH PRIDE

Irish Thoroughbred

and

Sullivan's Woman

Sign of Seven Trilogy
Blood Brothers • The Hollow • The Pagan Stone

Bride Quartet
*Vision in White • Bed of Roses • Savor the Moment • Happy
Ever After*

The Inn Boonsboro Trilogy
The Next Always • The Last Boyfriend • The Perfect Hope

The Cousins O'Dwyer Trilogy
Dark Witch • Shadow Spell • Blood Magick

The Guardians Trilogy
Stars of Fortune • Bay of Sighs • Island of Glass

Chronicles of The One
Year One • Of Blood and Bone • The Rise of Magicks

The Dragon Heart Legacy
The Awakening

EBOOKS BY NORA ROBERTS

Cordina's Royal Family
*Affaire Royale • Command Performance • The Playboy
Prince • Cordina's Crown Jewel*

The Donovan Legacy
Captivated • Entranced • Charmed • Enchanted

The O'Hurleys
*The Last Honest Woman • Dance to the Piper •
Skin Deep • Without a Trace*

Night Tales
*Night Shift • Night Shadow • Nightshade • Night Smoke •
Night Shield*

Suite 606
(with Mary Blayney, Ruth Ryan Langan, and Mary Kay McComas)

In Death

The Lost
(with Patricia Gaffney, Ruth Ryan Langan, and Mary Blayney)

The Other Side
(with Mary Blayney, Patricia Gaffney, Ruth Ryan Langan,
and Mary Kay McComas)

Time of Death

The Unquiet
(with Mary Blayney, Patricia Gaffney, Ruth Ryan Langan,
and Mary Kay McComas)

Mirror, Mirror
(with Mary Blayney, Elaine Fox, Mary Kay McComas, and
R. C. Ryan)

Down the Rabbit Hole
(with Mary Blayney, Elaine Fox, Mary Kay McComas, and
R. C. Ryan)

ALSO AVAILABLE . . .

The Official Nora Roberts Companion
(edited by Denise Little and Laura Hayden)

IRISH PRIDE

Irish Thoroughbred

and

Sullivan's Woman

TWO NOVELS IN ONE

NORA ROBERTS

St. Martin's Paperbacks

This is a work of fiction. All of the characters, organizations, and events portrayed in this book are either products of the author's imagination or are used fictitiously.

First published in the United States by St. Martin's Paperbacks, an imprint of St. Martin's Publishing Group.

IRISH PRIDE: IRISH THOROUGHBRED copyright © 1981 by Nora Roberts and SULLIVAN'S WOMAN copyright © 1984 by Nora Roberts.

For information, address St. Martin's Publishing Group, 120 Broadway, New York, NY 10271.

www.stmartins.com

ISBN: 978-1-250-78373-8

Our books may be purchased in bulk for promotional, educational, or business use. Please contact your local bookseller or the Macmillan Corporate and Premium Sales Department at 1-800-221-7945, ext. 5442, or by email at MacmillanSpecialMarkets@macmillan.com.

Printed in the United States of America

St. Martin's Paperbacks edition 2021

10 9 8 7 6 5 4 3 2 1

Irish Thoroughbred

CHAPTER 1

A delia Cunnane stared out the window without seeing the magic layer of clouds. Some formed into
mountains, others glaciers, flattening and thinning into
an ice-encrusted lake; but, for one experiencing her first
air journey, she found the view uninspiring. Her mind
was crowded with doubts and uncertainties that merged
with a strong pang of homesickness for a small farm
in Ireland. But both farm and Ireland were now very
far away, and every minute that crawled by brought her
closer to America and strangers. She knew, with a sigh
of frustration, that nothing in her life had ever prepared
her properly to cope with either.

Her parents had been killed in a lorry accident, leaving her an orphan at the tender age of ten. In the weeks
that followed her parents' death, Adelia had drifted
through a fog of shock, turning inward to ward off the
agony of separation, the strange and terrifying feeling of desertion. Slowly, a wall had been constructed
around the pain, and she had thrown herself into the
work of the farm with an adult's dedication.

Her father's sister, Lettie Cunnane, had taken over

both child and farm, running both with a firm hand. Although never unkind, neither had she been affectionate: She had possessed little patience or understanding for the unpredictable, often tempestuous child.

The farm had been the only common ground between them, and woman and child had built their relationship with the dark, fertile soil and the hours of labor it required. They had lived and worked together for nearly thirteen years; then Lettie had suffered a paralyzing stroke, and Adelia had been forced to divide her time between the duties of the farm and caring for an invalid's needs. Days and nights had merged together as she waged the determined battle to shoulder the increasing responsibility.

Her enemies had been the lack of time and the lack of money. When, after six long months, she was again left alone, Adelia was near the point of exhausted desperation. Her aunt was gone, and though she had worked unceasingly, the farm had had to be sold for taxes.

She had written to her only remaining relative, her father's elder brother, Padrick, who had emigrated to America twenty years previously, informing him of his sister's death. His answer had been immediate, the letter warm and loving, asking her to join him. The last sentence of the missive was a simple, gentle command: "Come to America; your home is with me now."

So she had packed her few belongings, sold or given away what could not be taken with her, and said goodbye to Skibbereen and the only home she had ever known. . . .

A sudden movement of the plane jolted Adelia back from memory. She sat back against the cushions of her seat, fingering the small gold cross she always wore around her neck. There was nothing left for her

in Ireland, she told herself, fighting against the flutters
of her stomach. Everything she had loved there was
dead, and Padrick Cunnane was the only family she
had left, the only link with what she had once had. She
pushed back a surge of sudden, unaccustomed fear.
America, Ireland—what difference did it make? Her
shoulders moved restlessly. She would manage. Hadn't
she always managed? She was determined not to be a
burden to her uncle, the vague, shadowy man she knew
only from letters, whom she had last seen when she'd
been barely three. There would be work for her, she
reasoned, perhaps on the horse farm her uncle had written of so often over the years. Her ability to work with
animals was innate, and she had absorbed a varied
knowledge of medicine through her experiences, her
skill being such that she had often been called on to aid
in a difficult calving or stitch up a rent hide. She was
strong, despite her diminutive stature—and, she reminded herself with an unconscious squaring of shoulders, she was a Cunnane.

Surely, she told herself with more confidence, there
would be a place for her at Royal Meadows, where her
uncle worked as trainer for the Thoroughbred racing
stock. There'd be no fields needing plowing, no cows
needing milking, but she'd earn her bread and butter if
she had to work as a scullery maid. She wondered suddenly, with a small frown, if they had scullery maids
in America.

The plane touched down, and Adelia disembarked
and entered the Dulles terminal in Virginia, where
she found herself gaping in confusion, fascinated by the
scene, confused by the babble of foreign tongues, the
odd mixture of people. Her eyes lingered over an East
Indian family in full native dress. She turned to observe
two teenagers in faded denims strolling by hand in

hand, followed by a scurrying middle-aged business-man clutching a leather briefcase.

Later, standing in the lobby, she looked around hoping to see a familiar face. Everyone rushing and hurrying, she thought. A body could be trampled and never seen again. . . .

"Dee, little Dee!" A man hurried toward her, a stockily built, compact man with a full thatch of curling gray hair, and she caught a glimpse of eyes as bright and blue as her father's before she was enveloped in a warm, crushing hug. The thought occurred to her that it had been a lifetime since anyone had held her so close.

"Little Dee, I would have known you anywhere." He pulled back and studied her face, eyes misty, smile tender. "It's like looking into Kate's face again—it's the image of your mother you are."

He continued to stare at her while she searched for her voice, his gaze taking in the deep, rich auburn hair falling in gleaming waves to her shoulders, the large, deep green of thickly lashed eyes, the tip-tilted nose and full mouth which Aunt Lettie had described as impudent, the face now of a startled pixie.

"What a beautiful sight you are," he said at last on a sigh of pure pleasure.

"Uncle Padrick?" she asked, finding a multitude of questions and emotions racing through her.

"And who else would you be thinking I might be?" He looked down at her with those well-remembered eyes, filled with love and laughter, and doubts, fears, and questions vanished in a wave of joy.

"Uncle Paddy," she whispered as she flung her arms around his neck.

As they drove along the highway from the airport,

Adelia stared about her in fresh amazement. Never had she seen so many cars, and all flying by at an outrageous speed. Everything moved so fast, and the noise, she marveled silently, the noise was enough to wake the dead. Shaking her head, she began to bombard her uncle with questions.

How far was it they were going? Did everyone drive so fast in America? How many horses were at Royal Meadows? When could she see them? Questions buzzed in her mind and through her lips, and Paddy answered them tolerantly, finding the soft lilt of her voice as sweet as a summer breeze.

"Where is it I'll be working?"

He removed his eyes from the road a moment and glanced at her. "There's no need for you to be working, Dee."

"Oh, but Uncle Paddy, I must," she disagreed, turning to face him. "I could work with the horses; I've a way with animals."

Thick gray brows drew together in a doubtful frown. "I didn't bring you all this way to be putting you to work." Before she could protest, he went on. "And I don't know what Travis would be thinking about me hiring my own niece."

"Oh, but I'd do anything." She brushed back masses of chestnut hair. "Groom the horses, muck out the stalls, cart hay—it doesn't matter." Unknowingly, she used her eyes in an outrageous manner. "Please, Uncle Paddy, it's crazy I'd be in a week, not having some sort of work to do."

Her eyes won the small battle, and Paddy squeezed her hand. "We'll see."

So engrossed had she been in their conversation and the fascinating stream of traffic that she had lost all track of time. When Paddy pulled into a drive and halted the car, Adelia gazed about her with new wonder.

"Royal Meadows, Dee," he announced with a sweeping gesture of his hand. "Your new home."

The entrance to the long, winding drive was flanked by two tall stone pillars, and bushes studded with the promise of flowering buds continued along its path as far as she could see. The grass was brilliantly green over softly rolling hills, and horses grazed lazily in the distance.

"The finest horse farm in all of Maryland, sure as faith," Paddy added with possessive pride as he proceeded along the curving drive. "And—in Pad-rick Cunnane's opinion—the finest in the whole of America."

The car rounded a bend in the drive, and Adelia caught her breath as the main house came into view. An immense structure, or so it seemed to her, with three magnificent stories of old and muted stone. Dozens of windows winked in the gleaming sun like large, clear eyes. Wide and boldly glistening, they were a sharp contrast to the stone's mellowness. Skirting the top two stories were balconies, the design of wrought iron as intricate and delicate as the finest lace. The house stood on a gently sloping lawn of close-cropped green, graced with bushes and stately trees just awakening from their winter sleep.

"Beautiful, isn't it, Dee?"

"Aye," she agreed, awed by its size and elegance. "The grandest house I've ever seen."

"Well, our house isn't so grand as this." He turned the car left as the drive forked past the stone building. "But it's a fine place, and I hope you'll be happy there."

Adelia turned her attention to her uncle with a smile

that transformed her face into a work of art. "I'll be happy, Uncle Paddy, as long as you're with me." Letting impulse guide her movements, she leaned over and kissed his cheek.

"Ah, Dee, I'm glad you're here." He took her hand in a firm grip. "You've brought the spring with you."

The car came to a halt, and Adelia turned to look out the front window, her mouth falling open at what greeted her eyes. An oval track commanded her view, and across from it stood a large white building, which Paddy identified as the stables. Fences and paddocks checker-boarded the area, and the scent of hay and horses drifted through the air.

In solemn amazement she gazed about, and the thought sped through her brain that she had not moved from one farm to another but from one world to another. At home, the farm had meant the earth, with its blessings and curses, a small barn in constant need of repair, a strip of pasture. Here, the space alone made her eyes widen, so much space to belong to one man. But as well as space, she recognized the efficiency and the order in fresh white buildings and split-rail fences. In the distance, where the hills began their soft roll, she saw mares grazing while their foals frolicked with the joy of spring and youth.

Travis Grant, she mused, recalling the name of the owner from Paddy's letters. *Travis Grant* knows how to care for what he owns. . . .

"There's my house." Now Paddy pointed out the opposite window. "Our house now."

Following his direction, she let out a cry of pleasure. The first story of the building was a large white garage, which she learned later serviced the trailers and trucks used for transporting the Thoroughbreds. Atop this was a stone structure, nearly twice as large as

the farmhouse in which she had spent her life. It was
a miniature replica of the main house, with the same
native stonework and glistening windows graced with
balconies.

"Come inside, Dee. Get a look at your new home."

He led her down a narrow, crushed stone path and
up the stairs to the front door, opening it wide and
nudging her ahead of him.

A bright, cozy room welcomed her, with pale green
walls and a shining oak floor. A brightly checked
sofa and matching chair invited her to sit in front of
the raised hearth when the weather was cool, or con-
template rambling hills through wide, sheer-draped
windows.

"Oh, Uncle Paddy!" She sighed, making an inadequate but expressive movement of her hands.

"Come, Dee, I'll show you the rest."

He led her through the house, her wide eyes growing larger with each new discovery, from the kitchen,
with its sunny yellow fixtures and spotless counters, to
the bath, where creamy ivory tiles made her dream of
languishing for hours in hot, soapy water.

"This is your room, darlin'."

He opened the door across from the bath, and Adelia stepped inside. It was not an overly large room, but
to her inexperienced eyes it was huge indeed. The walls
were painted a robin's-egg blue, and sheer white cur-
tains billowed and swayed at two open windows. The
soft blue and white was repeated in the flower print
of the bedspread, and a fluffy white rug lay on the
wooden floor. The mirror over the maple dresser reflected the expression of stunned pleasure on her face.
The knowledge that the room was to be hers brought
unaccustomed tears to her eyes. Blinking them away,
she turned and threw her arms around her uncle's neck.

Later, they strolled across the lawn toward the stables. Adelia had changed from the dress she had worn for the trip and was now clad in her more customary attire of jeans and cotton shirt, with her auburn curls pulled up and covered by a faded blue hat. She had convinced her uncle that rest was not what she needed, and that seeing the horses was what she wanted above all else. With her face glowing and eyes pleading, Paddy would have found it impossible to deny her anything.

Approaching the stables, they spotted a small group gathered around a chestnut Thoroughbred. The raised voices reached uncle and niece before their presence was noted.

"And what might be the problem here?" Paddy demanded.

"Paddy, glad you're back," a tall, husky man greeted him with obvious relief. "Majesty just had one of his spells. Gave Tom a bad kick."

Paddy transferred his attention to a small, spare young man seated on the ground, nursing his thigh and muttering.

"How bad is it, lad? Did you break anything?"

"Naw, nothing broke." Disgust was more evident than pain in both voice and face. "But I don't guess I'll be riding for a couple of days." Looking over at the dark chestnut, he shook his head with a mixture of resentment and reluctant amusement. "That horse may be the fastest thing on four legs, but he's meaner than a stomped-on cat."

"His eyes aren't mean," Adelia commented, and several pairs of eyes focused on her for the first time.

"This is Adelia, my niece. Dee, this is Hank Manners, assistant trainer. Tom Buckly, on the ground there, is an exercise boy, and George Johnson and Stan Beall, grooms." After introductions had been completed, Adelia quickly turned her attention back to the horse.

"They don't understand you, do they? Ah, but you're a fine fellow."

"Miss," Hank cautioned as she lifted a hand to stroke his muzzle, "I wouldn't do that. He's not in the best of moods to begin with, and he doesn't take to strangers."

"Ooch, but it's not strangers we'll be for long." Smiling, she stroked the length of his strong muzzle, and Majesty blew from wide nostrils.

"Paddy," Hank began in cautious warning, but the other man lifted a hand to silence him.

"A fine, beautiful horse you are. I've never seen another to compare with you, and that's the truth of it." She continued to speak as she ran her hands over his smooth neck and side. "You're built for running—strong, long legs and a fine, wide chest." Her hands moved over him freely as the horse remained still, ears at attention. She fondled his nose before resting her cheek against his neck. "I bet you're lonely for someone to talk to."

"I'll be switched." Hank observed Adelia's confident handling of the frisky colt and shook his head. "He's never let anyone do that before, not even you, Paddy."

"Animals have feelings as well, Mr. Manners." She brought her face from the Thoroughbred's neck and turned around. "He wants some pampering."

"Well, little lady, you certainly seem to have a way with him." He gave her a grin expressive of both amusement and admiration before turning his attention to Paddy. "He still needs to be exercised. I'll give Steve a call."

"Uncle Paddy." Adelia grabbed his arm on impulse,

eyes shining with excitement. "I can do it. Let me take him out."

"I don't think a little lady like you could handle a big fire-breather like Majesty," Hank put in before Paddy could speak, and Adelia drew herself up to the full of her five feet two inches and tilted her chin.

"There's nothing on four legs I can't ride."

"Is Travis back yet?" Paddy concealed his smile and addressed Hank.

"No." He eyed Paddy through narrowed lids. "You're not thinking of letting her take him out?"

"I'd say she's about the right size—couldn't weigh over a hundred pounds." He gave his niece a thorough survey, one hand rubbing his chin.

"Paddy." Hank's hand descended on his shoulder, only to be ignored.

"You're a Cunnane, aren't you, lass? If you say you can handle him, then by the saints you can." Adelia beamed at her uncle and told him firmly she was indeed a Cunnane.

"God knows what the boss is going to say when he finds out," Hank muttered, finding himself against a solid wall of family alliance.

"Just leave Travis to me," Paddy answered with calm authority.

With a shrug of his shoulders and another incoherent mutter, Hank resigned himself to Paddy's loss of common sense.

"Once around the track, Dee," her uncle instructed. "Pace him to what you can handle; I can see from the look of him he wants his head."

Pulling her cap lower, she nodded, watching the well-trimmed hooves paw the ground in impatience. With an easy vault she was in the saddle, and as Hank opened the wide gate she took Majesty onto the dirt track. Leaning forward, she whispered in his ear as he sidestepped and strained to be off.

"Ready, Dee?" Paddy called. As an afterthought he pulled out his stopwatch.

"Aye, we're ready." Straightening, she took a deep breath.

"Go!" he shouted, and horse and rider lunged down the track.

Crouching low over the Thoroughbred's neck, she urged him on to the speed for which he thirsted. The wind beat against her face, stinging her eyes, as they tore over the dirt at a pace she had never experienced, never imagined, but somehow had craved. It was a wild, exhilarating adventure; both horse and rider reveled in the unbridled sensation as they sped as one around the oval track, sun, wind, and speed their companions. She laughed and shouted to her partner, a new sense of freedom liberating her from the concerns and worries that had been a part of her life for so long. For a few short moments she was riding the clouds, away from pressure, away from responsibility, in a glorious haven that returned her to carefree childhood. When they came to the end of the run, she slowed the horse gradually to a halt and flung her arms around his gleaming neck.

"I'll be a son of a gun!" Hank said in simple astonishment.

"What were you expecting?" Paddy questioned, feeling as proud as a peacock with two tails. "She's a Cunnane." He held out the stopwatch for Hank to see. "Not a bad time either." With a final smile, he strutted over as Adelia slipped to the ground.

"Oh, Uncle Paddy!" Her eyes gleamed like emeralds against her flushed face, and she pulled off her cap, flourishing it in excitement. "He's the grandest horse in the world. It was like riding Pegasus himself!"

"That was nice riding, little lady." Hank extended his hand, shaking his head in admiration both for her ability and for the gleaming hair that now spilled over her shoulders.

"Thank you, Mr. Manners." She accepted his hand with a smile.

"Hank."

She grinned. "Hank."

"Well, Adelia Cunnane." Paddy slipped his arm around her shoulders. "Royal Meadows just hired another exercise boy. You've got yourself a job."

L ying in her bed that night, Adelia stared wide-eyed at the ceiling. So many things had happened, in so short a time, that her mind refused to relax and allow her body to rest.

After her ride on the Thoroughbred, she had been taken through the stables, introduced to more hands and more horses, shown into a tackroom that contained more leather than she had ever seen in one place at one time, and exposed to more people and more things than she believed she had ever been exposed to in her life. And all in the course of one day.

Paddy had prepared their dinner, firmly refusing assistance, and she had merely watched as he bustled around the kitchen. The stove, she decided, had more to do with magic than technology. And a machine that washed and dried the dishes at a touch of a button— marvels! Hearing about such things and reading about them was one matter, but seeing them with your own eyes . . . it was easier to believe in the Pooka and the little people. When, with a sigh, she said as much to her uncle, he threw back his head and laughed until tears flowed down his cheeks, then enveloped her in a hug as crushing as the one he had greeted her with at the airport.

They had eaten at the small dinette set in the kitchen window, and she had answered all his questions about Skibbereen. The meal was full of talking and laughing, and Paddy's eyes twinkled continually at her colorful descriptions and outrageous stories. She elaborated here and there, her hands working with her words, brows raising over guileless eyes as she stretched truth into an obvious exaggeration. Her uncle had noticed the faint shadows under them, however, and urged her to retire early, overcoming her protests with the deft suggestion that she had needed to be fresh in the morning.

So Adelia had obeyed, drawing a steaming tub and wallowing in unfamiliar luxury for what she knew Aunt Lettie would have considered a sinful amount of time. When at last she lay between the cool, fresh sheets, she found it impossible to relax. Her mind was full, crowded with new sensations, new images; and her body, so used to complete exhaustion before sleep, was unable to cope with the lack of physical exertion. Easing out of bed, she exchanged her nightdress for jeans and a shirt and, piling her hair once more under the absurd cap, slipped noiselessly from the sleeping house.

The night was clear, cool, and quiet, a vague breeze sweetening the air, only the bright, insistent call of a whippoorwill breaking the stillness. The light of the half moon guided her toward the stables as she strolled without thought of destination over the smooth new grass. The stillness, the familiar scent of animals, reminded her of home, and suddenly she felt a contentment and peace she had not even known she had lived without.

Hesitating outside the door of the large white stables, she debated whether she dare enter and spend the last of her evening with the horses. Having decided there was no harm in it, she was reaching out for the handle when an iron grip closed around her arm and whirled her around, and she was lifted off her feet for a moment like a rag doll.

"Just what do you think you're doing? And how did you get in here?"

She stared wordlessly at the owner of the harsh, angry voice, a vague shadow silhouetted in the dim moonlight, looming over her like an avenging giant. She searched for her own voice, but the combination of shock and pain had stolen it. Her words slipped down her throat as she felt herself being dragged into the building.

"Here, let's have a look at you," the voice growled as its owner switched on the lights. He spun her around, dislodging her cap, and the glory of her hair escaped its confinement to form a fiery cascade down her back.

"What the . . . you're a girl!" He released his firm hold and Adelia stepped back and began to give him both sides of her Irish tongue.

"Sure and it's observant you are to be noticing that—" She rubbed her arm vigorously while her green eyes glared up at her astonished assailant. "And who are you coming around grabbing innocent people and crushing their bones? A great, hulking bully you are, sneaking up on a body and dragging and pulling them about! A horsewhipping is what you're deserving for scaring the life from me and nearly breaking my arm in the process—"

"You may be pint-sized, but you're packed with dynamite," the man observed, obviously amused. He wondered as he looked over her softly rounded shape how he could have mistaken her for a boy. "From your accent I could make a guess that you're little Dee, Paddy's niece."

"I'm Adelia Cunnane, but it's not your little Dee I am." She regarded him with unconcealed resentment. "And it's not me who's having the accent. It's you!"

He threw back his head and roared with laughter, increasing Adelia's fury. "Oh, I am glad to have made you so happy." Folding her arms across her chest, she tossed her head, rich dark curls swinging wildly. "And who in the world are you, I'd like to know?"

"I'm Travis," he answered, still grinning. "Travis Grant."

CHAPTER 2

It was Adelia's turn to gape at her companion. As the mists of fury cleared from her eyes, she saw him clearly for the first time. He was tall and powerfully built, and the sleeves of his shirt were carelessly rolled above his elbows, revealing deeply tanned muscular arms. He had chiseled features, clear and sharp, and his eyes were so blue against the brown of his skin that they startled the casual onlooker. His hair was rich and full, thick black curls in a disarming disarray to his collar, and the mouth that continued to grin at her was well formed, showing strong white teeth.

This was the man she was to work for, this was the man she needed to impress, Adelia's brain registered numbly, and she had just raked him clean with her furious tongue. "Jakers," she whispered, shutting her eyes a moment and wishing she could disappear in a puff of smoke.

"I'm sorry we met under such, uh . . ."—he hesitated, his mouth twitching again—"confusing circumstances, Adelia. Paddy's been on top of the world since he made arrangements to bring you over from Ireland."

"I didn't expect to be meeting you till tomorrow, Mr. Grant." She clung desperately to pride and kept her voice even. "Uncle Paddy said you wouldn't be back."

"I didn't expect to find a half-pint fairy invading my stables," Travis returned, grinning once again.

Adelia straightened her spine and threw him a haughty look. "I couldn't sleep, so I came for a walk. I was thinking I might look in on Majesty."

"Majesty's a very high-strung animal," Travis admonished, his gaze roaming over her from top to bottom. "You'd best keep a respectable distance."

"And how will I be doing that?" she demanded imperiously, disconcerted by his masculine appraisal. "I'm to be exercising him regularly."

"The devil you are!" His eyes rose to hers and narrowed. "If you think I'd let a slip of a thing like you on my prize colt, you've lost your senses."

"I've already been on your prize colt." Anger returned, and her head tossed with it. "I rode around your track on him in fine time."

"I don't believe it." He took a step toward her, and her head was forced to tilt still further. "Paddy wouldn't let you up on Majesty."

"I'm not in the habit of lying, Mr. Grant," Adelia retorted with great dignity. "The boy, Tom, got a kick for his trouble, so I rode Majesty instead."

"You rode Majesty?" Travis repeated in slow, even tones.

"That I did," she agreed, then, noting the anger hardening the blue eyes, sped on. "He's a beauty, rides like the wind, but he's not bad-tempered. He wouldn't have been kicking Tom if the boy had understood him better." She was speaking rapidly, not giving Travis an opportunity to comment. "The poor thing just needed someone to talk to him, someone to show him he was loved and appreciated."

"And you can talk to horses?" Travis's lips curved on the question.

"Aye," she agreed, unaware of the mocking gleam that lit his eyes. "Anyone can if they've a mind to. I know animals, Mr. Grant. I worked with the vet back in Skibbereen, and I know a bit about healing as well. I would never do anything to bring harm to Majesty or any of your other horses. Uncle Paddy trusted me; you mustn't be angry with him."

He said nothing to this, only took his time studying her as her extraordinary eyes unknowingly employed their power. As his silence and intense regard continued, she felt a small tingle of fear, mixed with another sensation, strange and foreign, that she was unable to decipher.

"Mr. Grant," she began, swallowing pride to plead. "Please, give me a chance—a fortnight, no more." She took a deep breath and moistened her lips. "If you don't want me after that, just tell me, and I'll abide by your decision. I'll tell Uncle Paddy I'm not happy with the job, that I want to be doing something else."

"Why would you do that?" His head tilted as if to gain a new perspective.

"It's what I'd have to do," she returned with a shrug and a push at her tumbled hair. "Otherwise I'd be putting him in the middle. He's devoted to you and to this place—I know that from the letters he wrote me—but he's taken me on as his responsibility now. If I told him you had fired me, his loyalties would be torn in two. I'll not be the cause of that. Will you give me a two-week trial, Mr. Grant?" *Pride goeth before destruction,* she quoted silently, trying to remember Aunt Lettie's lectures on humility.

She stood, determined not to squirm under his silent contemplation, wishing he would not look at her as if he could read the thoughts running through her brain.

"All right, Adelia," he said at length. "You'll have your two-week trial, just between us."

A brilliant smile lit her face and she extended her hand. "Thank you, Mr. Grant. I'm grateful to you."

He accepted her hand, but his returning smile faded, a frown replacing it as he turned her palm up and examined it. Her hand was exquisitely small, fingers long and tapering, but it was rough and calloused from years of the abuse of labor. The continued contact was sending odd tingles through her body, and she looked down helplessly at the hand under his critical scrutiny.

"Is something the matter?" she asked in a voice she barely recognized.

He raised his eyes and looked into hers with an expression she could not fathom. "It's a crime for such a tiny hand to be as hard and rough as any ditchdigger's."

Unaccountably stung by his softly spoken words, she jerked her hand away, holding it behind her back. "I'm sorry they're not as soft as a lily, Mr. Grant. But it's not lady's hands I'll be needing for the job I'm doing for you. If you'll excuse me now, I'll be going in."

She moved past him quickly, and he watched her run like a rabbit across the grass and out of sight.

Birdcalls broke the night's slumber, and Adelia woke with the sun. She dressed quickly, happy with the anticipation of beginning her job, a job which was to her more of a magic wish granted than labor. She was sure she could prove herself to Travis Grant. A new home, a new life, a new beginning; she stared out at the infant sun and knew it would bring nothing but wonders.

The scent of frying bacon led Paddy to the kitchen, and he stood for a moment watching her movements while she remained unaware of his presence. She was humming an old tune he remembered from childhood, and she seemed to him the essence of shining, unspoiled youth.

"Sure and it's the most beautiful sight these old eyes have awakened to in many a year."

She turned to him, her smile dimming the sunlight into insignificance. "Good morning to you, Uncle Paddy. It's a fine, beautiful day."

While they were eating, Adelia casually mentioned that she had met Travis Grant the previous night during her nocturnal wanderings.

"I was hoping to introduce you myself this morning." He took a bite of crisp bacon and raised his brows. "What did you think of him?"

She tactfully kept her opinion to herself and answered with a move of her shoulders. "I'm sure he's a fine, good man, Uncle Paddy, but I wasn't with him long enough to make judgments." *Big, arrogant bully,* her mind added. "But I did tell him about Tom's accident, and that I'd been taken on as an exercise boy."

"Did you, now?" A slow smile formed as he added jam to his bread. "And what did he say to that?"

"He's smart enough to trust Padrick Cunnane's opinion." Her fingers crossed under the table, and she wondered if she had earned another black mark in Aunt Lettie's often mentioned Record Book of the Angels.

A short time later, Adelia stood in front of Majesty, rubbing his muzzle and holding an intimate conversation, unaware her actions were being observed by a pair of deep blue eyes.

"Morning, Paddy. I hear you've taken on a new hand."

Paddy broke off his conversation with Hank and greeted the tall, lean man. "Good morning to you, Travis. Dee told me she met you last night."

"Did she?" His lips curved as he continued to regard woman and horse.

"Wait till you see that little lady ride," Hank put in, shaking his head. "Could have knocked me over with a feather."

Travis inclined his head. "We'll soon see." He moved to where Adelia still stood speaking softly to the large Thoroughbred. "Hello again, half-pint. Does your friend ever answer you?"

She whirled, caught off guard, and regarded his amusement with indignation. "Aye, that he does, Mr. Grant, in his own way." She brushed past him to mount, and Travis stopped her with a hand on her wrist.

"Good Lord, did I do that?" He ran a finger over the dark smudge of bruises on her arm, and Adelia followed his glance before raising her eyes to his.

"That you did."

His eyes narrowed a moment, his fingers still light on her wrist. "We'll have to be more careful with you in the future, won't we, little Dee?"

"Not the first bruising I've had, nor likely to be the last, but you'll not be having any more occasion to be grabbing at me, Mr. Grant." With this, she swung herself astride Majesty and rode him onto the track. At Paddy's signal, the pair sprinted forward and galloped around the oval in a clean, steady rhythm.

"You wouldn't have been thinking I'd lost my senses hiring my niece, now, would you, lad?"

"I'll admit when she told me she'd been hired, I

had a moment of doubt about your sanity," Travis answered, keeping his eyes on the small woman glued to the speeding horse. "But I've always trusted your judgment, Paddy; you've never let me down."

Later that morning Adelia worked in the stables, insisting over Paddy's objections that she assist in the grooming of some of the horses. A sound behind her caused her to turn her head, and she encountered two small boys, one the mirror image of the other. She closed her eyes in mock alarm.

"Saints preserve us, sure and it's losing my mind I am! I'm seeing double."

The boys collapsed into giggles and spoke in unison. "We're twins."

"Is that the truth?" She breathed a deep sigh of relief. "Well, I'm glad to know it. I was afraid a spell had been put on me."

"You talk just like Paddy," one boy observed, eyeing her with unrestrained curiosity.

"Do I, now?" She smiled down at their identical faces. The boys were about eight, she hazarded, with snapping brown eyes. "The reason for that may be I'm his niece, Adelia Cunnane, just arrived from Ireland."

Two faces creased in two doubtful frowns. "He calls you little Dee, but you're not little, you're all grown up," one boy complained, the other nodding in agreement.

"That I am, as far as I ever will be, I'm afraid. But I was just a wee babe when I last saw Uncle Paddy, and I never did grow very tall, so I'm little Dee to him. And what might your names be?" she questioned, putting down the currycomb that she had been using.

"Mark and Mike," they announced, again in one voice.

"Don't be telling me who's who," she commanded, narrowing dark green eyes. "I'll guess; I'm mighty good at guessing." She circled them as they resumed giggling. "You'd be Mark, and you'd be Mike," she pronounced, placing a hand on each head. Two pairs of eyes stared at her in amazement.

"How did you know?" Mark demanded.

"I'm Irish," she stated simply, controlling a grin. "There's many of us from Ireland who's fey."

"Fey—what's that?" Mike chimed in, eyes wide and curious.

"That means I have strange, secret powers," Adelia claimed with a dramatic sweep of her hand. The two boys looked at each other and back at Adelia, suitably impressed.

"Mark, Mike." A woman entered the stables and shook her head in despair. "I should have known the pair of you would be here."

Adelia stared at the newcomer, stunned by her beauty and elegance. She was tall and slender, clad in a simple but, to Adelia's untrained eye, overwhelmingly beautiful outfit of dark blue slacks and white silk blouse. Black, silky hair curled back from her face. Soft, rose-tinted lips and a classic straight nose led to a pair of heavily lashed deep blue eyes that Adelia identified as Travis's.

"I hope they haven't been bothering you." The woman peered down in indulgent exasperation. "They're impossible to keep track of."

"No, missus," Adelia said, wondering if there had ever been a lovelier woman. "They're fine lads. We've just been getting acquainted."

"You must be Paddy's niece, Adelia." The generous mouth curved in a smile.

"Aye, missus." Adelia managed a smile of her own and wondered what it would be like to be as graceful as a willow limb.

"I'm Trish Collins, Travis's sister." She extended her hand and Adelia gaped at it in horror. After Travis's words the previous night she was self-conscious about the state of her hands, and her mind began to work swiftly.

How could she put her hard, rough hand into such a lovely, soft one! Yet there was no way out without being pointedly rude, so, wiping her palm on her jeans, she joined it with the one Trish offered. The other woman had noted Adelia's hesitation and concluded the reason for it when their hands met, but she made no comment.

At that moment, Travis entered the building, along with Paddy and a small, spare man Adelia did not recognize.

"Paddy!" The twins launched themselves at the stocky figure.

"Well, if it isn't Tweedledee and Tweedledum. And what mischief have you been up to this fine day?"

"We came to meet Dee," Mark announced. "She guessed which one of us was which."

"She's fey," Mike added soberly.

Paddy nodded, equally grave, his eyes twinkling as they met Adelia's over the two small heads. "Aye, that's a fact. There's been many a Cunnane who's had the sight."

"Adelia Cunnane"—Travis made introductions, a light smile playing over his mouth—"Dr. Robert Loman, our vet."

"Pleased to meet you, Doctor," Adelia greeted him, strategically keeping her hands behind her back.

"Rob's come to look over Solomy," Paddy explained. "She'll be foaling soon."

The pixie face lit with pleasure, and, looking down at her, Travis raised his brows. "Would you like to see her, Adelia?"

"Very much." She beamed him a smile, previous animosity forgotten.

"She's foaling quite late," Travis commented as the group walked down the long length of stalls. "A Thoroughbred's official birthday is January the first, and normally we breed with that in mind. We just acquired Solomy six months ago, and of course she was already in foal. She's from a good line, and the stud she was bred to is by the same sire as Majesty."

"Then you must have big hopes for the foal," Adelia returned, thinking of Majesty's style and speed.

"I think," he said with a smile, "you could safely say we had hopes for this foal." Placing a hand on her shoulder, he turned her toward an enclosure. "Adelia," Travis said with amused formality, "meet Solomy."

She sighed with delight at the animal, a dark, gleaming bay mare with a mane of flowing black silk. Running her hand down the stark flash of white on the forehead, she looked into dark, intelligent eyes.

"You're a fine, beautiful lady." The caressing of the smooth hide was met with a whinny of approval.

"I suppose you'd like a closer look," Travis observed, opening the stall door and gesturing for her to enter.

She preceded him and the vet into the stall, carrying on a low conversation with Solomy as she explored the swollen belly, probing with gentle, capable fingers. After a few moments she stopped and turned concerned eyes to Travis's laughing ones.

"The foal's turned wrong."

The blue eyes lost their laughter and studied her intently.

"Quite right, Miss Cunnane," Robert Loman agreed with a professional nod. "A quick diagnosis." Entering the stall, he too ran hands over the mare's belly. "We're hoping the foal will turn before she's full term."

"But you're not thinking it's likely; her time's almost here."

"No, we're not." He turned back to her, faintly surprised and greatly curious as to her knowledge. "We have to deal with the possibility of a breech. Have you had any training?"

"More doing than training." She shrugged, uncomfortable at having the attention focused on her. "I worked with a vet back in Ireland. I've done some birthings and some stitching and splinting."

She stepped out of the stall to stand beside Paddy, watching as the vet proceeded with his work. Paddy's arm slipped around her shoulders, and she rested her head against him.

"I hate to think what a hard time she'll be having. We had a mare that carried breech once, and I had to turn the babe." She sighed with the memory. "I can still see her poor, trusting eyes on me. How I hated to hurt her."

"You turned a foal by yourself?" Travis demanded, drawing her attention from the past. "That's a difficult enough job for a full-grown man, let alone a little thing like you."

She bristled, bringing herself up to the full of her meager height. "It may be that I'm small, Mr. Grant, but I'm strong enough to do what needs to be done." She glared up at him, her pride under attack, and stuck out her chin. "I'll tell you this: for all our difference in size I can work the day through with you!"

Stifling a snort of laughter, Paddy focused on a spot on the ceiling as Travis regarded her indignation with cool, steady eyes. After a moment, she turned and began to walk toward the front of the building.

"Did you really see a horse being born, Dee?" The twins tagged after her full of excitement.

"Many a time, and cows and pigs and the like." She took a small hand in each of hers and continued over the concrete floor. "There was a time I birthed twin lambs, and that was the prettiest sight. . . ."

Travis continued to stare after her as her voice trailed off in the distance.

The next few days passed easily for Adelia as she became accustomed to a new life and new surroundings. On the occasions she spoke to Travis, she continually struggled to hold back the tongue he seemed to have a habit of provoking. He stirred strange feelings in her, feelings she could neither comprehend nor prevent, and her defense against them took shape in a quick retort and flashing eyes. Though she gave herself nightly lectures on the evils of temper, when confronted with him during the daylight hours her vow of restraint slipped through her fingers.

She found herself watching him once as he strode toward the stables, his blue denim work shirt straining over broad shoulders as he moved over the grass. He seemed to eat up the ground with a careless vitality. There was a strange pull at her heart, and she sighed, then bit her lip in annoyance. It was only that he was such a fine, strongly built man, she told herself, lean and powerful. She dismounted from the Thoroughbred she had been exercising and rubbed his neck vigorously.

She had always admired strength and power, the same way she admired this strong, well-proportioned animal. Everyone she had met held Travis Grant in great respect and admiration. When he gave an order, it was carried out without question. Only Paddy, it seemed, had the right to advise or question.

But she was Adelia Cunnane, she reminded herself, and no man would get the better of her. She would not play peasant to his squire and pull her forelock when he passed by. She did her job, and did it well. He would have no cause to complain in that field. But she would speak her piece if she'd a mind to, and the devil take him if he didn't like it!

Late each afternoon, Adelia visited Solomy. She was sure the mare would deliver any day, and, knowing the birth would be a difficult one, she spent her visits comforting the mare and gaining her confidence.

"Soon you'll be having a fine, strong son or daughter," Adelia told her as she closed the stall door after her visit. "I'd like to take you and the babe and bundle you off with me. What do you think himself would do about that?"

"He might be tempted to have you hanged for horse thieving."

She spun around, her eyes encountering Travis's powerful form resting idly against the next stall. "It's a bad habit you have of sneaking up and scaring a body to death," she snapped at him, assuming that the uneven beat of her heart was the result of surprise.

"I do happen to own this place, Adelia," he returned in low, calm tones that only increased her agitation.

"That's a fact I'm not likely to forget. There's no need to remind me." She tilted her chin in defiance of him and the continuing flutter of her stomach, knowing

she should guard her words, and knowing the power to
do so was beyond her. "I give you your day's work, but
maybe you think I'm forgetting my place. Should I be
bobbing a curtsy, Mr. Grant?"

"You impudent little wench," Travis muttered,
straightening from his relaxed position. "I'm getting
a bit weary of being stabbed by that sharp tongue of
yours."

"Well, it's sorry I am about that. The best advice I
can give is that you not be conversing with me."

"That's the best idea you've had." He grabbed her
around the waist, lifting her a foot off the ground as
their eyes warred with each other. "I've been wanting
to do this since the first time you slashed at me with
your sharp Irish tongue."

He crushed her mouth with his, cutting off a heated
retort. Too surprised by his action to resist immediately, Adelia began to experience unfamiliar and disturbing sensations, a heat and weakness that she might
feel on a day spent working in the field. His hands were
like steel around her small waist, holding her body suspended in the air while his lips assaulted hers, entering
her mouth with his tongue in a kiss that was both devastating and totally foreign to any she had ever known.

Pressed hard against him, lips joined, she felt his
warmth, his essence, seeping into her, demanding and
receiving her merging. She could feel the authority in
the arms that held her, taste the knowledge on the lips
that claimed hers, and body and mind surrendered to
both. Unable to combat the turbulence of the unex-
plored, she felt it whirl her like a cyclone, spinning her
toward the sun until the heat threatened to become fire.

And as each of her senses were assaulted and conquered, he continued to explore her mouth, feasting on
it as a man who knew a woman's flavor. He took, and

she knew nothing of the richness of the banquet she gave him, warm and ripe and fresh.

After a lifetime, he released her, dropping her back to the ground as she stared at him mutely, eyes huge with confusion.

"Well, half-pint, this is the first time I've seen you at a loss for words." He mocked her openly, the lips that had just conquered hers lifted in a smug, satisfied smile.

His taunt broke the strange hold over her mind and tongue, and her eyes lit with molten green fire. "You son of the devil," she began in a rich explosion, and what followed was a raging stream of Irish curses and dire predictions delivered in so strong an accent that it was nearly impossible to comprehend the words.

When her imagination had at last run dry, and she could only stand staring at him breathlessly, he threw back his head and laughed until she thought he would burst.

"Oh, Dee, you're a fabulous sight when you're breathing fire!" He took no trouble to hide his amusement, an infuriating grin glued to his face. "The madder you get, the thicker the brogue. I'm going to have to provoke you more often."

"I'm giving you warning," she returned in an ominous voice, which only widened the grin. "If you ever molest me again, it's more than my tongue you'll be feeling."

Lifting her head, she strode out of the stables, clutching the last threads of her dignity around her.

She said nothing to Paddy about her scene with Travis, and instead banged around the kitchen as she prepared dinner, uttering incoherent sentences about great arrogant beasts and strong-arm bullies. Her fury with Travis was intermingled with fury with herself.

The fact that his touch had brought both excitement and unexplained pleasure angered her further, and she berated herself for the uncontrollable attraction she felt for him.

CHAPTER 3

By the next day, Adelia's anger had faded. She was not given to prolonged periods of ill humor; rather, she exploded like a burst of flame, simmered, then slowly cooled down. There remained, however, a disturbing new awareness, an awareness both of herself and the unfamiliar longings of womanhood, and of the frustrating, attractive man who had released them.

She managed to avoid any face-to-face contact with Travis during the morning, going about her duties in the normal fashion while she kept a cautious eye alert for his approach. Duties complete, she strolled back for her daily visit with Solomy. Instead of leaning over the low barrier to greet her, as was Solomy's habit, Adelia found her lying on her side in the hay, breathing heavily.

"By all the saints and apostles!" Rushing inside, she knelt beside the raggedly breathing mare. "Your time's come, darlin'," she crooned, running her hands over the large mounded belly. "Just rest easy now. I'll be back." Springing up, she sped from the stables.

She spotted Tom in the far paddock and, cupping

her hands, shouted, "Solomy's time's here. Get Travis—call the vet. Be quick!" Without waiting for an answer, she ran back inside to comfort the laboring horse.

She was murmuring and stroking the sweating hide when Travis and Paddy joined her. Soft words and gentle hands had calmed the mare, whose deep brown eyes were riveted on Adelia's dark green ones.

Travis knelt beside her, his hands joining hers on the gleaming skin, and though Adelia spoke to him, her eyes never left the mare's.

"The foal's still the wrong way; it must be turned, and quickly. Where's Dr. Loman?"

"He's had an emergency—can't be here for half an hour." His voice was clipped, his own attention on Solomy.

She turned her head and captured his gaze. "Mr. Grant, I'm telling you she doesn't have that long. The foal has to be turned now, or we'll lose them both. I can do it; I've done it before. It's God's truth, Mr. Grant, she hasn't much time."

They stared at each other for a long moment, Adelia's eyes wide and pleading, his narrowed and intense. Solomy let out an agonizing whinny as a new contraction began.

"There, my love." Adelia switched her attention back to the mare, murmuring words of comfort.

"All right," Travis agreed, a long breath escaping through his teeth. "But I'll turn it. Paddy, call in some of the men to hold her down."

"No!" Adelia's protest caused the mare to start, and she spoke quietly again, using hands and voice to soothe. "You'll not bring a bunch of bruisers in here forcing her down and frightening her." Again she raised her eyes to Travis's and spoke with calm assurance. "She'll hold for me; I know how."

"Travis," Paddy intervened as he started to speak. "Dee knows what she's about." Nodding, Travis moved off to scrub his hands and arms.

"Have a care," she warned as he prepared to begin. "The babe's hooves will be sharp, and the womb can close on your hand quickly." Taking a deep breath, she lay her cheek against the mare's, hands circling the damp flesh in a steady rhythm as she began to croon in quiet Gaelic.

The mare shivered as Travis entered her, but remained still, listening to Adelia's comforting voice.

The air seemed to grow closer, heavy with Solomy's breathing and the mystical beauty of the ancient tongue Adelia murmured. It brought a heavy warmth to the spring afternoon, isolating them from all but the struggle for life.

"I've got him," Travis announced, sweat running unheeded down his face. His breath came quickly, and he muttered a steady stream of soft curses, but Adelia heard nothing, giving herself over to the mare. "It's done." He rested back on his heels, turning his attention to the woman at his side. She gave no sign to him, only continued her slow, rhythmic crooning, hands gently caressing, face buried in the mare's neck.

"Here it comes," Paddy cried, and she turned her head to watch the miracle of birth. When the foal finally emerged into the world, both woman and horse sighed and shuddered.

"It's a fine, strong son you have, Solomy. Ah, sure, and there's no more beautiful sight in the world than an innocent new life!"

She turned her glowing face to Travis and gave him a smile that rivaled the sun. Their eyes met, and the look deepened until it seemed to Adelia that time had stopped. She felt herself being drawn into fathoms of dark blue, unable to breathe or speak, as if some invisible shield had descended, insulating them from all but each other.

Can love come in an instant? her numbed brain demanded. Or has it been there forever? The answer was forestalled as Robert Loman arrived, shattering the magic that had held her suspended.

She stood up quickly as the vet began to question Travis on the colt's delivery. A wave of giddiness washed over her as she rose, and she sank her teeth into her lower lip to combat the weakness. Keeping the mare calm had been an enormous strain, almost as if she had experienced each pang of labor, and the unexpected rush of emotion when Travis had held her eyes had left her drained and dizzy.

"What is it, Dee?" Paddy's voice was full of concern as he took her arm.

"Nothing." She placed her palm to her spinning head. "Just a bit of a headache."

"Take her home," Travis commanded, regarding her closely. Her eyes were bright and enormous against her pallor, and she appeared suddenly small and helpless. Rising, he moved toward her, and she stepped back, terrified he would touch her.

"There's no need." She kept her voice calm and even. "I'll just go up and have a wash. I'm fine, Uncle Paddy." She smiled into his frowning face, avoiding Travis's at all costs. "Don't you worry." Stepping from the stall, she moved quickly from the building, filling her lungs with fresh, clean air.

That evening found Adelia quiet and pensive. She was unused to confusion and uncertainty, characteristically knowing what needed to be done and doing

it. Her life had always been basic, the fundamental existence of meeting demands as they came. There had
been no room for indecision or clouded reasoning in a
world that was essentially black or white.

She lingered in the kitchen after dinner, reasoning with herself with firm common sense. The foaling had been difficult, the strain emptying her body of
its strength, and the sight of the new colt had fogged
her brain. These were the reasons she had reacted so
strongly to Travis. She could hardly be in love with him;
she barely knew him, and what she did know was not
altogether to her taste. He was too big, too strong, too
self-confident, and too arrogant. He reminded her of a
feudal lord, and Adelia was too Irish to have any liking
for landed gentry.

However, after her work was done and self-analysis
complete, she remained oddly weary and disturbed.
Sitting down on the floor at Paddy's feet, she laid her
head in his lap with a deep sigh.

"Little Dee," he murmured, stroking the thick auburn curls. "You're working too hard."

"What nonsense," she disagreed, snuggling deeper
into the still newness of comfort. "I haven't worked a
full day since I arrived. The day would not nearly be
over yet if I was back on the farm."

"Was it hard for you, lass?" he asked, thinking she
might now be ready to talk of it.

Again Adelia sighed, moving her shoulders restlessly. "I wouldn't say hard, Uncle Paddy, but everything changed after Mother and Da died."

"Poor little Dee, such a wee thing to be losing so
much."

"I thought my world had ended when they died,"
she whispered, hardly aware she was speaking aloud.
"I'm thinking I died myself for a time, so angry and

frightened I was, then numb, feeling nothing. But I began remembering how they were together. No two people could have loved each other more. Such a fine, full loving they had, even a child could see it."

So engrossed were the man and woman in the words being spoken that neither heard the sound of feet climbing the stairs. Travis halted in his action of knocking, dropping his hand as he watched the poignant picture, and Adelia's words drifted through the screen.

"The only thing I could give them was the farm, and it was all I had left of them. Poor Aunt Lettie, she worked so hard and I was a constant cross for her to bear." She laughed as memory flickered through her mind. "She never could understand why I had to ride so fast. 'Sure and it's your neck you'll be breaking,' she used to call after me, shaking her fist. 'Who'll be helping with the plowing if you bash in your head on the road?' Then when I'd have one of my rages and go off shouting and cursing—and it's often, I'm afraid, I did just that—she'd cross herself and start praying for my doomed soul.

"Jakers, but we worked." With a long breath she shut her eyes. "But it was too much for one woman and a half-grown girl, and not enough money to hire help, and none to be made without it. Do you know how it is, Uncle Paddy, when you see the thing you need, but the closer you get the further away it is? Always moving away from you, always just out of your reach. Sometimes, when I look back, I can't tell one day from the rest. Then Aunt Lettie had that stroke, and how she hated to be lying there helpless day after day."

"Why did you never let me know how things were?" Paddy questioned, looking down at her dark head. "I could have helped you—sent you money, or come back myself."

She raised her head and smiled at him. "Aye, that's just what you would have done, and to what good? Throwing your money away, taking yourself from the life you'd chosen . . . I'd not have had that for a minute, and neither would Aunt Lettie, or Mother and Da. The farm's gone, just as they are, and so is Ireland. Now I have you, I'm not needing another thing."

Looking into his eyes, seeing the concern and regret written there, she wished suddenly she had kept her own counsel. "How is it, Padrick Cunnane, that a fine, handsome man like yourself never took a wife?" Her grin turned impish, and devils danced in her eyes. "There must have been dozens of ladies willing. Have you never found a woman to love?"

He touched her cheek, giving her a wistful smile. "Aye, lass, that I did, but she chose your father."

Deep green eyes filled with surprise that melted into sympathy. "Oh, Uncle Paddy!" She flung her arms around him, and Travis turned from the door and walked silently down the stairs.

The next morning the air seemed to sigh with spring, whispering promises of flowers and cool, leafy trees. To Adelia it brought memories of other springs. Spring was the time the earth asked to be replenished and grew pregnant with new life. Her world had always revolved around the earth, its gifts and hardships, its demands and promises.

From the balcony of Paddy's house she surveyed the land that was Travis's. It seemed to stretch on and on with the easy, gentle roll of a calm sea. Green and brown waves were dotted not with boats but with finely sculptured Thoroughbreds. It ran through her mind that she had no conception of what lay over the last hill. This land was still a stranger. From the moment of her arrival in America she had seen little else but what belonged to Travis Grant.

Over the pure, sweet air floated an occasional whinny or the quick call of a bird. But for this, there was silence. There was no strident call of rooster announcing the new day, no fields turned up waiting to receive seeds, no weeds demanding uprooting. All at once homesickness washed over her so intensely that she could only shut her eyes and weather the storm.

So much is gone, she thought, and her hands hugged her elbows as if in comfort. I'll never be able to go back, never see the farm again. Sighing, she opened her eyes and tried to shake off the melancholy. There's nothing to be done about it; the bridges are burned. This is home now, and if it's not really mine, it's the closest I'll come.

"Where are you, lass?"

Adelia started slightly as Paddy's arm slipped around her; then she sighed again and rested against his shoulder. "Back on the farm, I suppose. Thinking about spring planting."

"It's a day for it, isn't it? The air's cool, and the sun's warm." He gave her shoulder a small squeeze, then clucked his tongue as if in regret. "I've got to go into town today. It's a pity."

"A pity?"

"I was hoping to get some seeds in around the walkway. Thought I might make a flower bed in front of the house, too." He shook his head and sighed. "Just don't know when I'll find the time."

"Oh, I'll do it, Uncle Paddy. I've plenty of time." Drawing away, she looked at him with such innocent acceptance of his trumped-up excuse that he nearly broke into a grin.

"Little Dee, I couldn't ask you to do all that on your day off." He creased his face into doubtful lines and patted her cheek. "No, it's too much. I'll get to it as soon as I find a bit of time."

"Uncle Paddy, don't be silly. I'd love to do it." Her smile was blooming again, chasing the clouds from her eyes. "Just show me what you want done."

"Well . . ." He permitted her to argue a few more minutes before allowing himself to be persuaded.

Armed with a myriad of seed packs and a small spade, Adelia stood on the patch of lawn surrounding Paddy's house and mentally mapped out her landscaping. Petunias along the walks, asters and marigolds against the house, impatiens for the border. And sweet peas, she thought with a smile, for the trellis she had asked Paddy to buy. In the fall, she decided, I'll plant bulbs, as many as the ground will hold. Daffodils and tulips. Satisfied with her planning, she began to turn the earth.

The sun grew warmer, and her sleeves were soon pushed past her elbows. In the distance she could hear the sounds of men and horses going through their daily routine: a shout, laughter, the thud of hooves on dirt. But soon, lost in her planting, she drifted apart. Softly, she began to sing a song remembered from childhood, the words soothing and familiar. The scent of fresh earth eased the ache with which she had awakened.

A shadow fell across her. Twisting her head, she dropped the spade nervously as Travis looked down at her.

"I've made you stop. I'm sorry."

He seemed impossibly tall as he stood over her. She craned her neck and squinted against the sun. It

glowed in an aura around his head, and for one fanci-
ful moment she thought he looked like a knight on his
way to vanquish dragons.

"No, you just startled me." Picking up the spade,
Adelia told herself she was a fool and began to work
again.

"I didn't mean the planting." He crouched down
beside her, his shoulders brushing hers. "I mean the
song. It sounded very old and very sad."

"Aye, it's both." She inched away, carefully patting soil over seeds. "A lot of Gaelic songs are old and
sad."

Folding his legs under him, he sat easily on the grass
and watched her. "What's it about?"

"Oh, love, of course. The saddest songs are always
about love." She lifted her head to smile at him. His face
was close, his mouth a breath away. The spade hung
suspended in her hand as she only stared, wondering
what she would do if the whisper of space was gone and
his mouth found hers.

"Is love always sad, Adelia?" His voice was as soft
as the breeze that danced around them.

"I don't know. I . . ." She felt the weakness growing
stronger and tore her eyes from his. "We were talking
about songs."

"So we were," Travis murmured, then brushed back
the hair that curtained her face. She swallowed and began digging with renewed interest. "I never thanked
you properly for your help yesterday with Solomy."

"Oh, well . . ." Moving her shoulders, she kept her
eyes on the ground. "I didn't do that much. I'm just glad
Solomy and the foal are well. Do you like flowers, Mr.
Grant?" she asked, needing to change the subject.

"Yes, I like flowers. What are you planting?" His
voice was casual as he lifted a package of seeds.

"All different kinds," she told him, this time able to raise her head and smile. "They'll be a lovely sight by summer. Your soil's rich, Mr. Grant; it wants to give." She squeezed a handful of earth, then held it out in her palm.

"You'd know more about that than I." Taking her fingertips, he studied the soil in her hand. "You're the farmer."

"I was," she amended and tried to free her hand.

"I'm afraid I don't know much about planting— vegetables or flowers." He ignored her attempts to pull her fingers away and brought his eyes to hers. "I suppose it's a gift."

"It just takes time and effort, like anything else. Here." Concluding that if she gave him something to do, her hand would be released, she held out some seeds. "Just drop a few in and cover them up. Don't crowd them," she instructed as he obeyed. "They want room to spread. Now you cover them up and let nature take over." Smiling, she absently brushed a hand across her cheek. "No matter what you do, nature has the last word in any case. A farmer knows that here the same way a farmer knows that in Ireland."

"So, now that I've put them in," he concluded with a grin, "I just sit back and watch them grow."

"Well," she said, tilting her head and giving him a sober stare, "there might be a thing or two more, like watering or weeding. These seeds will take quick, and the flowers will pop up before you know it. I'm putting in sweet peas there." She pointed across the lawn, forgetting that she still held the soil in her other hand. "When the breeze comes up at night, the scent will drift through the windows. There's something special about sweet peas. They start off so small, but they'll just keep climbing as long as there's something to hold on to. There should be a rosebush," she murmured almost to herself. "When the scents mingle together, it's like nothing else on earth. Red roses, just starting to open up."

"Are you homesick, Dee?" The question was low and gentle, but her head whipped back around in surprise.

"I . . ." Shrugging, she bent her face to her work again, uncomfortable that he had read her emotions so clearly.

"It's quite natural." He lifted her chin with his hand until their eyes met again. "It's not easy to leave behind everything you've ever known."

"No." Moving her shoulders again, she turned away and began to spread marigold seeds. "But I made the choice, and it truly was what I wanted. It's what I want," she amended with more firmness. "I can't say I've been unhappy a moment since I got off the plane. I can't go back, and I don't really know if I'd want to if I could. I've a new life now." Tossing back her hair, she smiled at him. "I like it here. The people, the work, the horses, the land." Her hand made a wide, encompassing gesture. "You've a beautiful home, Mr. Grant; anyone could be happy here."

He brushed a trace of dirt from her cheek and returned her smile. "I'm glad you think so, but it's your home, too."

"You're a generous man, Mr. Grant." She kept her gaze level with his, but her smile was suddenly sad and sweet. "There's not many who'd say that and mean it, and I'm grateful to you. But for better or worse, the farm was mine." Sighing, she traced a finger through the soil. "It was mine. . . ."

*   *   *

L ate the next morning when Adelia turned one of the Thoroughbreds she had been exercising over to a groom, Trish Collins approached her with a friendly smile. "Hello, Adelia. How are you settling in?"

"Fine, missus, and good morning to you." She regarded Trish's dark beauty with fresh admiration. "And where are the lads this morning?"

"In school, but they'll be here tomorrow. They're half crazy to get a look at the new foal."

"A beautiful sight he is."

"Yes, I've just had a peek at him. Travis told me how marvelous you were with the mare."

Her mouth dropped open a moment, surprised and inordinately pleased that Travis should have praised her. "I was glad to help, missus. Solomy did all the work."

"Call me Trish," she requested with a shake of her head. "Missus makes me feel old and crotchety."

"Oh, no, missus, you're not old at all," she blurted out, horrified.

"I wouldn't like to think so. Travis and I won't be thirty-one until October." Trish laughed at the stricken face.

"So you're twins as well," Adelia concluded, feeling more at ease. "I suppose that's why I saw your brother's eyes the first time I met you."

"Yes, we do bear a strong resemblance to each other, which is why I constantly tell him how handsome he is." She smiled at Adelia's light, musical laugh. "Am I holding you up? Are you busy?"

"No, missus." At the raised brow, she amended, "No, Trish. I was about to take my break and fix a cup of tea. Would you like one?"

"Yes, thank you, I would."

They paused at the top of the stairs to the garage

house as Adelia bent to pick up a long, narrow white box. "Now, what might this be?"

"Flowers would be my guess," Trish concluded, indicating the printed name of a local florist.

"What would they be doing here?" She frowned down at the box as they stepped inside. "Someone must have left them at the wrong house."

"You might open them and find out," Trish suggested, amused by the frown of concentration. "As your name's on the box, they just might be for you."

Auburn curls danced as she shook her head and chuckled. "Now, who'd be sending me flowers?" Setting the box on a table, she opened the lid and gave a small cry of pleasure. "Oh, just look! Have you ever seen such a sight?" The box was filled with long-stemmed roses, deep blood red, their half-closed petals soft as velvet to her hesitant fingers. Lifting one out, she held it under her nose. "Ah," she breathed and passed the bloom to Trish. "Straight from heaven." Then, shrugging, she returned to practical matters. "Who would they be for?"

"There should be a card."

Locating the small white note, Adelia read it silently, and her green eyes widened as she read the words a second time. She brought her gaze from the slip of paper to meet an openly curious regard. "They're for me." Her voice mirrored disbelief as she handed Trish the card. "Your brother sent them to thank me for helping with Solomy."

"'Dee, to thank you for your help with the new foal. Travis,'" Trish read aloud, and added under her breath, "You certainly wax poetic on occasion, brother."

"In my whole life," Adelia murmured, touching a silky petal, "no one has ever given me flowers."

Trish looked over quickly, observing the shimmering eyes and the stunned pleasure passing over Adelia's features. Pushing tears back, Adelia spoke on a sigh. "This was a lovely thing for your brother to do. I had a rosebush at home—red roses they were, too. My mother planted it." She smiled, feeling incredibly happy. "It makes them that much more special."

Later, they walked back to the stables. As they drew near, Travis and Paddy emerged from the building, and the Irishman greeted them both with a beaming smile.

"Travis, we've died and gone to heaven. Sure and it's two angels coming to greet us."

"Uncle Paddy." Adelia tweaked his cheek. "Living in America hasn't lessened your gift for blarney." Looking up at the man who towered above the rest of them, she treated him to the pure, honest smile of a child. "I want to thank you for the flowers, Mr. Grant. They're lovely."

"I'm glad you liked them," he answered, enjoying the smile. "It was little enough after what you did."

"Here's something more for you, Dee." Paddy reached into his pocket and withdrew a piece of paper. "Your first week's wages."

"Oh," Adelia said with a grin. "It's the first time I've been paid in money for doing anything." She frowned at the check, confused, and Travis's brows rose in amusement at her expression.

"Is something wrong with it, Adelia?"

"Yes . . . no . . . I . . ." she stumbled, and brought her eyes to Paddy.

"You're wondering what it is in pounds," he concluded, grinning merrily.

"I don't think I figured it right," she answered, embarrassed under Travis's gaze.

Chuckling, he did some mental arithmetic and told her. Confusion changed to astonishment and something close to terror.

"What would I be doing with that kind of money?"

"First time anyone around here complained about being overpaid," Travis commented and received a baleful glance.

"Here." Adelia turned her attention back to her uncle and held the check out to him. "You take it."

"Now, why would I be doing that, Dee? It's your money; you earned it."

"But I've never had so much money at one time in my whole life." She sent him a pleading look. "What will I do with it?"

"Go out and buy some of those female trappings and folderol," he suggested vaguely, waving his hand, then pushing the check back at her. "Treat yourself to something. The good Lord knows it's about time."

"But, Uncle Paddy—"

"Why don't you buy yourself a dress, Dee?" Travis inserted with a grin. "I'm curious to see if you've got legs under those jeans."

Adelia's head snapped up, and she eyed Travis with a dangerous gleam. "Aye, I've legs, Mr. Grant, and I've been told a time or two it's not a trial to look at them. But you'll not have to be worrying yourself; it's not dresses I need to tend your horses."

His grin only widened as he gave a negligent shrug. "It doesn't matter to me if you want to be taken for a boy."

Her wrath increased as he had meant it to, and her eyes fired sharp green daggers. "There's only one who ever made that mistake, he being an ill-mannered, bad-tempered brute of a man without a brain working in his empty head."

"Shopping's a marvelous idea," Trish broke in, deciding it was time to play peacemaker. "As a matter of fact, Travis"—she smiled and fluttered her lashes—"Dee's taking the rest of the day off so we can do just that."

"Oh, really?" he returned dryly, folding his arms across his chest.

"Yes, *really*. Come on, Dee."

"But I haven't finished. . . ."

Trish linked her arm through the still protesting Adelia's and propelled her to a late-model compact. Before she had time to think things through, Adelia had an account at a local bank, a checkbook, and more cash than her apprehensive brain could comprehend.

"Now"—Trish backed the compact from its parking space—"we're going shopping."

"But what will I buy?" She stared at Trish's clear profile in complete consternation.

Stopping at a red light, Trish turned to her anxious face. "When's the last time you bought something for yourself for the fun of it? Have you ever bought something because you wanted it instead of just needing it?" The light changed, and as she joined the flow of traffic she sighed at Adelia's blank expression. "Don't misunderstand. I'm not saying people should just throw their money away, but it's high time you did something for yourself." Glancing at Adelia's furrowed brow, she smiled and shook her head. "You can afford to slow down, Dee, take a day off, buy something foolish, stretch your wings, take a breath." She grinned as Adelia merely stared at her. "The sky will not fall if Adelia Cunnane takes time off to have some fun."

No one was more surprised than Adelia when, in fact, she did have fun. The large mall fascinated her with its various small specialty shops and large department stores. There were more clothes than she had ever seen, in colors and soft materials that had her staring and touching in frank admiration.

While Adelia gazed around her, Trish examined garments critically, going from rack to rack, dismissing dozens of dresses, skirts, and blouses, occasionally removing an item and hanging it over her arm. Finding herself in a changing room, Adelia could only stare at the garments Trish had placed on a hook. Then, taking a deep breath, she stripped off her shirt and jeans and slipped on a soft jersey dress in muted shades of green.

The silky material felt strange and wonderful to her skin, clinging to gentle curves and falling gracefully below her knees. She gaped at the stranger in the mirror, her hand seeking the cross at her throat to assure herself that she was still the same person.

"Dee," Trish called from outside the curtain, "have you got one on yet?"

"Aye," she answered slowly, and Trish pulled the curtain aside, smiling in triumph at the reflection in the full-length mirror.

"I knew that dress was you the minute I saw it."

"It doesn't feel like me," Adelia mumbled, then turned to face Trish directly. "It's beautiful, but what would I do with so grand a dress? I exercise horses. I work in a stable—"

"Dee," Trish interrupted firmly. "Whatever your occupation, you're still a human being; you're still a woman, an exceptionally beautiful woman." Adelia's eyes widened, and her mouth opened to protest, but before the words could be uttered Trish took her by the shoulders and turned her to face her reflection. "Look at yourself, really look," she ordered in no-nonsense terms, then shifted to gentler tones. "There'll be times when you'll want only to be a woman; this dress is for those times. Now," she said with practical authority as she released her, "try something else on."

For the rest of the afternoon Adelia allowed Trish to take command. For the first time in more than a decade, she permitted someone else to make all the decisions, and somehow she found she was having fun. They halted in front of a cosmetics counter, and Trish began spraying scents until Adelia grumbled in protest.

"This." Trish selected one of the bottles she had sampled. "Light and delicate, with just a touch of spirit." Paying for the cologne, she handed the package to Adelia. "A present."

"Oh, but I can't!"

"Yes, you can. Friends get pleasure from giving presents. Now, that marvelous skin of yours doesn't need any help, but I think we'll accent your eyes—and some lipstick, nothing too dramatic." She stopped and laughed. "I'm bullying you, aren't I?"

"Aye," Adelia agreed, feeling caught up in a genial whirlwind and finding she liked it.

"Well, you needed it," Trish said firmly. "Is there anything else you want?"

She hesitated, then blurted out quickly, "Something for my hands. Your brother said I've hands like a ditchdigger's."

"That man!" she exclaimed in disgust. "He's the epitome of tact and diplomacy."

"Trish, hello!"

Adelia turned to see a flash of amazing silver-blond hair before Trish was enveloped in an exuberant embrace. Adelia's first startled impression was of lavish curls and musky scent.

"I'm so glad to see you, darling." A high, bubbly voice drifted with the scent. "It's been weeks."

"Hello, Laura." With an affectionate smile, Trish

disentangled herself. "It's good to see you, too. Laura
Bowers—Adelia Cunnane."

"How do you do, Mistress Bowers." The greeting
was returned with a flash of beautiful white teeth before Laura's attention returned to Trish.

"Darling, how is that fabulous brother of yours?"

"Fabulous," Trish returned, giving Adelia a quick
grin of mischief.

"Don't tell me he's not pining after Margot?" Laura
sighed and gave a flutter of extensive lashes. "I was so
hoping to offer him my comfort. Not even a tear or two
to be dried?"

"He seems to be bearing up under the strain," Trish
returned. Hearing the unexpected sarcasm, Adelia
glanced at her in surprise.

"Oh, well, if he doesn't need comfort," Laura continued, obviously not affected by Trish's tone, "he's still
at loose ends, so to speak. If dear Margot overplayed
her hand by whisking off to Europe, I for one am not
above volunteering to fill the gap. Heard from her
lately?"

"Not a peep."

"Well, then, I'll take it that no news is good news."
She gave Trish a wink and tossed her brilliant curls.
"Such a gorgeous man. Do you know Travis, Adelaide?"

"Adelia," Trish corrected before Adelia could do so
herself. "Yes, Dee knows Travis very well."

"Charming man," Laura bubbled. "Now that Mar-
got's out of the picture, at least temporarily, I'll just have
to give him a ring. Do tell him I'll call, won't you?"
With another flurry of curls, she pecked both of Trish's
cheeks. "I hate to, darling, but I simply must run. Don't
forget to give Travis my very best. So nice to have met
you, Amanda."

Adelia opened her mouth, then closed it again as Laura scurried off in a wave of musk.

"Sorry, Amanda." Trish grinned and patted Adelia's cheek. "Laura's really very sweet and basically kind, but she's a bit short of brains."

"She has such beautiful hair." Tearing her gaze from Laura's retreating coiffure, Adelia turned back to Trish. "I've never seen hair that color before. She must be very proud of it."

Trish laughed until she was forced to wipe away tears as Adelia looked on in puzzlement. "Oh, Dee, I adore you! Come on, we'll get that hand cream; then I'll buy you a cup of tea."

Waiting patiently while her mentor weighed the pros and cons of various lotions, Adelia reflected on Laura Bowers's conversation. *Margot,* she repeated, nibbling absently on her bottom lip. Who is this Margot, and what is she to Travis? For a moment she struggled with the urge to ask Trish outright, then, remembering her manners, she kept silent. *Perhaps he's in love with her.* This thought brought such a sharp, unexpected pain that she nearly gasped aloud. *But he's not,* a part of her insisted. If Travis Grant were ever to love a woman, he would never let her go. He would go to the ends of the earth to bring her back. Unless, of course, he had been rejected. His pride would never allow him to pursue a woman who had refused him. But who would ever refuse such a man? *It's not my concern,* she told herself fiercely, forcing herself to concentrate on Trish's detailed description of various hand lotions.

At last Trish was satisfied. Adelia was suitably outfitted and had all the cosmetics that Trish thought were necessary. Laden with parcels, the two women headed back to the car. For once, Adelia was reduced to

silence. She sat bolt upright on the front seat as Trish
drove swiftly over the winding country roads. She
was even too excited to enjoy the rolling hills and the
horses grazing in the meadows, now softly outlined by
the sinking afternoon sun.

Paddy was there to open the door when Adelia burst
in with her new treasures.

"Little Dee, you're looking as happy as the first time
you rode Majesty round the track," he said, observing
her flushed, happy face.

"This was nearly as exciting, Uncle Paddy." She
laughed and stepped through the doorway. "Never have
I seen so many clothes, so many people. Do you know,
I think everyone in America is in a constant hurry, driving, rushing through the stores—nothing ever seems to
move slowly. This place Trish took me was amazing—
all these shops in one big building, and it had foun-
tains, right inside." She sighed, then shrugged and
grinned. "I know I should be ashamed for squander-
ing money the way I did, but I'm not. I had a fine
time."

"It was due time, lass, due time." He kissed her
cheek as they entered the living room.

"Well, Paddy, she's lost her innocence." Travis rose
from an armchair and grinned down at Adelia and
her packages. "Trish corrupted her. I knew I shouldn't
have let that sister of mine get hold of her."

"Your sister is a wonderful lady, Mr. Grant." Adelia
tossed back her head to meet his eyes, chestnut curls
falling back from her face. "She has a sweet and generous soul, and a good deal more in the way of manners
than some I could name."

His brow lifted, and he glanced over her head to
look at Paddy as the older man struggled not to grin.

"It appears Trish has a champion, and one I don't think I care to challenge." He shifted his gaze back to Adelia's irate face. "At least," he added with a slow, enigmatic smile, "not today. . . ."

CHAPTER 4

Saturday dawned sunny and unseasonably warm. The trees were now in full leaf, and the air carried the sweet scent of flowers as spring approached midterm. Adelia sang happily as she groomed Fortune, a sturdy three-year-old colt who listened with approval to her high, lilting voice as she brushed him.

"Dee! Dee!" She whirled around to see Mark and Mike scurrying into the stables. "Mom said we could come down and see you, and the new foal, too."

"Good day to you, gentlemen; it's pleased I am to have you visiting me."

"Will you show us the foal?" Mike demanded, and she smiled at his enthusiasm.

"That I will, Master Michael, as soon as I've finished with my friend here. Now." She set down the brush and reached a hand into her back pocket. "Where is it that I put that hoof pick?" Her pockets were empty, and she searched the ground, frowning. "It's the little people at work again."

"We didn't take it," Mark objected.

"People are always blaming kids for everything," Mike complained righteously.

"Oh, but it's not children I'm speaking of," Adelia corrected. "It's leprechauns."

"Leprechauns?" the twins chorused. "What's a leprechaun?"

"Could it be you're telling me you've never heard of leprechauns?" she asked in amazement. The boys shook their identical heads, and she folded her arms across her chest. "Well, your education's sadly lacking, lads. It's a sorry thing to remain ignorant of the little people."

"Tell us, Dee," they demanded, pulling at her hands in excitement.

"That I will." She hauled herself up to sit on a bench as the two boys squatted on the floor at her feet. "Now, the leprechaun is a strange fellow, his father being an evil spirit and his mother a fairy fallen from grace. By nature he's a mischief-maker. He only grows to be about three feet high, no matter how old he happens to be. Some say he likes to be riding on sheep or goats, so a man knows, if his stock is tired and weary of a morning, that the little people have been up to their tricks and using them for some errand where they didn't want to travel on foot. They can be lazy when they've a mind to.

"They love to be making mischief about the house as well. Why, a leprechaun'll make a pot boil over on the stove, or keep it from boiling at all, as his whim suits him. Or he'll steal the bacon or toss the furniture about for the sheer love of the confusion. Other times he'll drink his fill of the milk or poteen and fill up the bottle with water.

"Now," she continued, her eyes bright with excitement as the two boys clung to her words, "to catch a

leprechaun would bring certain fortune to the one who
had the wit to hold him. The only time you can catch
him is when he's sitting down, and he never sits unless
his brogues want mending. He's forever running about
so that he wears them out, and when he feels his feet
on the ground, he sits behind a hedge or in the tall grass
of a meadow and takes them off to mend them. Then"—
she lowered her voice to a dramatic whisper, and the two
heads inched forward—"you creep up, quiet as a cat,
and grab him tight in your arms." She flung her arms
around an imaginary leprechaun and shouted, "'Give
me your gold,' you say. 'I've got no gold,' says he."

Releasing her invisible captive, she gave the boys
a roguish smile. "Now, there's gold by the ton, and
that's the truth of it, and he can tell you where it's to
be found, but he won't till you make him. Now, some
try choking him or threatening him, but, whatever you
do, you mustn't for a moment take your eyes from him.
If you do that, he's gone in a flash, and you'll not be
seeing him again. The scheming devil has a pocketful
of tricks for getting away, and he can charm the birds
from the trees if he's a mind to. But if you hold your
ground and keep your eye on him, his gold is yours, and
your fortune's made."

"Did you ever see a leprechaun, Dee?" Mark asked,
bouncing with excitement.

"By the saints, I thought I did, a time or two." She
nodded sagely. "But I never got close enough before
they had vanished, quick as you please. So"—she
jumped from the bench and tousled two dark heads—
"unless I'm finding me one who's traveled to America,
I'll have to be working for my living." She picked up
a hoof pick from the bench. "And that's what I'm doing now, or I'll be fired for laziness and be begging for
pennies."

"We wouldn't let it come to that, would we, boys?"

Adelia spun around, her color rising as she met Travis's mocking smile. The thumping in her heart she attributed to surprise, and she was forced to swallow nervously before speaking.

"It's a habit you're making of creeping up on a body and frightening the wits from them, Mr. Grant."

"Maybe I mistook you for a leprechaun, Dee." His grin was annoying, but she refused to be baited and bent to lift Fortune's hoof.

He led the twins down to visit the new foal, and she set down the horse's leg and watched his broad back retreat down the passage.

Why did he always send her into a flutter? she wondered. Why did her pulses begin to race at a speed that rivaled Majesty's whenever she looked up and met those surprisingly blue eyes? She leaned her cheek against Fortune's sturdy neck and sighed. She'd lost, she conceded. She'd lost the battle, and though she fought against it, she was in love with Travis Grant. It was impossible, she admitted. Nothing could ever develop between the owner of Royal Meadows and an insignificant stablehand.

"Besides," she whispered to the understanding colt, "he's an arrogant brute of a man, and I don't believe I like him one little bit." Hearing the boys approach, she bent quickly and lifted another hoof for cleaning.

"Run along outside, boys. I want a word with Dee." At Travis's command, the twins scrambled past, chattering and exclaiming over the foal. She set down the horse's leg and straightened to face him, the color fading from her cheeks.

Blast my cursed tongue, she thought in desperate condemnation. Aunt Lettie told me a thousand times where my temper would take me.

"I—have I done something wrong, Mr. Grant?" She stammered slightly and bit her lip in frustration.

"No, Dee," he answered, slowly searching her troubled face. "Did you think I was going to fire you?" His voice was oddly gentle, and she felt a tremor at the unfamiliar tone.

"You did say I could have a fortnight, and I've a few days left before—"

"There's no need for a trial," he interrupted. "I've already decided to keep you on."

"Oh, thank you, Mr. Grant," she began, overcome with relief. "I'm grateful to you."

"Your way with horses is quite phenomenal, a strange sort of empathy." He stroked Fortune's flank, then fixed his eyes on her again. "It would be impossible to complain about your work, except that there's too much of it. I don't want to hear about you cleaning tack at ten o'clock at night anymore."

"Oh, well . . ." Turning back to the bench, Adelia gave intense concentration to placing the hoof pick in its proper spot. "I just—"

"Don't argue, and don't do it again," he commanded, and she felt his hands descend to her shoulders. "You know, you seem to split your time between working and arguing. We'll have to see if we can find another outlet for all that energy."

"I don't argue, exactly. Well, perhaps sometimes." She shrugged and wished she had the courage to turn and face him. The decision was taken out of her hands as she found herself being turned, then lifted until she once again sat on the bench.

"Perhaps sometimes," Travis agreed, and she found it disconcerting that his smile was so close, his hands still circling her waist.

"Mr. Grant," she began, then swallowed as he

reached up to pluck her cap from her hair, freeing the rich cloud of auburn. "Mr. Grant, I've work to do."

"Mmm." His comment was absent as he became involved with the winding of curls around his fingers. "I've always had a fondness for chestnuts." Grinning, he gave her hair a firm tug until her face lifted to his. "A very particular fondness."

"Would you like to check my teeth?" Seeking a defense against a swift wave of longing, Adelia stiffened and sent him what she hoped was a lethal glare. His burst of unrestrained laughter caused the glare to light with green fire, and she struggled to slide from the bench.

"Oh, no." He held her still with minimum effort. "You should realize by now that I find it impossible to restrain myself when you start spitting fire."

He took her mouth quickly, one hand still tangled in her hair, the other slipping under her shirt to claim the smooth skin of her back. She found her second trip through the storm no less devastating than the first, and while her will melted under its force, her senses sharpened. The scent of leather, horses, and masculinity rose and surrounded her, a strange, intoxicating scent she knew she would always associate with him. She could feel his strength as he plunged her deeper into the kiss, demanding every drop of sweetness from her mouth. Hard and seeking, his lips parted hers, his tongue teasing hers into mobility until she was pliant and yielding against him.

For the first time she felt the pain and demand of womanhood, the slow ache growing in the center of her being and spreading to encompass her entirely, until there was nothing but the need and the man who could assuage it. She heard a soft moan as her lips were freed, not aware it was her own weak protest at liberation, and her lids opened slowly to reveal eyes dark and slumberous with desire.

"I find," Travis commented in a low, lazy voice, "that is a more productive use of time than arguing."

Adelia watched his eyes drop to the lips still warm from his and felt his hand tighten on her hair. It relaxed slowly, and a smile moved across his face as his eyes rose to hers. "It also appears to be the only way to shut you up for any amount of time."

He dropped her cap back on her head, then traced her cheek with his finger. "I find Irish tempers have definite advantages."

He strode away, and Adelia contemplated his long, graceful stride in confusion, reaching up one hand to press the cheek his finger had touched.

Pushing away a puzzle she could not solve, she spent the rest of the day in a state of euphoria. She was staying. She had found her place on the mammoth horse farm, and an uncle who wanted as well as needed her, and a job that was a dream realized. And at least, she thought happily, she would be close to Travis, seeing him almost daily, feeding her need on the sight of his tall, powerful form, on a few snatched words of conversation. That was enough for the present, and the future was something to be faced when it arrived. . . .

Long after her uncle had retired, Adelia remained wide awake. She had tried to relax with a book, but her spirits were too high for sitting idly, and she closed it and slipped outside.

She decided to walk to the stables, promising herself she would not touch one bridle but merely look in on the horses. The night remained warm, the sky blanketed with stars, so clear and vivid that she reached up, imagining she could pluck one from the soft, black curtain. At peace with the world, she meandered toward the large white building.

Entering, she switched on a low light to dispel the unrelieved darkness. She had gone no more than twenty feet when a soft moaning sound caught her attention, and she whirled in the direction of an empty stall. A man lay in a crumpled heap, and she caught her breath in alarm.

"Merciful heavens!" She hurried in and bent over him. "What's happened? Oh!" she uttered in disgust and stood, hands on hips. "You are drunk, George Johnson, and a pitiful sight indeed. You smell like a poteen factory. What do you mean drinking yourself into such a state and lying about in the stables?"

"So, it's pretty little Dee," George mumbled thickly, hauling himself into a half-sitting position. "Did you come for a visit? Come to share my bottle?"

Adelia had found herself avoiding the groom. She had often found his eyes on her, and his leering smile had caused her to recoil instinctively. Now, however, she was angry and disgusted, and she took no pains to hide it.

"No, I'll not be sharing a bottle with the likes of you—I've no patience for drunken sods. Haul yourself up and be on your way. You've no business in here with your mind fuddled with whiskey."

"Giving orders now, little Dee?" He struggled to his feet and faced her. "Too good to drink with me?" He raked her from head to foot with bleary eyes, pausing on the swell of her breast and moistening his lips. "Maybe you don't want to drink when there's more interesting things to do." He grabbed her shoulders and closed his mouth over hers, the strong smell of whiskey assaulting her senses as she pushed against him.

"You filthy pig of a man!" she spat, infuriated that

he had touched her. "You great, sniveling, drunken buzzard, don't you ever put your hands on me again. You guzzling serpent, I'll kick you into next week if you touch me again." She ranted at him until he grabbed her with such force that her breath caught in her throat.

"I'll do more than touch you." His hand clamped over her mouth, and he pushed her down roughly in the straw-filled stall. She fought in wild fury, kicking and scratching as his hands began to bruise her body, choking back the sickness that rose as his lips violated hers. Her blouse ripped away from the shoulder, the sound exploding in her ear. Anger gave way to terror, and she struggled more violently. Her nails dug into his arms, tearing his skin, and as he cursed with pain and raised his head, her scream pierced the still night.

A hand slapped hard across her cheek, numbing her face as he closed his palm over her mouth again. She continued to thrash out as his free hand captured her breast and moved over her with cruel purpose. Her strength was ebbing, and she realized she was helpless against the violation that was to come. He was tugging at her jeans, his drunkenness causing his fingers to fumble at the snap. The hand over her mouth was depriving her of air, and a foggy dimness floated in front of her eyes.

Please, somebody, help me, she prayed desperately as nausea swamped her. Suddenly, she was released from his crushing weight. She heard a muffled curse and the soft thud of flesh on flesh. Crawling to the stall's opening, she breathed deep to force back the queasiness. *Travis,* she thought dizzily, as she made out his powerful figure in the dimly lit stable.

He was beating the smaller man with a ruthless determination, knocking him to the floor with crushing blows, only to drag him up again by the shirtfront and send him sprawling once more. George offered no resistance; indeed he could not, she realized as her mind cleared. He was already unconscious. Still, Travis's fist pounded, pulling the man up on his watery legs again and again. He's killing him, she thought suddenly, and sprang to her feet, running toward them.

"No, Travis, you're killing him!" She grabbed the hard, muscular arm. "For the love of God, Travis—you're killing him!"

He jerked back, and for a moment she feared he would brush her off like a fly and finish the man who now lay in a motionless heap on the stable floor. As he turned to face her, Adelia stepped away, frightened by his expression of rage. His face seemed to be carved from granite, his eyes steely blue and penetrating as he stared at her. She trembled at the strong, harsh mask and offered up a silent prayer that she would never have that deadly fury directed at her.

"Are you all right?" His voice was clipped, his eyes boring into hers.

"Aye." She swallowed convulsively, dropping her eyes from his stare. "Oh, Travis, your hands!" Without thought, she took them in her own. "They're bleeding; you'll have to tend to them. I have some salve that's—"

"Damn it, Dee." He yanked his hands away from hers, taking her by the shoulders and tilting her head back so her eyes once more met the icy fury in his. He surveyed the torn blouse, the bruises already in evidence on the creamy skin, the rich hair tousled around her pale face. "How badly did he hurt you?" His voice was low and uneven.

Dee struggled to keep her own voice calm and not give way to the hysteria bubbling below the surface. "Not badly—he just frightened me. He only hit me once." Travis's face suffused with color, dark and angry at her words, his hands tightening uncontrollably on her shoulders. "Is he alive?" she asked, her voice barely audible. Travis let out a long breath, released her, and turned to study the crumpled form.

"Yes, more's the pity. Heaven knows he wouldn't have been if you hadn't intervened. The police will see to him now."

"No!" Her cry of protest brought Travis's attention back to her.

"Adelia . . ." he began slowly. "The man tried to rape you, don't you understand?"

"I know very well what his intentions were." She hugged herself to control the spasmodic trembling assailing her. "But we can't call the police." She rushed on as Travis made no protest. "I don't want Uncle Paddy to know about this. I won't have him worrying and upset because of me. I'm not hurt, and I won't have Uncle Paddy upset—I tell you, I won't!" Her voice rose, and he slipped a gentle arm around her shoulders.

"All right, Dee, all right," he soothed, tightening his grip around her shuddering. "I'll call a couple of men and have him taken off the property. No police." He began to lead her from the stables. "Come on, I'll take you home."

The room began to lurch sickeningly as a roaring sound filled her brain, the dim light ebbing until she could barely see. "Travis." Her voice sounded strange and far away over the deafening roar in her head. "I'm sorry, but I'm going to faint." As she spoke, the darkness closed in and swallowed her.

Adelia opened her eyes slowly, experimentally. There was something cool and wonderful on her forehead, and someone was stroking her cheek and speaking her name. She sighed and closed her eyes again, enjoying the new sensation of pampering, before opening them once more to focus on her surroundings.

The room was lit with a warm glow, the walls a cool, soft ivory trimmed with carved dark wood. She made out a wingback chair and a dark mahogany table on which stood an antique globed lamp that softly lit the room. Her eyes traveled over to the man who knelt beside her and rested on Travis's face.

"I'm in the main house," she stated matter-of-factly, and his expression of concern was transformed into an amused smile.

"Leave it to you not to say the usual 'Where am I?'" He removed the wet cloth from her head and sat down beside her on the long sofa. "I don't know anyone else who could calmly announce she was sorry, she was going to faint, and then proceed to do so."

"I've never fainted before in my life," she told him, mystified. "I'm sure I don't like it."

"Well, your color's better now. I've never seen anyone go so white. You scared the daylights out of me."

"I'm sorry." She gave him a weak smile and sat up. "It was a foolish thing to do, and—" She stopped suddenly as her hand went to her throat, only to find the cross that always hung there missing. "My cross," she stammered, looking down to where her hand rested. "I must have lost it in the stables. I've got to find it." He pushed her back firmly as she attempted to rise.

"You're in no shape to go out there now, Dee," he began, but she cut him off, struggling against his hold.

"I've got to find it. It can't be gone." Her color had drained again, and he pushed her back on the sofa.

"Dee, for heaven's sake, you'll fall flat on your face."

"Let me go. I can't lose it."

He tried to keep his words soothing, feeling helpless against her rising hysteria. He had seen her flaming angry and deeply moved, but never incoherently
desperate, and he struggled to hold both her and his own
temper in check. "Dee," he said shortly, giving her a
small shake. "Get a grip on yourself. It's just a cross."

"It was my mother's. I've got to have it—it's all I
have left of her. It's all I have." She was trembling violently, and he drew her into the warm circle of his arms
and began the ageless comfort of rocking.

"I'll find it for you, don't worry. I'll go back and find
it tonight."

Resting against his strong shoulder, she felt strangely
content, and both panic and the threatened tears dissolved. "Do you promise?"

"Yes, Dee, I promise." He rubbed his cheek against
the silk curtain of her hair, and she wondered suddenly
what it was about a man that made it so good to be
held by one—or was it just one man? Sighing, she
allowed herself another moment's luxury pressed
against him.

"I'm all right now, Mr. Grant." She drew herself
away as far as his arms would permit. "I'm sorry I acted
like that."

"You don't have to be sorry, Dee." His hand lifted
to brush back the full, thick waves that tumbled around
her face. "And it was Travis before; let's leave it at that.
I rather like the way you say it."

She felt her pulse respond to his soft words and
gentle touch, her awareness of him growing until she
thought her veins would burst from the pressure.

"I—Is it that you're implying I have an accent?" Her
brows lifted in mock censure as a defense against the
suddenly dangerous atmosphere.

"No. I'm the one with the accent."

His smile drew one of her own, but the innocent intimacy only heightened her confusion, and she felt her color rise in an unaccustomed blush, her lashes sweeping down like fragile shutters. He grinned at the uncharacteristic shyness before he rose and moved to a small bar across the room.

"I think you could use a drink before I take you home." He lifted a crystal decanter. "Some brandy?"

"Brandy's a stranger to me, but perhaps if you've some Irish . . ." She sat up straighter, grateful for the distance between them.

"I'd be hard pressed not to with Paddy as my trainer," he commented, pouring a small measure of whiskey into a glass. "Here." He walked back to her and offered the glass. "This should steady you and keep you from falling into my arms again."

She took the glass and downed its contents without a shudder as Travis watched with uplifted brows. He looked down at the empty glass she handed him before bursting into gales of laughter.

"And what would you be finding so funny?" Tilting her head, she regarded him with curious eyes.

"That a half-pint like you could down two fingers of whiskey as though it were a cup of tea."

"Aye, well, it comes with the blood, I suppose. I'm not one that drinks often but, when I do, I can handle my liquor—which is more than can be said of that slimy pig of a groom." He turned back to set the empty glass on the bar so that she was unaware of the hardening of his features. "Travis . . ." she said, hesitating over his name, and he turned, relaxing his face into calm lines. "I'm grateful to you for what you did." Standing, she moved until she stood in front of him.

"I'm owing you, Travis, though God Himself knows how I'll ever repay you."

His eyes were intense for a moment, brooding over the face she turned up to his; then his features relaxed into a smile, and he ran his finger down her cheek. "Perhaps one day I'll call in the debt."

The sun streamed onto the kitchen table as Adelia removed the postbreakfast clutter. She was grateful Paddy had noticed nothing amiss, having been fast asleep when, late and disheveled, she had arrived back home. He had greeted her that morning with his usual cheery smile, and she had mirrored it, firmly blocking the memory of her night's encounter from her mind. Hearing footsteps approach the kitchen, she closed the door on the dishwasher.

"I'm just coming, Uncle Paddy. I've got the buttons all figured out now. It's amazing how— Oh!" She stopped as she turned and saw Travis leaning against the doorway. "Good morning." She pushed at her hair as her thought processes skidded to a halt.

"How are you?" He walked toward her, eyes traveling in an intense survey.

"I'm f-fine, just f-fine," she stammered, and despised herself. Will I always behave like this when he comes on me unexpectedly? she demanded of herself, and determinedly offered a slight smile. His hand cupped her chin, and Adelia held very still as he searched her face.

"Are you sure?"

She nodded; then, realizing she had been holding her breath, she let it out slowly. "I'm fine, really." Her eyes traveled past him, and he read her concern easily.

"Paddy's already gone. I told him I needed to speak

with you for a minute." Releasing her chin, Travis reached into his pocket and pulled out her cross and chain.

"Oh, you found it!" Her face lifted to his, illuminating the room more brilliantly than the sun. "Thank you, Travis, for troubling. It means a great deal to me."

"There's no need to thank me, Dee, and it wasn't a question of troubling." He tucked a strand of hair behind her ear in a gentle gesture that threatened to dissolve her knees. "The clasp is broken. I'll have it repaired for you."

"You don't have to do that. I can—"

"I said I'll have it repaired." His voice was firm, and her brows drew together at the underlying anger in his tone. Letting out a long breath, he slipped the cross back into his pocket, then carefully framed her face with his hands. "Adelia, I'm responsible for what happened last night. No, don't argue," he commanded as her mouth opened to contradict. "What happens to you—to the people who work for me—" he amended, "is my responsibility. I wanted you to know I'd found your cross, so you wouldn't worry. I'll have the chain repaired and get it back to you as soon as possible."

"All right," she murmured, finding currents of pleasure brushing along her skin as his hands continued to cup her face as if it were something fragile and precious.

He smiled, and his thumb traced her lips with a teasing lightness. "At times, Dee, you can be surprisingly docile. Then, just when I think you've been halter broken, you start bucking again."

Drawing away, Adelia straightened her shoulders. "I'm not a mare to be pulled about on a lead line."

Smile became grin. Travis tousled her hair before

taking her hand and pulling her from the room. "Maybe you'll find it depends who's holding the line."

The days passed slowly for Adelia as the two main men in her life were absent for a time. Paddy had accompanied Majesty to Florida in preparation for the Flamingo Stakes. She found, for one who had always taken her own self-sufficiency for granted, that the nights grew longer without Paddy's company. The house seemed large and quiet and empty. Alone in the evening, she reflected how easily a heart could be lost to another. In less time than it takes for the moon to go from full glory to a sliver of light, love had swept over her, leaving her vulnerable. Love for Paddy, a sweet, full warmth of belonging, and love for Travis, an aching, spreading need.

She built a fire, though the spring air was kind through open windows, and curled up in front of its company, her head resting on the arm of her chair. Paddy would be home the next day, and she found the knowledge comforting, for with his presence there would not be so many hours alone, so many hours to think. Travis would not leave her thoughts or her heart, and seeing him daily brought as much torment as it did delight.

As the fire grew soft and low in the grate, her mind drifted to him, her lashes fluttering down to conceal her dreams, her hair falling in a curtain against her cheek.

"Dee." She stirred in the twilight world of dreams, sighing as a hand brushed through her hair. "Dee, wake up."

Lids opened slowly, and eyes misted with sleep focused on Travis. Her hand lifted to touch his cheek before fantasy was completely dimmed. "Oh." Dropping her hand, she struggled to sit up, pushing back her hair to look up at him. "Travis." She felt fresh color warm her sleep-flushed cheeks and pulled the neck of her faded blue robe closer together. "I must have fallen asleep."

"If I could have understood how anyone could be comfortable in that position, I would have left you alone." Smiling, he moved from his crouched position to sit on the arm where her cheek had rested.

Desperately aware of his nearness, Adelia pushed far into the corner of the chair, her hands clasped in her lap. "I was just thinking that Uncle Paddy would be home tomorrow," she said with partial honesty.

"Yes. I'd like to have gone with him, but I just couldn't get away." He laid a finger under her chin and lifted it. The dying power of the fire danced in her hair. "You've missed him."

"Aye." Her smile spread as her eyes traveled over his face. "And Majesty as well." His smile answered hers, and as the moment grew long, she felt the need to abort the contact. "I'm sorry Majesty didn't win his race." Her fingers smoothed the skirts of her robe.

"Hmm?" His hands were exploring the flickers of light in her hair, and she repeated her statement in a rush of words.

"Oh, well, he placed and made a good run. Winning takes time, Dee." With a laugh, Travis ruffled her hair. "Time, patience, and strategy. . . . Look, I have something for you." Reaching into his pocket, he drew out her cross. "I didn't have the opportunity to give it to you earlier today."

"Oh, Travis, thank you." She lifted her face again to smile. "It means a great deal."

"I know." Instead of handing it to her, Travis opened

the clasp and slipped the chain around her neck. His
fingers on her skin were warm and gentle, and Adelia
lowered her eyes, struggling not to tremble. "Better?"
he asked when the clasp was secured, and she nodded,
swallowing before the words would come.

"Much better, thank you, Travis."

He studied her bent head a moment; then, taking
her hand, he pulled her to her feet. "Come on, close the
door behind me and go to bed. You're tired." Reaching the door, he paused, one hand on the knob. "You
look like a child." Her chestnut hair hung loose and
heavy over the shoulders of her robe, and he ran a hand
down the length of it. "A child can't be bundled off to
bed without a goodnight kiss," he said softly. Before
she could step away, his hand had circled her neck, his
mouth lowering to linger on her cheek while her lips
parted in hunger. Her hunger was to go unsatisfied,
for his mouth barely brushed her other cheek. As in a
dream, she watched him straighten, then turn to leave,
closing the door gently behind him. . . .

With Paddy's return Royal Meadows threw itself into preparing Majesty for the Blue-Grass
Stakes. The race was a preliminary for the most pres-
tigious race in the country, the Kentucky Derby. Majesty's record was impressive, and his good showing in
Florida had hopes running high for his next venture on
the track.

Adelia leaned on the fence surrounding the track,
chin resting on crossed arms, as Steve Parker, the young
jockey, raced Majesty around the large oval. There had
been an immediate liking between her and the small
man, an easy rapport born of a mutual love of horses.

She watched their progress around the track, enjoying their fluid harmony.

Pushing the button on the stopwatch he was holding, Paddy let out a loud whoop of approval before he handed it to Travis. "If he runs like that in Kentucky, there's not another horse will come within five lengths of him at the finish. He holds the turns like a lover."

"Aye, and he runs for the sheer love of it," Adelia murmured, sighing as Steve brought the colt toward them in a slow walk.

"Let's hope he loves it as much in Kentucky," Travis put in and sauntered over to speak to his jockey.

"Are you excited about your first race, little Dee?" Paddy asked, ruffling her hair.

"You might say I'm a bit excited," she returned with a grin. "My eyes will be glued to the television; not even a ton of dynamite could blast me away."

"Television?" Paddy repeated, the skin crinkling around his eyes as he narrowed them. "What's put it in your mind about television? You'll be coming with us."

"Coming with you?" She stared back in confusion.

"Of course, Adelia." She spun around at Travis's voice, her eyes making contact with his hard chest before she tilted her head back to meet his calm, controlled gaze.

"Now, why would I be doing that?"

"Because," he answered evenly, "I say so."

"Is that the way of it?" she demanded, infuriated by the tone of command in his voice. "Well, if it's a groom you need, there's others who've been here longer. Stan or Tom deserves to go more than me."

"But, Dee," Steve protested with a wide grin as he joined them, "you're much prettier than those two. I'd rather look at you—you'll give me inspiration."

"Inspiration, is it?" she returned, amused by the compliment. "You're mad as a hatter." She turned to Travis again, shifting her eye level by several long inches. "I think you'd best take one of the men," she began, but he cut her off, narrowing his eyes and grabbing her hand.

"Excuse us," he called over his shoulder as he began to stride off, dragging Adelia in his wake. When at last he stopped some distance away, she rounded on him furiously.

"What the devil do you mean racing off like that and carting me behind you?" she panted, outraged. "Your legs are almost as long as my whole body, and I had to fair run to keep up with you."

She glared up at him, a picture of righteous indignation.

"I prefer to argue in private, Adelia," Travis said coolly, meeting her mutinous face with nonchalant command. "I run Royal Meadows and I give the orders." Even through her own anger, Adelia could see the signs of temper held in check; his eyes hard and direct, he was suddenly the essence of the master. "I will not have you countermanding my orders privately, and most certainly not publicly." His words annoyed her further simply because she knew he was right. "You're going to have to get it through that stubborn head of yours that you are no longer in solitary control of what is to be done. Now, I believe the issue here is your presence in Kentucky," he went on calmly, his face expressionless.

"I was telling you—"

"I'm telling you," he interrupted imperiously. "You're going."

Her eyes flashed at the order. Why, she thought, if

it's God's pleasure for me not to be forever bursting with temper did He give me such a demanding one?

"Majesty responds better to you than anyone else," Travis went on. "I want you tending to him." Anger receded slowly at his words, and she dropped her eyes, staring at the ground while she considered his statement. "You'll come to Kentucky because it suits me to have you there, and I'm accustomed to having what suits me." His smile spread in a rapid change of mood as her head snapped up with fresh anger. His hands claimed her waist, then trailed slowly upward, resting on the sides of her firm young breasts as her anger faded into confusion. Lingering, his thumbs caressed in a slow circle, then trailed once in a lazy arch over the subtle curves, pausing at their fullness before moving to rest under their soft swell. Her lips parted, but she found no strength to protest against the unfamiliar intimacy, her body responding to his touch, eclipsing her will. She felt herself rising from the ground, and her hands went to his shoulders automatically to compensate for the loss of gravity.

"Put me down." The order emerged as a trembling whisper, and his smile grew wider before his mouth lowered.

"In a minute."

His mouth was dominant and sure, and her fingers dug into his shoulders as the force of the kiss held her in its prison. With a final flash of lucidity, she knew she could never fight Travis on these terms. Then all was lost in the dark demand of need.

"Steve's right," he murmured, his teeth nibbling at her lip and sending shooting sparks of flame through her veins. "You are prettier than Tom or Stan."

With a final hard, brief kiss, he dropped her back

to the ground, to stride away with casual arrogance, whistling the first few bars of "My Wild Irish Rose." Adelia stood gaping after him, trembling with a confusing mixture of indignation and longing.

CHAPTER 5

Adelia found herself on a plane for the second time in her life. This plane, however, was vastly different from the crowded economy section of the passenger jet in which she had traveled over the Atlantic. Now she was passing over the relatively short distance between Maryland and Kentucky in the lush comfort of Travis's specially equipped private jet. Adelia's attitude during this flight was also a marked variation from her first. She stared, mesmerized, from the window, fascinated by the topography of far-distant West Virginia.

She looked down on patchworks of green and umber dotted by small houses, toy-train cities, and gray ribbons of roads snaking and winding to connect them. There were rivers and pine-topped mountains, their colors soft from her eagle view, and she thought with pleasure that the world was indeed a wondrous place. Engrossed in her new discoveries, she did not notice when Travis sat next to her.

"Enjoying the view, Dee?" he asked at length, smiling at the way she pressed her forehead to the glass like a child at a bakery window. She started at his voice, then turned her head to face him, pushing back the chestnut curls that spilled over her face at the movement.

"Merciful heavens, you're forever surprising me. You move like the wind through a willow."

"Sorry. I'll practice stomping." He grinned and shifted in his seat to regard her more directly. "I've often thought you move like one of those fairies Ireland's so famous for, or maybe one of your leprechauns."

"Oh, well, it can't be both. A leprechaun's not considered a fit associate for a reputable fairy."

"Only a disreputable fairy," he returned, amused at the sobriety of her statement.

"Aye, and for the most part they're on their good behavior, hoping to be readmitted to Paradise on the last day."

"Tossed out, were they?"

"When Satan was rebelling, they stood back from the fighting, not wanting to take sides till they knew how it would end. But since that was their only offense, they were banished to earth instead of tossed into the pit with the rebels."

"Seems fair," Travis concluded with a nod. "As I recall, they have the rather awesome power to turn one into a dog or a pig or something equally undesirable, but are normally disposed to good deeds if treated with the proper respect."

"That's right," she agreed. "How did you know that?"

"Paddy saw to the holes in my education." He leaned over her, smiling, and she pressed back into the cushions, green eyes growing wide. "Relax." His voice tightened in annoyance. "I'm not going to eat you." He fastened the seat belt around her waist and leaned back. "We'll be landing in a minute."

"So soon?" She controlled her voice to casualness while the beating of her heart vibrated in her ears.

"That's right," he answered, matching her tone as he secured his own belt. "You've been staring down at Kentucky for some time now."

With amazing organization and economy of movement, the plane was landed, Majesty was unloaded and transferred to a waiting van, and the travelers were on their way to Churchill Downs.

Adelia's impression of Louisville was vague. Her mind was in the back of the van with Majesty. She worried that he might be frightened and confused by the strange sights and long transport. When she voiced her concern, she was rewarded with a deep, full laugh from Travis. The ominous gleam in her eye was ignored as, chuckling, he informed her that Majesty was a seasoned traveler and took it in his stride.

Her irritation had faded by the time the van reached the extensive stables at Churchill Downs. Travis immediately confirmed the arrangements that had been made for Majesty's stall space and feed.

Travis Grant was well known and highly respected in racing circles. Adelia noted that he was greeted with warmth by the men and women milling around the stable area. He stood head and shoulders above the group, exuding power and a virile masculinity that, she observed with a rude stab of jealousy, was obviously appreciated by the women who greeted him. Infuriated with herself for her own weakness, Adelia turned sharply back to Majesty and led the gleaming colt into his stall.

Time passed swiftly as she tended to the animal's needs, brushing and soothing as she kept up a flow of one-sided chatter. As she was completing her duties, she heard loud footsteps approaching and turned around to see who was causing the din.

"Loud enough?" Travis grinned at her with unexpected boyishness.

"Aye," she agreed and gave him a solemn nod. "You sounded like a herd of great African elephants. You're a funny man, Travis," she commented, tilting her head to the side and studying him.

"Am I, Dee? How?"

"There's times you're like the local squire tossing orders about, and the steel in your eyes could freeze a man in his tracks. Then I think you're a hard man. But then sometimes . . ." Faltering, she shrugged and turned back to Majesty.

"Don't stop now." Deliberately, he turned her back to face him, a faint smile playing on his mouth. "You've intrigued me."

She was uncomfortable now and wishing with a full heart that she would learn to think before speaking. But Travis ignored her expression of embarrassment, hands light but firm on her shoulders, eyes demanding her elaboration.

"Sometimes . . . I've seen you laughing and talking with the men, or carting one of the twins about on your shoulders. And I see the way it is between you and Uncle Paddy, and the way you treat your horses. I think then maybe there's a gentle side, and maybe you're not so hard, after all." She finished in a rush, wishing she had never started, and turned back to give Majesty unnecessary additional attention with the brush.

"That's very interesting," he commented, taking the brush from her hand and continuing the grooming himself. "She's spoiling you," he addressed Majesty, running an affectionate hand along his flank. "She'd stand in here rubbing you down for the next hour if I let her."

She tore her eyes from Travis's fingers as they

stroked the rich chestnut hide. "I don't spoil him; it was just love and care I was giving. We all need that from time to time."

He turned his head and met her eyes with a long, level look. "Yes, we all need that from time to time."

That night, awake in the unfamiliar hotel room, Adelia tossed and turned, ultimately rolling over and pounding her innocent pillow. Love was decidedly uncomfortable, unpredictable, and unwelcome. Sighing, she hugged the pillow she had just beaten, determined to erase incredibly blue eyes from her dreams.

The next morning Adelia had her first real look at Churchill Downs. Leading Majesty from the stables, she stopped as she came to the track, her companion waiting with calm indulgence as she stared in open amazement.

The grounds were enormous, the wide mile-and-a-quarter track encircling a grass field bordered by fences and graced with well-shaped shrubs and flower beds of brilliant color. Moving her eyes over the vast expanse of stands, she wondered somewhat whimsically who would be left to tend to the outside world when they were filled with people. The tops of the stands were roofed, crowned with spires, she noted.

"Something wrong, Dee?" Her observations were interrupted by Travis's question, and she jumped in surprise. "Sorry," he said without bothering to conceal a grin. "Forgot to stomp."

"I should be getting used to it by now." She sighed and began to lead Majesty along once more. "What a grand place this is." Her hand swept in an expressive arch as he fell into step beside her.

"It's one of my favorites. The architecture's basically the same as it was when it was built over a hundred years ago. And, as you well know, it's the most famous track of all because it is here that the Derby is run. And the Derby, everyone remembers. On the first Saturday in May, this ribbon of track is gold, and for a few minutes the world stops, and it's only the race." He turned to her with a smile. "It all comes down to the challenge at the turn for home, when the goal is still a quarter of a mile away. Since eighteen seventy-five the best horses have run here, and the best horses have won here. It's not only the classic race, it's a breeders' race, and there isn't anyone in the States who wouldn't rather produce a winner in this than in any other contest. The winner of a Derby becomes the horse to beat for the rest of the season; the magic stays with him. And this," he continued, giving Majesty a friendly slap on the flank, "is one who likes to win."

"Aye, that he does," she agreed, giving Majesty an indulgent smile. "And he's not shy about his own capabilities. He's feeling pretty sure of himself. He wants the Blue Grass Stakes out of the way so he can move on to the Derby."

"Does he?" The corner of his mouth tilted as Majesty nuzzled Adelia's shoulder. "And how do you feel?" His finger touched her cheek, and she turned to face him. "Do you want the prep race out of the way so you can dive into the Derby?"

"I'm not ready for the first one yet." Adelia shrugged, nearly stumbling as Majesty's head nudged at her back. "It's him that's in the hurry. But I like the looks of this place." Again, she encompassed Churchill Downs with a sweep of the hand. "I like knowing it hasn't changed much in all these years." She began to walk again, at Majesty's urging. "Never did I think to see such a place."

"There are other tracks that are perhaps more eye-catching," he commented, following her fascinated gaze. "At Hialeah in Florida, they have hundreds of pink flamingos in the center-field lake."

Stopping, she turned to him with wide eyes. "I should like to see that."

"I'm sure you will," he murmured, twining his fingers in the ends of her long, silky waves. Then, pulling the brim of her cap down over her eyes, he repeated in a lighter tone, "Yes, Dee, I'm sure you will."

The week moved swiftly, hours crammed with duties and activities. Most of Adelia's time was given to Majesty's care, talking and fondling as much as grooming and seeing to his more practical needs. She spent much of her free time with Steve Parker, teasing him about his girlfriends or watching from the rail as he accustomed Majesty to the track. Other times she spent with Paddy, discussing the Thoroughbred's qualities and the style of the other colts who would compete in the qualifying race.

"The colt that wins is automatically eligible for the Derby," he informed her, giving Majesty a thorough examination as she watched from the stall door. "Of course, Travis nominated this fellow right after he was born, the same way he's entered Solomy's foal, and kept up with the nomination as he got older. He knows when he's got a winner. Travis is a man who keeps one eye on the future."

"He's good with the horses," Adelia commented. The obvious pride and affection in Paddy's voice warmed her. "You can see he cares for them; it's not just a matter of the money they'll bring him."

"Aye, he cares," Paddy agreed, giving Majesty an affectionate slap on the flank. "And he's fierce on the matter of using painkillers or drugs as others have been known to do. If one of Travis's horses isn't up for the race, he doesn't run and that's that. Of course, money's not a problem with Travis, but it wouldn't make any difference if it was, because that's the man he is. Now, he has a practical side as well." He moved from the stall to join Adelia and slipped an arm around her shoulders. "Investments—and he's mighty crafty about them. He knows how to take a purse or the sale of a foal and turn it into more. He's got the touch," Paddy added with a wise nod. "And a time or two, he's stretched my pennies for me, though not on as grand a scale as his. Travis takes care of his own." Squeezing her shoulder, Paddy led Adelia out into the flash of sunlight. She remained silent, thinking of this new aspect of the man she loved.

The sky was overcast on the day of the Blue Grass Stakes. The air was heavy. Lead-gray clouds lay thick as a blanket overhead. Tension seemed to start at Adelia's brow and spread down to her toes; the stillness of the air weighed like a stone at the nape of her neck. To take her thoughts off the coming race she kept both hands and mind busy. Glancing up she saw Travis enter the building. She smiled as he approached.

"I believe that, if you could, you'd get into the silks and ride him today."

"The truth of it is," she began, finding the ease of his smile soothing, "I think I'd be less terrified that way. But I don't think Steve would care for it."

"No." The syllable was accompanied by a slow,

grave nod. "I don't think he would. Come up to the stands with me. Paddy'll take over now."

"Oh, but—" Her objection was neatly cut off as he captured her arm and propelled her to the door. "Wait!" she cried and pivoted to run swiftly back to Majesty, throwing her arms around his neck and whispering in his ear.

When she rejoined Travis, he stared down at her, both amused and frankly curious. "What did you tell him?"

She gave him a mysterious smile for an answer. As they approached the stands, she dug into her back pocket and thrust some bills into his hands. "Will you place a wager for me? I don't know how to go about it."

"A wager?" he repeated, looking down at the two dollars in his hand. Looking up, his features were entirely too serious. "Who do you want to bet on?"

"Majesty, of course." She frowned at the question, her expression lightening as she recalled some of the terms she had heard tossed around the stables. "To win . . . on the nose."

To his credit, Travis's features remained grave. "I see. Well, let's see . . . his odds are five to two at the moment." Brows drawn, he studied the odds board. "Now, number three there is ten to one, but that's not too long for a gambler. Number six is two to one; that's rather conservative."

"I don't know about all that," she interrupted with a frustrated wave of her hand. "It's just all a bunch of numbers."

"Adelia." He said her name slowly, giving her a small pat on the shoulder. "One must never bet unless one knows the odds." Ignoring her, he glanced up at the flashing numbers. "It's three to one on number two, a

nice safe choice for win, place, or show. It's eight to five
on number one."

"Travis, you're making my head spin with all of
this. I just want to—"

"And fifteen to one on number five." He looked
down at the two crumpled bills. "You could amass a
small fortune if that one came in."

"It's not for the money." Her breath came out in
one impatient huff. "It's for the luck."

"Ah, I see," he returned with a solemn nod before
the grin escaped and spread. "Irish luck is not to be
scoffed at."

Though she scowled quite fiercely for a moment,
he slipped his arm over her shoulders and led her to
the two-dollar window.

Before long, she was standing next to him and gaping openly at the masses of people filling the stands.
The enormous stadium would hold one hundred and
twenty-five thousand, Travis had informed her, and to
her astonished eyes there seemed to be no less than
that. Several people greeted Travis, and she felt an occasional twinge of discomfort as eyes often passed
over her in speculation. Embarrassment was soon
eclipsed by excitement as post time approached. She
watched the horses step onto the track, her eyes immediately focusing on Majesty and the rider in brilliant
red and gold silks on his back. As Majesty's name was
announced, Adelia closed her eyes, finding the combination of excitement and nerves nearly overpowering.

"He looked ready," Travis commented casually,
then laughed as she jolted at his words. "Relax, Dee,
it's just another race."

"I'll never be easy about it if I see a hundred," she
vowed. "Oh, here comes Uncle Paddy. Is it going to
start?"

For answer, he pointed, and she watched the horses being loaded into the starting gate. Her hand clutched at the cross at her neck, and she felt Travis's arm slip over her shoulders as the bell sounded and ten powerful forms lunged forward.

It seemed to her a mass of flying hooves and thunderous noise, the pack clinging together in one speeding block. Still, her eyes were glued on Majesty as though he were racing alone. Her hand reached up of its own accord to grasp the one on her shoulder, tightening as she urged the colt to greater speed. Steadily he moved forward, as if following her remote-control command, persistently passing one, then another, until he emerged alone from the field. Suddenly the long legs increased their stride, streaking across the dirt track until his competitors were left with the sight of his massive hindquarters as he lunged under the wire.

Travis's arm encircled her, and Adelia found herself crushed to his hard chest, sandwiched between his lean body and her uncle's stocky frame. It was like being caught fast between two unmoving, loving walls, and she found the sensation torturously wonderful, a heady mixture of scents and textures. Her uncle's voice was raised in excitement in her ears, and her head was snuggled, as if it belonged, against Travis's chest. Majesty's win, she decided, closing her eyes, was the best present she had ever had.

Every man, woman, and child in Louisville ate, slept, and breathed the Kentucky Derby. As the days dwindled, the very air seemed to shimmer with anticipation. Adelia saw Travis sporadically. Their conversations revolved around the colt, the only personal aspect of their relationship being the abstracted pat on

the head he would give her from time to time. She began to think that quarreling with him had had its advantages, and she relieved her frustrations by spending
more time with Majesty.

"You're a fine, great horse," she told him, holding
his muzzle and looking into his intelligent eyes. "But
you mustn't let all of this go to your head. You've a job
to do come Saturday, and it's a big one. Now, I'm going
out for a few minutes, and I want you to rest yourself,
then perhaps we'll see about a currying."

Satisfied with Majesty's silent agreement, Adelia
stepped out of the stables into the bright May sun and
found herself surrounded by reporters.

"Are you the groom in charge of Royal Meadows'
Majesty?" The question was fired out by one of the people who suddenly cut her off from the rest of the world
with a wall of bodies. The sensation was disconcerting,
and she was thinking wistfully of the dim solitude of
the stables when she heard another voice.

"You don't see many grooms that look like this one."

She rounded on the man who had spoken, squint-
ing against the sun to see more clearly. "Is that the
truth, now?" she demanded, discomfort replaced by annoyance. "I thought red hair was common enough in
America."

The group roared with laughter, and the man at
whom her remark had been directed responded with a
good-natured grin. Questions were fired at her, and for
a few moments she surrendered to the pressure and answered, valiantly attempting to keep one query separate from the next.

"By the saints!" She threw up her hands in dismay,
shaking her head. "You're all speaking in a muddle."
Pushing the brim of her cap back from her head,
she took a deep breath. "If it's more information

you're wanting, you'd best ask Mr. Grant or Majesty's trainer." She pushed through them with determination, turning when she felt a hand on her arm and finding herself facing the reporter who had made the personal observation.

"Miss Cunnane, sorry if we were a little rough on you." He smiled with considerable charm, and Adelia found herself smiling back.

"No harm was done."

"I'm Jack Gordon. Maybe you'd let me make it up to you by taking you out to dinner tonight."

She was both surprised and flattered by the invitation, gaining the pure feminine pleasure of having an attractive man pay her specific attention. He was, however, a stranger, and she was opening her mouth to decline when a voice sounded behind her.

"Sorry, my groom's off limits."

She whirled around to see Travis watching them, blue eyes cool and direct. Fury bubbled inside her, reflecting plainly in her flashing eyes.

"Don't you have some work to do, Adelia?" he asked with an imperial lift of brows. The eyes that met his told him without words what she thought of his question before she wheeled around and stalked to the stables.

Some fifteen minutes later, Travis disengaged himself from the avid reporters and joined her. She watched as he strode toward her, hands carelessly thrust in the pockets of slim-fitting jeans.

"Don't you know better than to make dates with strange men, Adelia?" His tone was deliberate, superior, and infuriating.

"My personal life is my own affair," she raged at him. "You've no right to interfere."

"As long as you're in my employ and responsible for my horses, your life is my affair."

"Aye, Master Grant," she tossed back, undaunted by the narrowing of his eyes. "I'll be certain to ask your permission before I take my next breath." Her foot stomped in temper. "I didn't arrive on this earth yesterday. I can take care of myself."

"Were you taking care of yourself in the stables a couple of weeks ago?" She paled at this and turned away. With a muttered curse, he turned her around to face him. "Dee, I'm sorry. That wasn't fair."

"No, it wasn't." She jerked away, eyes bright with angry tears. "But it doesn't surprise me you'd be saying it. You've a habit of putting me in my place, Master Grant, and I've been reminded there's work to be done. So be off with you and let me be about it." Removing her cap, she dropped a curtsy. "If it please Your Honor."

"I've had just about enough, you green-eyed witch," he muttered, taking a step toward her. "I'd like to haul you over my knee for the spanking you deserve, but I'll get more out of this sort of punishment."

He had her crushed against him with a speed that allowed her only a short gasp of protest before his mouth descended, hard, then demanding, then possessing, in rapid succession. When he lifted his mouth, she felt him drawing her soul through her eyes.

"I'm not going to make a habit of this," he muttered and took her lips again, his fingers tangling in her hair, then moving over her back until she thought she would perish from the heat.

Feather-light tremors followed the trail of his hand along her spine, touching her with an exquisite fear. She felt the pressure of his arms bending her back, his mouth hard on hers, demanding not response but submission. She became aware of her own slightness, a fragility she had never known was part of her, as his strength overpowered even the thought of struggle. Lucidity drifted from her, leaving only the feel of a hard body and a demanding mouth, which took from her until it was impossible even to breathe.

Drawing away, Travis held Dee steady as she staggered. He stood a moment looking down thoughtfully into her flushed face. "You know, Dee," he said at length, his voice as calm and unperturbed as she was ruffled and confused, "you're too little to possess such a dangerous temper."

Flicking a friendly finger down her nose, he strode out into the sunshine.

The day of the Derby was an advertisement for spring, warm with a soft, scented breeze under a clear, cloudless sky. The perfection of the weather meant nothing to Adelia, whose nerves were so tightly coiled that it could have easily been midwinter. Seeing Travis several times during the morning and early afternoon, she was both envious and annoyed by his calm, easygoing manner while she remained a massive bundle of quivering nerves. Between the lingering sensation of her last encounter with him and the prospect of the race, she found functioning at even borderline normality an effort. Waiting through the preliminary races was sheer torture.

She found herself beside Travis in the stands, thinking that if the race did not begin soon, she would have to be carted away and locked up until it was over.

"Here." Adelia glanced down at the glass he offered before raising her eyes to his.

"What is it?"

"A mint julep." Taking her hand, he placed the glass in it and curled her fingers around it. "Drink it," he commanded, then smiled at the frown she gave it.

"The purpose is twofold. One, it's traditional, and you can keep the glass to remember your first Derby. And two," he continued, grinning, "you need something to calm your nerves; I'm afraid you're going to keel over."

"So am I," she admitted and sipped gingerly from the glass. "Travis, I would swear there are more people here than the last time. Where do they all come from?"

"Everywhere," he returned easily, following her fascinated gaze. "The Run for the Roses is the most important race of the season."

"Why do they call it that?" she asked, finding the combination of conversation and mint julep soothing.

"The winner's draped with a blanket of red roses in the Winner's Circle, and the jockey gets an armful. So," he concluded and lifted his own glass, "it's the Run for the Roses."

"That's nice," she approved, lifting the brim of her cap further on her head. "Majesty will like red roses."

"I'm sure he'll be crazy about them," Travis agreed with suspicious sobriety, and Adelia's dignified retort was interrupted by the first strains of "My Old Kentucky Home."

"Oh, Travis, the parade's starting!" She fastened her eyes on Majesty and the small man on his back, clad in colorful red and gold silks. The others with their brilliant contrasts of blues and greens and yellows paled before her eyes. To her there was not another animal to compare in power and beauty with Travis's Thoroughbred colt—and, judging by the way Majesty pranced, he agreed completely.

"Saints preserve us, Uncle Paddy," she murmured as he appeared at her side. "My heart's pounding so I'm sure it'll burst. I don't think I'm made for this."

Her eyes never left Majesty's form as he was loaded into the gate. Her senses swam with the blare of the trumpets and the roar of the crowd. With a swiftness that took her breath away, the doors were released and the horses sprang forward in a turbulent herd.

Her eyes followed the colt as he galloped with steady assurance around the track. She was not even aware that as the bell had rung she had grabbed Travis's hand in a viselike grip, squeezing tighter as each heart-pounding second passed. The air shivered with the voice of the crowd, individual calls and shouts melding into one trembling roar. She rode every inch of the track on Majesty's back, feeling the rush of wind on her face and the strong rhythm of the colt's gait under her.

As they rounded the second turn, Steve brought Majesty to the inside rail, and the colt took his head and left the field with long, smooth strides. The gap between the chestnut and his nearest competitor widened with what appeared to be effortless ease as he streaked down the back stretch into the home stretch and under the wire more than four lengths in the lead.

Without hesitation, Adelia threw herself into Travis's arms, clinging with a joy she could only express physically by babbling incoherent and self-interrupted sentences to both him and her uncle, who was improvising an enthusiastic jig beside her.

"Come on." Travis tossed an arm around Paddy's shoulders. "We've got to get down to the Winner's Circle before the crowd's too thick."

"I'll wait for you." Adelia pulled back, stooping to retrieve her dislodged cap. "I don't like all those reporters staring and snapping and jumping all over me with their questions. I'll wait on the outside and take Majesty along when it's over."

"All right," Travis agreed. "But tonight, we celebrate. What do you say, Paddy?"

"I say I've just acquired a strong yearning for champagne." The two men grinned at each other.

That evening, Adelia stared at the reflection in the full-length mirror of her room. Her hair lay full and lush on her shoulders, shining like newly minted copper against the muted greens of her dress.

"Well, Adelia Cunnane, look at you." She smiled with satisfaction into the mirror. "There's not a one back in Skibbereen who'd be knowing you in such a dress, and that's the truth of it." A knock sounded at her door, and she plucked her key from the dresser. "I'm coming, Uncle Paddy."

Opening the door with a dazzling smile, she was not greeted by her merry-faced uncle but by an incredibly attractive Travis in a dark dinner suit, the white silk of his shirt startling against his deep tan. They stood silently for a moment as his gaze roamed over her, from shining hair and deep green eyes to the soft, rounded curves outlined by the clinging jersey. His gaze rose to her face again, but still he did not smile.

"Well, Adelia, you're astonishingly beautiful."

Her eyes widened at the compliment, and she searched for something suitable to say. "Thank you," she finally managed. "I thought you'd be Uncle Paddy."

His eyes continued to hold her in the doorway, and she moistened her lips with the tip of her tongue in an innocently inviting gesture. "Paddy's meeting us downstairs with Steve."

The single-minded intensity with which she was being studied was rapidly stripping her of all composure, and her words tumbled out quickly. "We'd best be joining them—they'll be waiting."

Travis merely nodded, a slight inclination of his

head, and she took a step toward him, only to stop nervously when he made no move to let her pass. Raising her eyes from his shirtfront to his face, she opened her mouth to speak, only to find her mind a vacuum. He gazed down at her for another unnerving moment, then held up a single red rose, placing it in her hand.

"Majesty sent it. He says you're fond of red roses."

"Oh." He was not smiling with the whimsy of his words, and her mind fidgeted for something to ease the sudden awareness, the physical strength of his gaze. "I didn't know you talked to horses."

"I'm learning," he answered simply, and ran a finger over her bare shoulder. "My teacher's an expert."

She dropped her eyes to the bloom in her hand, thinking that twice in her life she had been given flowers, and both times they had come from Travis, both times they had been red roses. She smiled, knowing she would never again see a red rose without thinking of him. That was a gift more precious than jewels. Open and innocent, her smile lifted for him.

"Thank you, Travis, for bringing it to me." On impulse, she rose to her toes and kissed his cheek.

He stared down at her, and for a moment Adelia thought she saw some hesitation, some indecision, flicker in his eyes before his features relaxed into a smile.

"You're welcome, Dee. Bring it along—it suits you." Taking the key from her hand, he placed it in his pocket and led her to the elevator.

The celebration dinner was a new experience for Adelia. The elegant restaurant, the unaccustomed dishes, and her first encounter with champagne combined to give her a glowing sense of unreality. The tension brought on by the few moments alone with Travis was dispelled by his casually friendly attitude during the meal. It was almost as though the awareness that had passed between them had never taken place. The evening drifted by in a haze of happiness.

The following week, however, found her back in Maryland in jeans and cap, busily fulfilling her duties and thrusting elegant meals and fancy dresses from her mind. Long hours of grooming, exercising, and training filled the days, giving her little time to dwell on the strange new emotions Travis had aroused. She avoided the reporters who were often hovering around the track and stables, not wishing to be cornered again and bombarded with questions. At night, however, she was less successful in avoiding the dreams that assaulted her awakened senses.

Days passed into weeks, and although Adelia gave all the Thoroughbreds love and attention, she continued to dote on Majesty.

"Don't forget yourself just because you've had your picture in some fancy magazines," she admonished him, failing to keep her voice stern as she completed his grooming.

Paddy strolled into the stables and laid a hand on her shoulder. "Keeping him in line, are you, little Dee? Don't want him too big for his breeches, do we?"

"That we don't." Turning, she smiled at her uncle, then studied him carefully. "You look tired, Uncle Paddy. Aren't you feeling well?"

"I'm fine, Dee, just fine." He patted her rosy cheek and winked at her. "I think I'll sleep for a week when the Belmont's come and gone."

"You've earned a rest; you've been working hard and long. You're a bit pale. Are you sure—"

"Now, don't fuss," he interrupted with a good-natured scowl. "Nothing worse than a fussing woman. Just be keeping your mind on this lad here." He patted

Majesty's side. "Don't you worry about Paddy Cunnane."

She let this pass, vowing silently to keep her eye on him. "Uncle Paddy, is the Belmont important?"

"Every race is important, darlin', and this is one of the top. Now, this fellow here, with that barrel of a chest"—he inclined his head toward Majesty and winked again—"he'll do well there. It's a long race, a mile and a half, and that's what he was bred for. A distance runner, and one of the finest. Not like Fortune, mind you; he's a sprinter and can beat almost anything at a shorter distance. Travis is smart enough to breed horses with both distance and sprinting in mind. That's why he put Fortune in the Preakness at Pimlico, and he was second by half a length. And that's just fine. But this one's for the Belmont." He shook Majesty's head lightly by the muzzle. "And so are you," he added, giving Adelia a pat on the head.

"Me? Am I going as well?"

"That's right. Hasn't Travis told you?"

"Well, no. I haven't seen much of him since we got back from Kentucky."

"He's been busy."

Her answer was absent as she considered the wisdom of attempting to refuse. Recalling the result of her previous attempt, Adelia thought New York might be a fine place to visit.

Belmont Park, on Long Island, was alive with reporters. Adelia managed to stay in the background the majority of the time and, when cornered, she escaped as soon as possible. She was unaware of the speculation about her and her relationship with the owner of Royal Meadows' Majesty. The casual attire of jeans and shirt did nothing to conceal the appeal of her beauty, and her reluctance to speak with the press added a mystery that acted as a meaty bone to the hungry pack of reporters. At times she felt hounded and wished she had stood firm and refused to come. Then she would see Travis as he moved toward the stables, hands in pockets, hair ruffled by the breeze. She would admit, though it brought little comfort, that she would have gone mad had she been left behind.

Newspapers and nagging reporters were not in Adelia's thoughts as she joined Travis for the third time in the crowded stands. She noticed, with some discomfort, that Belmont and its occupants were more sophisticated than Churchill Downs. There, size had been offset by an old-world charm, the soft, lazy accent of Louisville. Somehow, Belmont seemed more vast, more intimidating, and beside the sophistication of the elegantly groomed women who occupied the stands and clubhouse, Adelia felt inadequate and naive.

Silly, she told herself and straightened her shoulders. I can't be like them, and they're certainly taking no notice of me, in any case. Most of these fine ladies can't keep their eyes off Travis. I suppose these are the kind of ladies he sees at his country club, or takes out for a quiet dinner. Depression threatened to settle over her like a black cloud, but she took a deep breath and blew it away.

Adelia had lectured herself that by this time she should be accustomed to the tension and the crush of people, but as post time drew closer she felt the familiar anxiety and undeniable excitement capture her. She could find neither words nor ability to speak, and stood gripping the rail with both hands as Majesty strutted to the starting gate. He was impatient, she observed, sidestepping and lifting his front legs in small, nervous prancing steps as Steve struggled to control him, urging him forward into his place in the starting gate.

"I'll have to bring you to the track more often, Dee." Travis gave her shoulder a small squeeze. "In a couple of months, you'll be a veteran."

"I'll never be a veteran, I'm afraid, because each time it seems like the first. I can hardly bear it."

"I'm going to keep bringing you in any case," he informed her, tangling his fingers for a moment in the ends of her hair. "You bring the excitement back. I believe I'd been taking it for granted."

She turned to him, nonplussed by the gentle tone of his voice, and had opened her mouth to speak when the bell shrilled with the roar of the crowd. Brilliant silks were now a soft blur as Thoroughbreds thundered around the track. After the first turn the field dispersed, transforming from a single mount of speeding legs to a zigzagging cluster of gleaming bodies. To Adelia, Majesty seemed to weave his way through them like a fiery comet, passing one after another until he bore down on the leader. Then, as if a switch had been flicked, came the power, the lengthening of stride, the rippling of muscles, the steady increase of his lead, until Majesty flew down the home stretch, capturing the coveted Belmont with power and style.

The crowd went wild, cheering and shouting with one deafening voice. Adelia's feet left the ground as Travis lifted her, swinging her in circles as she clung to his neck. He continued to hold her as Paddy's arms came around them both, drawing them all together in joy and excitement. The words shouted were senseless to her, and she told herself later that it was the temporary insanity of the moment that had caused her to meet Travis's lips with hers. Even on later reflection, she was unclear who had initiated the kiss, but she knew she had responded. She had flung her arms around his neck, and the thrill that had coursed through her had eclipsed even the rushing flurry of the race. When her feet touched the ground, and Travis lifted his mouth from hers, her head was still spinning with light and color, her body trembling with the backlash of emotion, the tidal wave of sensation. She could do no more than stare up at him. For a moment, it was the same as the day the foal had been born, and the crowded, noisy stands of Belmont Park faded into a solitary, private world. She was oblivious to the throng and the curious stares, aware only of his arms around her, and the feeling that she was slowly, helplessly drowning in his eyes.

"We'd best be going down, lad." Paddy made a business of clearing his throat before he laid a hand on Travis's shoulder. Her knees weakened as his eyes left hers to meet her uncle's. She felt the sudden dizziness and disorientation of one who had been awakened from a dream too quickly.

"Yes." Travis grinned, the quick-spreading grin of a boy. "Let's go congratulate the winner. Come on." Spinning Adelia around, he began to lead her away.

"I'm not going down there," she objected, making a futile attempt to hold her ground.

"Yes, you are," he disagreed, not bothering to glance back at her. "I let you have your way before, not this time. You're coming down to help Majesty accept his flowers, white carnations this time, and one's for you."

Her sputtering objections and attempts to disentangle herself went unheeded, and she found herself in the Winner's Circle with the others.

There were microphones and the flash of lights, and she faded into the background as far as possible. She was still shaken by the intensity of need that had flowed through her in Travis's embrace, a strong, wild desire to belong to him completely. It was like being assailed with an unquenchable thirst, and the sensation terrified her. Her morals were deeply rooted, a melding of religious and personal beliefs. She knew, however, that her longing for Travis, her love for him, made her weak, and any resistance would melt as quickly as springtime snow if he pressed his advantage.

She must stay away from him, she determined, avoid situations where they would be alone and she would be vulnerable to his experience and her frailty. As she glanced over at his tall, lean frame, their eyes locked, and she trembled. Her lashes swept down, and she realized helplessly what a rabbit feels when cornered by a strong, sleek fox.

CHAPTER 6

B ack at the hotel, Adelia accompanied Paddy to his room, having no wish to be alone with her thoughts. Travis walked down the carpeted hall with them, pausing at the doorway as she slipped through.

"I've made reservations for us." His teeth flashed in a grin. "Steve's doing his own celebrating with a little lady who's been dogging his footsteps since the Derby."

"Ah, Travis." Paddy sat down heavily on the bed. "You'll have to do without this tired old man. I'm weary to the bone." He gave a smile and a shake of his head. "I've had all the excitement I can stand for today. I'll play lord of the manor and have my dinner in bed like royalty."

"Uncle Paddy." Adelia moved closer, dropping a hand on his brow. "You're not feeling well. I'll stay with you."

"Go on with you." He made a dismissing gesture with his hand. "Fussing like your grandmother used to. It's tired I am, not sick. The next thing I know you'll be pouring some strange remedy down my throat or threatening me with a poultice." He glanced up at Travis with a long-suffering sigh. "She's a worrisome bundle, lad. Take her off my hands and give these old bones a rest."

With a nod of masculine understanding, Travis turned to Adelia. "Be ready in forty-five minutes," he stated simply. "I don't like to be late."

"'Do this, do that,'" she fumed, throwing up her hands. "Never a 'will you' or 'may I.' I'm not in the stables now, Travis Grant, and I don't fancy being ordered about." She tossed back her fiery curls and folded her arms across her chest.

Travis raised a quizzical eyebrow before he moved to the door. "Wear that green thing, Dee. I like it." He closed the door against any possible further outbursts.

Dee was ready at the appointed time, having been cajoled by her uncle to leave him and celebrate Majesty's victory. Telling herself she was only going out with the arrogant brute for Paddy's sake, she zipped herself into the green dress as a knock sounded at her door. Muttering disjointedly about the devil's own spawn, she swung open the door and glared.

"Good evening, Adelia," he greeted her, obviously unconcerned by her warlike stance. "You're looking lovely. Are you ready?"

She glowered at him for another moment, wishing she had something handy to throw at him. Tilting her chin, she stepped into the hall, closing the door with force behind her.

She clung to her stubborn silence as the taxi drove through surging traffic, but Travis remained unperturbed, chatting amiably and pointing out various spots of interest. He was making it very difficult for her to keep her anger on the boil.

Defiance wavered as they entered the restaurant, grander than she could ever have imagined. Wide-eyed, she gazed around her at the sophisticated patrons in their evening dress. She allowed herself to be led unresisting to a quiet corner table, greatly impressed by the elegance of the maitre d'. Softly lit and situated for privacy, the table sat high above the throbbing city, the lights blinking and speeding below a direct contrast to their quiet seclusion. She glanced up as their waiter requested her choice of cocktail, then looked across at Travis with a helpless shake of her head. Smiling, he ordered champagne.

"It's a shame we couldn't bring Majesty with us," she commented, then grinned, animosity forgotten. "He did all the work, and we're drinking the champagne."

"I very much doubt he'd appreciate it even if we took him back a bottle. For a Royal steed, he has the taste of a peasant. So"—he paused, allowing his finger to rub gently over her hand as it rested on the cloth—"it's up to us to drink to his victory. Did you know, Adelia, the candlelight scatters gold through your eyes?"

Surprised by his sudden observation, she merely stared, greatly relieved when the arrival of the champagne saved her from inventing a response.

"Shall we have a toast, Dee?"

Lifting the slender-stemmed glass, she smiled, more at ease. "To Majesty, the winner of the Belmont Stakes."

His lips curved as he copied her gesture. "To winning."

"Hungry?" he asked after an interlude of quiet conversation. "What's your pleasure?"

"Well, it won't be mutton and potatoes," she mur-

mured absently, sighing at the strange workings of the
world that had shifted her into a new life. Her attention
came to a full stop as she glanced over the menu, her
eyes lifting to his, wide and astonished.

"Is something wrong?"

"It's robbery, sure as faith; there's not another word
for it!"

He leaned forward, taking both her hands in his
and grinning at her anxious expression. "Are you
sure there's no Scots blood in you?" Adelia opened
her mouth to retort, highly insulted, but he raised her
hands to his lips, causing the words to die before they
were born. "Don't get your Irish up, Dee." He smiled
over their joined hands. "And overlook the prices. I'm
able to deal with them."

She shook her head. "I can't look at it again—it
makes my head spin. I'll have what you have."

Chuckling, he ordered the meal and more wine as
his hands held hers captive. When they were once more
alone, he turned her hands over, examining her palms,
ignoring the sharp jerk she made to release herself.

"You're taking better care of them," he murmured,
rubbing his thumb over her skin.

"Aye," she retorted, embarrassed and resentful.
"They're not quite as bad as a ditchdigger's these days."

He raised his eyes to hers, watching her a moment without speaking. "I offended you that night. I'm
sorry." His gentle tone tilted her balance, and she felt
the familiar weakness flowing into her.

"It doesn't matter," she stammered and shrugged
and tugged at her hands again. He ignored both verbal
and physical protests.

"You have fascinating hands. I've made quite a study
of them. Small, exquisite, and totally capable—the
three rarely go together. Capable Adelia," he murmured

before his eyes fastened on hers again with an intensity that caught her off guard. "You had a bad time on that farm, didn't you?"

"I—no. No, we got along."

"Got along?" he repeated, and she felt his eyes searching her face for the words she was not saying.

"We did what needed to be done." She spoke lightly, not sure what it was he wanted from her. "Aunt Lettie was a strong, stubborn woman, and not one to be beaten easily. I often thought it strange how little she was like Da," she continued, her expression drifting into introspection. "And now I see how little she was like Uncle Paddy, for all she was their sister. Perhaps it was the demands of having to take on me and the farm that left her so little time for the gentler things. Such small things: a kiss goodnight, a word of affection . . . a child can starve with a full plate."

She brought herself back with a shake of the head, surprised by her own words and uneasy under his glance. She groped for some way to turn the subject. "I only had the farm to concern me; she had the farm and me, and I think I was more trouble than the farm." She smiled, willing him to lighten his features with one of his own. "She told me a time or two I had too loose a grip on my temper, but, of course, I've tightened the hold now."

"Have you?" At last the smile curved his mouth.

"Oh, aye." She gave him a solemn and guileless nod. "I'm a very mild sort of person."

The smile spread to a grin as their meal was set before them. As they ate, conversation drifted into generalities, an easy flow of words, as undemanding and soothing as the wine that accompanied the food.

"Come," he said suddenly and rose. "Dance with me."

Before she could voice agreement or protest, she found herself being led to the dance floor and enfolded in his all too familiar arms. Her first stiffness at the contact melted as she relaxed against him, surrendering herself to his movements and the quiet music. Surely, she decided, allowing both mind and body to float, everyone's entitled to a taste of heaven. Tonight I'm taking mine. Tomorrow will come, all too soon.

The night was magic, as if a fairy had granted her a wish, and the very briefness of it heightened her senses. She tucked all the sights and sensations into a corner of her mind to be treasured and sighed over when day broke the spell.

It was late when they stepped into the warm night, and though Adelia's eyes were heavy, she wished the evening were just beginning. Clinging to the last enchanted minutes, she made no objection when Travis drew her close to his side in the cab.

"Tired, Dee?" he murmured, his lips brushing the top of her head so lightly she was not sure she hadn't imagined it.

"No," she said in a sigh, thinking how right her head felt cushioned against his shoulder.

He laughed softly, his voice slow and warm, and his fingers stroked through the silk of her hair until her mind drifted into the world of half-dreams.

"Dee?" She heard her name but, loath to rouse herself from the heavenly comfort, she made a small murmur of protest. "We're back," Travis announced, lifting her chin with his finger.

"Back?" Her heavy lids opened, and she stared at the face so close to hers, dreams and reality mixed into confusion.

"At the hotel," he explained, brushing tumbled hair back from her face.

"Oh." She sat up, realizing the dream was over.

He was silent on the elevator ride to their floor, and Adelia used the time to regain her grip on reality. They moved to her door, and Travis removed her key from his pocket to unlock it as she raised her head to thank him. The smile she meant to accompany her thanks faded as she met his eyes. The concentrated, steady look caused her to step backward, only to find herself trapped against the doorframe, while he closed the distance without seeming to move at all. His hand slipped beneath the curtain of her hair, while he caressed her neck in a slow, lazy motion. They gazed silently at each other; then, very slowly, he lowered his head and pressed his mouth to hers in a kiss that was as soft as a summer breeze, unlike the others he had given and ultimately more devastating. She clung to the lapels of his jacket, trying to steady her world, but soon gave up all such efforts and moved her arms to encircle his neck, rising on her toes to meet him demand for demand.

His lips moved to trail along her face, brushing easily along cheeks and closed lids as if savoring the taste. Trembling heat was replaced by a new and poignant languor, a weak giddiness induced by a far more potent potion than champagne. Her hands moved to tangle in his hair as her body melted to his, submitting to whatever he would ask, willing to give whatever he would take.

She felt his hunger when his mouth took hers again, the hardness of his body as he pressed her more urgently against him, and with a moan of pleasure at the new demand, she drew him yet closer. The longing to be possessed, insistent and clamorous, raged through her like fire. She strained against him, her heart throbbing and echoing in her ears as she felt him devour what was offered, then demand more.

Abruptly he released her mouth, his hand moving to brush against her cheek and linger a moment, and she closed her eyes again, inviting his lips to claim hers.

"Goodnight, Dee," he murmured, and giving her a nudge into the room, he closed the door between them.

Adelia stared at the smooth, empty panel, bringing her hands to burning cheeks. Stunned both by her unprecedented actions and by the sudden rejection, she found it impossible to move. She had offered, and he had refused. Even in her inexperience, she knew her willingness could not have been mistaken for anything other than full surrender. But he had not wanted her, not completely. Her own standards had dissolved in his arms, but he had walked away and left her alone. And how else could it be? she asked herself, shutting eyes tight on threatening moisture. I could never be anything to him but a groom for his horses. Someone who amuses him from time to time. He was only being kind to me, trying to show me a pleasant evening. She trembled once. *I should be content with that and stop searching for what can never be mine.* Glancing down at the soft folds of her dress, Adelia reminded herself she was not Cinderella, and in any case it was long past midnight.

They boarded the plane the next morning in a warm, light drizzle. Again, reporters hounded them. Adelia scurried up the ramp, leaving the men to deal with them. Shaking raindrops from her hair and her cream-colored skirt, she pressed her face to a window and watched Travis disengage himself from the press.

During the flight, she skimmed through a magazine, reluctant to enter into conversation. Travis's attitude toward her that morning had been casual, friendly, and vaguely preoccupied, and the stirring need in her that lingered from their previous evening made it a strain for her to mirror his mood.

When he disappeared into the forward cabin with Steve, she let out a deep breath and began to pace the lounge. What am I to do? she asked herself desperately. How can I control the way he makes me feel? I'll be making a fool of myself over him; he's bound to see the way I love him. Then he'll be feeling sorry for me, and I couldn't stand that. I'll just have to find a way to keep more distance between us.

Her gaze wandered over to her uncle, all thoughts of her problem fleeing her mind as she observed the unhealthy cast to his normally ruddy skin.

"Uncle Paddy." She moved to him, cupping his face in her hands and studying him carefully. "You're not well. What is it?"

"Nothing, Dee." The strain in his voice drew her brows together. "I'm just tired."

"You're like ice." She knelt down in front of him so that their faces were level. "You see a doctor the minute we get home. It won't be long now. I'll fetch you a cover and a cup of tea."

"Now, Dee, I'm just feeling my age." He stopped and grimaced in pain.

"What is it?" she demanded, hands already searching to comfort. "Where are you hurting?"

"Just a twinge." The words came out in jerks before he began to gasp for air.

"Uncle Paddy! Merciful heaven, Uncle Paddy!" She clutched at him as he collapsed, falling forward out of the chair and into her arms.

She was not even aware that she shouted for Travis over and over, desperately, helplessly, as she lowered her uncle onto the floor. But suddenly he was there, brushing her hands aside, his head lowering to the stocky chest.

"Tell John to radio ahead for an ambulance," he called to Steve over his shoulder, his hands beginning to push in a steady rhythm on Paddy's chest. "He's had a heart attack."

With a moan, Adelia clutched Paddy's hand to her own heart as if to transfer her strength. "Travis, in the name of heaven—Travis, is he dying? Oh, please, he can't be dying."

"Stop it," he commanded sharply, the words as effective as a slap. "Pull yourself together. I can't deal with this and hysterics as well."

One breath came and went quickly, then she took several more, deep and steady, her hand clutching and unclutching convulsively over Paddy's. Slowly the hysteria was buried under a wall of control, and she began to stroke her uncle's head and speak in soft, reassuring tones, though she knew he probably couldn't hear her.

Seconds dragged and minutes crawled with Travis continually monitoring the unconscious man's pulse, only Adelia's murmurs breaking the silence. She felt the change in the plane's speed and the loss of altitude, heard the whine of the landing gear and felt the jerk of wheels on ground, but her flow of words continued, and she kept her uncle's hand firmly in hers.

She watched through a haze of unreality as paramedics worked on him before transferring him to the waiting ambulance. As she made to join them, Travis took her arm, telling her they would follow in the car. She went without protest, her mind and heart encased in the numbing ice of fear.

She responded only in vague monosyllables to his attempts at consolation, and after a glance at her pale, waxen features, he concentrated on weaving through the traffic toward the hospital.

The long wait began in a small, cheerless lounge scattered with ancient magazines that some read to pass the time and others stared at in desperation. Adelia did neither, but sat, still as a stone, her hands gripped together in her lap, neither moving nor speaking as Travis paced the room like a caged tiger. Her mind was screaming in protest, searching for the power to pray as fear devoured her. Her control was tight, stretching at the seams like an ill-fitting coat as the minutes passed.

When at last a white-coated figure approached, Travis whirled and advanced on him. "You're Padrick Cunnane's family?" the doctor asked, glancing from the tall, powerful man to the small, pale woman.

"Yes." His answer was curt as he too glanced at Adelia. "What's going on? How is he?"

"He suffered a coronary—not a massive attack. He is conscious now, but his condition is aggravated by anxiety over someone named Dee."

Adelia brought her head up. "I'm Dee. Is he going to die?"

The doctor studied the pale, composed features and took a step closer to her. "We're doing all we can to stabilize his condition, but his own anxiety is a factor in his recovery. His concern is focused on you. I'm going to let you see him. You must do nothing to upset him; persuade him to relax." He turned back to the dark man whose eyes were fixed on the woman. "Are you Travis?" At his nod, the doctor continued. "He wants to see you, too. Come with me."

Travis took Adelia's hand and lifted her from the chair, leading her after the retreating white coat.

"Five minutes," the doctor cautioned, and led them into the Cardiac Care Unit.

Her hand tightened in Travis's as she saw her uncle in the hospital bed, wires and tubes joining him to machines that whirled and buzzed. He was pale and drawn and suddenly old, and her mind screamed in revolt as she struggled for control.

"Dee." The voice was weak and unsteady, and she moved close to take his hand in hers.

"Uncle Paddy." Kissing the hand, she held it to her cheek. "Everything's going to be fine. They'll be taking good care of you, and soon you'll be home again."

"I want a priest, Dee."

"All right, don't worry." A cold hand gripped and squeezed her heart, and she felt the trembling start in her knees but forced it away.

"It's you I'm worried for. You can't be left all alone again, not again." His voice was rasping, and she soothed and murmured. "Travis . . . is Travis here?" He continued to fret, and she turned, fear shining from her eyes.

"Right here, Paddy." He moved to stand next to Adelia.

"You've got to take care of her for me, Travis. I'm giving her to you. She'll be all alone if anything happens to me. Such a wee thing she is and so young. It's been too hard for her . . . I should have been there for her before. I was going to make it up to her." He made a feeble gesture with his free hand. "I want your word you'll be taking care of her. I can trust you, Travis, with what's mine."

"I'll take care of her; you have my word." His answer was calm and steady, his hand closing over the two that were joined. "You don't have to worry about Dee. I'm going to marry her."

The relaxation in the taut face was visible, his breathing slowing. "You take care of my little Dee, then. I want to see the two of you married. Will you bring a priest here, and let me see it done?"

"I'll arrange it, but you'll have to relax and rest. Let the doctors do their job. Dee and I will be married right here this afternoon. All I need is a judge to sign a waiver of the two-day waiting period."

"Aye, I'll rest till you come back. Till you come back, Dee." She forced her lips into a smile and placed a kiss on his brow before she followed the doctor and Travis from the room. She whirled on him as soon as the door closed behind them.

"Not here," Travis commanded, gripping her arm. "Is there somewhere private we can talk?" he asked the doctor in calm tones. After directing them to an office, the doctor closed the door and discreetly left them alone.

CHAPTER 7

Adelia jerked out of Travis's hold as the door shut, fear and despair bubbling into fury. "How could you do that? How could you tell Uncle Paddy you were going to marry me? How could you lie to him that way?"

"I didn't lie, Adelia," Travis returned evenly. "I have every intention of marrying you."

"What are you thinking of, saying such things?" she continued as if he had not spoken. "It's cruel, with him lying there sick and helpless and trusting you. You had no right to make such a promise. You'll break his heart, you—"

"Get hold of yourself," Travis commanded, taking her shoulders and administering a brisk shake. "I told him what he needed to hear, and by God you'll do what he wants if it helps save him."

"I'll not be a party to such a cruel lie."

The grip on her shoulders increased, but she was beyond physical pain. "Doesn't he mean anything to you? Are you so selfish and hardheaded that you can't make a small sacrifice to help him?" She flinched as if he had struck her and turned blindly away, her hands gripping the back of a chair. "We'll stand in that room this afternoon, and we'll be married, and you make him believe it's what you want. When we know he's strong enough, you can get a divorce and end it."

She drew her hands over her eyes, pain washing over her in turbulent waves. *Uncle Paddy lying there half dead—Travis telling me we're marrying and divorcing in the same breath. Oh, I need someone to tell me what to do,* she thought frantically.

To be his wife, to belong to him—she'd wanted it so badly that she hadn't even dared to think of it, and now he was telling her that it was going to happen, that it *had* to happen. She was hurt beyond words. It would have been easier to go through life without him than to be his wife for an hour without his love. *Divorce*—he had said it so easily. He was talking of divorce before he had even put the ring on her finger. Taking a deep breath, she tried to force herself to think clearly, but she was too overcome by the bleak realization that he was not talking of a real marriage, a marriage of love, that he didn't want her for herself, but rather for her uncle's sake. There must be another way. There had to be another way. She swallowed painfully to steady her voice, "I'm Catholic. I can't get a divorce," she said dully.

"An annulment, then."

She stared at him in horrified silence, "An annulment?"

"Yes, an annulment. It should not be any problem if the marriage isn't consummated. It will simply be a matter of a little paperwork." He spoke in calm, businesslike tones, and her hands tightened on the chair as she attempted to fight her way through to reason. "For Pete's sake, Dee," he said impatiently, "can't you go through the motions of a ceremony for Paddy's sake? It won't cost you anything. It could make the difference between his living and dying."

He took her shoulders again, spinning her around, checking his anger as he studied the transparent glow to her skin, the fear in her eyes that stared back at him. He could feel the trembling begin under his hands and watched as she shut her eyes and tried to stem it. He muttered an oath, then drew her against him and wrapped his arms around her. "I'm sorry, Dee. Shouting at you is hardly going to make it any easier, is it? Come on, sit down." Leading her to a sofa, he sat beside her, keeping her close inside his arms. "You've been hanging on to control for too long; have a good cry. Then we'll talk."

"No, I don't cry. I never cry. It doesn't help." She held herself rigid in his grasp, but he continued to hold her close. "Please, let me go." She felt her control slipping and struggled against the arms that would not give way. "I have to think. If I just knew what to do . . ." Her breath came in short gasps, the trembling no longer controllable, and her hands clutched at his shirtfront to keep from falling. "Travis, I'm so afraid."

She burst into violent sobs, and his arms tightened around her. Once the tears escaped, she could not stop them. Held in check for more than a dozen lonely years, they now flowed freely down her face pressed into Travis's chest. He kept silent, one hand stroking her hair, and let the storm run its course.

The sobs lost their force, subsiding to soft whimpering, until she lay quiet in his arms, empty and spent. She gave one long, shuddering sigh. "I'll do whatever you think has to be done."

* * *

How Travis arranged the paperwork so quickly, she never questioned. She had been too numb to deal with technicalities. The only stand she had made was to refuse to leave the hospital even for a quick rest or a meal. Determinedly, she had planted herself in the waiting room and refused to budge.

She signed her name on the license where she was told, greeted the slender young priest who would make her Travis's wife, and accepted a handful of flowers from a friendly nurse who claimed a woman couldn't be a bride without a bouquet. She smiled at this, a small, frozen smile that hurt her cheeks, knowing she was not really a bride. Legally she would bear the name of the man she loved, but the vows they would exchange would mean nothing to him. The words and motions were only a charade to bring comfort to a sick man.

They stood side by side in the stark room, surrounded by machines, the air heavy with the smell of medicine, and became husband and wife. Adelia repeated the priest's words in a calm, clear voice and looked blankly at the signet ring Travis slipped on her finger before closing her fist over it. It hung loose on her finger and lay like a stone on her heart. In less than ten minutes it was all over, and she accepted his light, brief kiss without demur.

Adelia Cunnane Grant bent over and kissed her uncle's brow. He smiled up at her, his eyes lighting with a suggestion of their usual merriment. She knew in that instant that Travis had been right.

"Little Dee," he muttered, seeking her hand and clinging to it. "You'll be happy now. Travis is a good man."

She forced a smile and patted his cheek. "Aye, Uncle Paddy. You'll rest now, and we'll be able to bring you home soon."

"I'll rest," he agreed, and his eyes raised above her head to meet Travis's. "Treat her with care, lad . . . she's a Thoroughbred."

They drove home in silence. The sun broke through patches of clouds to filter on the road. Adelia watched the play of light and kept her mind a blank. Pulling up in front of the main house, Travis broke the heavy silence.

"I called ahead and informed my housekeeper of the wedding. She'll have prepared your room by now. Your things have been brought over."

She frowned. "I'm not—"

"For the time being," he cut in, his eyes narrowing, "you are my wife, and as such you will live in my house. We'll keep separate bedrooms," he added in a tone that caused her mouth to shut quickly. "We will, however, maintain the outward appearance of a married couple. There is no reason for the present that anyone other than you and I know of this arrangement. Explanations now would only complicate matters."

"I see. You're right, of course."

He sighed at the strain in her voice and went on in gentler tones. "I'll make it as easy on you as possible, Dee. I only ask that you play your part; otherwise you'll be free to do as you please. There'll be no need for you to work."

"I can't work with the horses?" Adelia broke in, eyes widening in dismay. "But, Travis—"

"Adelia, listen to me." He cupped her face in his hand. "You can do as you like. You don't even know what that means, do you?" His brows drew together at her blank, bewildered face. "If you want to work with the horses, you're free to do so, but not as my employee, as my wife. You can spend your time lounging around the country club or cleaning out stalls—it's up to you."

"All right." Slowly, she unclenched the fists that

were tight in her lap. "I'll do my best to make it easy on you as well. I know you were right to do this for Uncle Paddy, and I'm grateful to you."

He stared at her for another moment, then shrugged and slipped from the car.

When they entered the house, a plump, gray-haired woman bustled into the hall to greet them, wiping her hands on a full, white apron.

"Hannah, this is Adelia, my wife."

Warm hazel eyes inspected Adelia and smiled in approval. "Welcome, Mrs. Grant. It's about time a lovely young thing lured my Travis to the altar." Adelia murmured something she hoped was appropriate. "I'm sorry to hear about Paddy; we're all fond of him." The treacherous tears started again, and Adelia closed her eyes against them. "Oh, the poor thing's dead on her feet. Travis, take her up; the room's ready for her."

She started the climb up the staircase, which seemed to take on the proportions of Mount Olympus. Without a word, Travis swept her into his arms and carried her up the remaining steps and down a long, carpeted hallway. Entering a bedroom, he crossed the floor and laid her on a huge four-poster bed.

"I'm sorry." She lifted her hand and dropped it again. There seemed to be nothing further to say.

He sat next to her and brushed the hair from her cheeks.

"Adelia, when will you learn weakness is not always a flaw? Darned Irish stubbornness," he muttered, frowning down at her. "I'd swear nothing else kept you on your feet this long. There hasn't been a whisper of color in your cheeks for the past six hours."

She stared up at him, wanting to pull him down to her and feel the comfort of his warmth. He turned abruptly and moved to a large cherrywood wardrobe.

"I don't know where Hannah put your night clothes." Pulling open the double doors, he exposed the meager contents. "Good heavens, is this all you have?"

She tried to snap at him but found gathering the strength too great an effort. Moving over to a mirrored triple dresser, he began opening drawers, muttering and swearing, and she lay back and watched him, too weary to be embarrassed that he should handle her clothes with such familiarity.

He pulled out a plain, high-necked cotton gown and, after a brief disparaging scrutiny, brought it to her. "Tomorrow, for heaven's sake, go shopping and buy some clothes."

"Don't you order me about, Travis Grant." She sat up, unable to keep quiet any longer, and snapped at him with a ghost of her usual spirit.

He stared down at her without expression. "While we're married, Adelia, we'll be expected to socialize, and you'll have to dress properly. We'll see to it tomorrow. Now, can you manage to change by yourself, or do you need some help?"

Snatching the gown from his hands, she spoke stiffly. "I can manage very well."

"Good. Change and get some rest. You won't do Paddy any good if you make yourself ill." Without waiting for her reply, he turned and strode from the room, shutting the door behind him.

Too tired to appreciate the beauty of the light, airy room, she slipped off the skirt and blouse which had served as her wedding dress and pulled the cotton nightgown over her head. Folding down the mint-green spread, she crawled between the smooth sheets and fell instantly into the deep, dreamless sleep of exhaustion.

* * *

The birds woke her, as was their habit, chattering and chirping outside the window. Opening her eyes, she focused on the unfamiliar surroundings and remembered. She relaxed the fist that had remained tight over her wedding ring throughout the night, while her eyes made a slow survey of the room. She had thought her bedroom in the garage house large, but she estimated this would hold two rooms that size. The walls were muted green and white striped paper, trimmed with dark woodwork. The furniture was cherry, both the large wardrobe and dresser in which Travis had rummaged the evening before, and a small writing desk, two night tables, and a small pie-crust table which served a tufted-back chair. On the small table was a vase bursting with fresh flowers. Their scent drifted to her as she sat up in bed, hugging her knees close. She sighed as she gazed at the tall French windows which led to the balcony, thinking she had never seen such a lovely room. *How happy I could be here if only Uncle Paddy was well, and Travis . . .* She tried to clear her mind of such negative thoughts. Thrusting back the covers, she jumped out of bed.

After showering and dressing in her only remaining skirt, she ventured downstairs, hoping she could locate the kitchen in the strange house which was now her home.

"Good morning, Dee." Travis appeared from a room off the downstairs hall, which she later learned was his office. "Feeling better?"

"Aye," she answered, suddenly shy and uncertain in front of the man who was her husband. "I don't know when I've slept so long."

"You were exhausted." She kept herself still as he lifted her chin and examined her face like a parent seeking to find signs of ill health in a child. "Your color's back," he said at length and smiled.

"I'm fine." She managed to remain passive as his hand continued to hold her chin. "I was wondering if I could call the hospital . . . and see if Uncle Paddy—" Her hands fluttered, then clung together in front of her.

"I've already called; his condition has stabilized." His hands moved to rest on her shoulders. "He spent a peaceful night."

A tremor passed through her. She shut her eyes and buried her face against Travis's chest. After a moment, she felt his arms encircle her lightly. "Oh, Travis, I thought he was going to die. I was afraid we would lose him."

He held her away until she tilted her head to look up at him. "He's going to be all right, with a little time and care, and no worries." His features relaxed. "Of course, when he gets home, he'll have to slow down. We'll have to bully him into it."

"Aye." Her smile was like the stars through the clouds. "But there's two of us."

"So there are," he murmured, then tousled her hair. "I imagine you're starving. I couldn't wake you for dinner last night."

"I feel like I haven't eaten in a week." With a sigh, she pushed at the hair he had just ruffled. "If you'll show me the kitchen, I'll start breakfast."

"Hannah's seeing to it," he informed her, taking her arm and leading her into a large dining room. Noticing the expression on her face, he whispered confidentially in her ear as he pulled out a chair, "Don't worry, I've been eating her cooking all my life."

"Oh, I didn't mean—I meant no disrespect. It's only that I'm not used to having someone fix my meals." Her expression bordered on horror, and he leaned back in his chair and laughed.

"Don't look so stricken, Dee. Hannah will think I'm beating you already."

"Well, I wouldn't want you to think that I meant . . ." She fumbled for something to say which would release her from her awkwardness. "The room you gave me is lovely. I want to thank you."

"I'm glad you like it."

At his careless response, she was grateful for Hannah's entrance with a steaming breakfast platter.

"Good morning, Mrs. Grant. I hope you're feeling better after a good night's rest." She set the platter on the table and Adelia smiled up at her.

"Thank you, I feel fine." She was careful not to start at her new title.

"Hungry though, I'll be bound." Nodding, she studied the pixielike face. "Travis told me you ate next to nothing yesterday, so I'll expect you to do full justice to your breakfast."

"You should be warned, Dee, not to trifle with Hannah," Travis put in from across the table. "She can be ferocious. Personally, she terrifies me."

"Don't you listen to his nonsense, Mrs. Grant." She sent Travis a scowl before giving her attention back to Adelia. "You'll be busy for a while with Paddy in the hospital, but once you're settled, you let me know how you want things done. For now, if it's agreeable, I'll just plan your meals around your visits to the hospital."

"I—whatever you think best."

"We'll have plenty of time to talk about it," the housekeeper concluded. "Now, you get to your breakfast while it's hot." With this she bustled from the room.

Adelia listened to Travis's breakfast conversation, answering only when it was required, while she slowly took in her surroundings. The dining room was large with dark wainscoting and elegantly patterned wallpaper. The furniture was heavy, gleaming oak. Everywhere was the glow of silver and glimmer of crystal.

"Travis," she said suddenly, and his brows rose in acknowledgment as he sipped his coffee. "I don't fit into all this. I haven't the way or the experience to know what's expected of me. I don't want to be an embarrassment to you, and I'm mortally afraid I'll do or say something horrible, and—"

"Adelia." The one word stopped her rambling. She saw from his expression that she had already made a mistake. From the way his face was set, she waited for him to rant at her, but when he spoke, his voice was calm and precise. "You will not embarrass me, you could not embarrass me. Relax and be what you are, that's what's expected of you."

They lapsed into silence. Adelia toyed with the remainder of her eggs. "By the way," Travis began, and she raised her eyes and saw he was smiling, "you've had your picture in the paper."

"My picture?"

"Yes." His smile widened at her frowning expression. "Two pictures, as a matter of fact. There's one of you and Steve with the two of you sitting on the paddock fence, and there's one of you and me taken after the Belmont Stakes."

Color flooded her cheeks as she realized the contents of the second picture. "I don't know why they kept following me around with their cameras and their pencils."

"I can't imagine," Travis returned, his lips curving again. "It appears that the press has had a splendid time speculating about the romances of my attractive groom. . . ."

Her eyes widened, and the color ebbed and flowed again. "Are you meaning . . . Oh, what a passel of nonsense! Steve and I are friends, and you and I . . ." She faltered, sputtered, and fell into excruciating silence.

"Married, Adelia, is what we are, friends or not." With what she thought was a very odd smile, he drained his coffee and rose. "I don't suppose it will sound like such a passel of nonsense to the press when our current relationship is leaked to them. I can keep it out of the papers for a while, but we'll have to deal with it sooner or later. . . . I take it you're done since you've been playing with your fork for the last ten minutes." Securing her arm, he brought her to her feet. "Now, if you'll take that frown off your face, I'll drive you to the hospital."

A ny anxiety Adelia still harbored was dispelled by the appearance of her uncle. The color on his cheeks, which had appeared a ghastly gray the day before, was now closer to his normal, ruddy hue. His eyes twinkled as Travis brought her into the room. His voice was weak rather than booming, but steady and unforced. When he complained about being hooked up to blasted, noisy machines, her concern melted into laughter, and, kissing the hand she held in hers, she felt the last vestige of tension dissolve.

After a short visit, Travis drew her into the hall. "You won't be able to stay too long this time. The doctor says he tires easily and needs his rest. That, and seeing you, is the best medicine he can get."

"I won't tire him, Travis," she promised. "He's looking so much better, I can hardly believe my eyes. I'll only stay a little while more. As soon as I see he's tiring, I'll go."

He looked down at her smiling face, his fingers tangling absently with the ends of her hair. "I have to get back now, but Trish will be along soon to take you shopping." His hand dropped, and he stared past her as if suddenly preoccupied. "She'll know just what you need, and if you like, she can bring you back here for a while longer this afternoon."

"It's kind of you to be doing all this, Travis." She touched his arm to bring his attention back to her. "I don't know how to repay you for all that you've done already."

"It's nothing." He shrugged off her thanks and, drawing out his wallet, handed her some bills. "I've made arrangements for you to charge whatever you need. Trish will be there to see to the details, but you'll need some cash as well."

"But, Travis, it's so much. I can't . . ."

"Don't argue, just take it." He closed her hands over the bills in a final, impatient gesture. "Give it to Trish to hold for you, and for heaven's sake, Dee," he added with exasperation, "buy yourself a purse. I'll see you this evening."

He strode down the long corridor, leaving Adelia staring after him.

CHAPTER 8

When Trish arrived, she greeted Paddy with an affectionate kiss and told him firmly that anyone could see he was faking and enjoying being the center of attention. After a brief visit, she hurried Adelia out into the corridor and hugged her with enthusiasm.

"I'm so happy about you and Travis." Her eyes shone with affection. Adelia began to feel the first weight of guilt. "Now I have the little sister I always wanted." Adelia was treated to yet another hug. "Jerry sends his best." She referred to her husband, her face wreathed in smiles. "The twins went wild when I told them that Dee was now their aunt. They claim that makes them Irish and soon they'll be fey, too."

Adelia responded with smiles and agreeable murmurs, hating herself for the deception and wishing with all her heart that she could confide in the woman whom she felt was a true friend. But she had given Travis her word and she would keep it.

Hooking her arm through Adelia's, Trish began to stroll toward the elevator. "Travis has given me firm instructions to see that you buy a complete wardrobe."

She grinned with obvious pleasure as the elevator began its slow descent to the ground floor. "Of course I told him that I would be more than happy to follow orders and spend his money with abandon."

"He said you should hold this for me." Dee handed Trish the wad of bills, which she accepted and placed absently in her tan leather bag.

"This is going to be fun."

Adelia smiled faintly.

If Adelia was under the impression that this shopping expedition would follow along the lines of her first, she was soon enlightened to the contrary. Trish ignored department stores for the more exclusive shops. Adelia began to feel as if she were caught in the backlash of a tropical storm. She was whirled through shops while Trish made selections, dismissed or accepted articles with a nod or murmur to the sales clerks. Purchases mounted into an alarming mountain, leaving Adelia dizzy and confused.

Evening dresses that shimmered and flowed, sportswear Adelia considered suitable for royalty, soft, cobwebby lingerie that seemed too fragile to be real; all were tried on, inspected thoroughly by Trish's critical eye, then approved or rejected. Italian shoes and handbags, French scarves and negligees were included with a nod for foreign craftsmanship.

"Trish, surely Travis didn't mean for me to buy all this," Adelia objected, looking uneasily at the stacks of boxes and bags. "One person couldn't live long enough to wear all those clothes."

"You'd be surprised," Trish murmured absently as she surveyed a long, sweeping evening gown in brilliant green silk. "You'll be doing a lot of traveling, and there are parties and official functions . . ." Her voice trailed off as she held the gown in front of Adelia and narrowed her eyes in consternation. "Travis was very specific. He told me to see to it that you have everything necessary and to ignore the arguments you were sure to give me. That is precisely what I'm doing. Here." She thrust the gown into Adelia's hands. "Go try this on. Green is your color."

"We can't buy anything else," Adelia stated flatly, attempting to hold her ground. "There'll be no room in the car for us when the packages are put in."

"Then, little sister, we'll hire a van." Giving her a shove into the dressing room, Trish gave her attention to a white linen blouse.

L ate that afternoon, Adelia stared at the packages that lay piled high on her bed. With a weary sigh, she turned and left the room. Hannah greeted her as she stood in the downstairs hall, unsure whether she should stay in the house or seek out Travis at the stables.

"Mrs. Grant, how's Paddy?"

"He's looking just wonderful. I left him only an hour ago."

"You poor thing, you look all in."

"I've been shopping. I think cleaning out the entire stable would be less of a chore."

Hannah chuckled. "A cup of tea is what you need. Just sit down and I'll bring you one."

"Hannah." She stopped the plump woman before she could bustle away. "Could I . . . would you mind if I came into the kitchen and had one with you?" She made a small, helpless gesture with her hands. "I'm not used to being waited on."

The round face brightened, and a motherly arm slipped around Adelia's waist. "Just you come with me, missy. We'll have a nice cup of tea and a little chat."

It was there Travis found them together an hour later. He stood in the doorway watching in amused amazement as Adelia and Hannah worked on dinner preparations, chattering like lifelong partners.

"Well, well, well, a miracle in this day and age." Two heads turned toward him as he gave his brief, charming grin. "I never thought I'd live to see the day when you'd let anyone work in your kitchen, Hannah." He glanced from his housekeeper to the small woman at her side. "What kind of Irish charm did you use on her, Dee?"

"Just her charming self, you young rascal," Hannah stated with great dignity. "Now, missy"—she removed the vegetable parer from Adelia's hand—"you just run along now and keep that man out from under my feet. He's always been a nuisance in the kitchen."

Travis grinned again, serenely unperturbed. "Come out on the terrace, Dee," he invited and captured her hand. "It's too nice to stay indoors."

He led her out through wide French doors and onto the smooth stone surface of the terrace. The sweet scent of plants and flowers filled the June evening. The sun still cast a warm golden light, scattering shadows on the stone.

"So, Dee," he began, seating her in a striped cushioned chair and dropping down in an identical one across from her, "did you get everything you needed?"

"Everything?" she repeated. She closed her eyes and shuddered. "Never in my life have I ever seen so many clothes, much less put them on. Trying on this, taking off that." Opening her eyes again, she met his wide smile with a look of disdain. "You won't be smiling when you have to build another room to hold them all. Your sister is a stubborn woman, Travis Grant. She just kept tossing things at me and shoving me into dressing rooms. I couldn't make her listen to reason."

"I thought Trish might be helpful."

"Helpful?" She gave a long-suffering sigh. "I felt like I was being blown about by a whirlwind. Packages growing like a great mountain, and Trish smiling and finding something else. She had a fine time," she added, mystified.

"Yes, I imagine she did. I don't see her having much trouble filling out your wardrobe." He smiled at the picture and leaned back in his chair.

"Travis," she began after a small pause, "whatever will I do with all those things?"

"You might try wearing them," he suggested. "It's the usual procedure."

"That's fine for a time. I understand I can't go about in my old clothes with things as they are now. But after, when . . ." She stumbled and searched for the right words. "When things are back as they were before, I—"

"The clothes are yours, Adelia," he interrupted with a quick gesture of his hand. "You'll keep them whatever happens. I certainly have no use for them." Rising, he paced the length of the terrace and stared out over the smooth expanse of lawn.

Adelia sat silently, concerned by his anger and bewildered over how she had caused it. She stood and approached him, laying a tentative hand on his arm. "I'm sorry, Travis. That sounded ungrateful; I didn't mean it to. Everything's happening so fast. I don't want to take advantage of what you're doing for me."

"One can hardly call it taking advantage when it's like pulling teeth to get you to accept anything." His shoulders moved and he turned to face her. "Adelia," he said with a sigh somewhere between impatience and amusement, "you are so artless."

She did not question the ambiguity of his words, so relieved was she that his anger had faded and he was smiling at her again.

"I have something for you." Reaching into his pocket, he drew out a small box. "My signet ring was fine in an emergency, but it looks big enough to fit on your wrist."

"Oh." She found nothing else to say as she opened the box and found a small band studded with winking diamonds and glowing emeralds.

He removed the large, masculine ring from her finger and replaced it with the jeweled wedding band. "I'd say that suits a bit better."

"It fits," she murmured inadequately, overcome with the longing to throw her arms around him and cry out her love.

"I've studied those hands enough to make an educated guess as to your ring size." He spoke lightly and, dropping her hand, moved back to his chair.

Swallowing the obstruction in her throat, she followed him. "Travis." She stood in front of his chair, feeling the strangeness of looking down at him. "Travis, you're doing all the giving, and I have nothing for you. I want to . . . Is there nothing I can do for you? Is there nothing you want from me?"

He met her eyes with a long, unfathomable stare until she thought he would not speak at all. "For now, Dee," he said at length, "the best thing you can do for me is to accept what's given and not question it."

She sighed at his answer. "All right, Travis, if it pleasures you."

He stood and took her hand, a finger running over her wedding band. "Yes, it pleasures me. Come inside

and we'll eat, and I'll tell you how Majesty sulked for
you today."

The next two weeks passed quickly, Adelia's days
full between the hospital and the stables. Paddy
was moved into a regular hospital room. No longer at-
tached to machines, he improved daily, complaining
vigorously about being stuck in bed and poked with
needles. The easy friendliness of the men at the stables and the soothing routine of riding and grooming
brought a sense of normalcy back to Adelia's life, and
at times she almost forgot she was Mrs. Travis Grant.

Travis was kind and casually affectionate, speaking of Paddy's recovery and on the general topic of
horses when they took meals together. He left Adelia
free to pursue whatever project she chose, making no
demands, his attitude tolerant, generous, and distant.
She was aware of a subtle change in their relationship,
and she found it did not please her. He never raised his
voice or criticized, and he never touched her in any
way unless strictly necessary. She wished fervently that
he would yell at her or shake her, or do something to
lose his cool, composed manner. Their relationship was
now far less personal than it had been when they had
been employer and employee.

She was returning to the house one afternoon, wondering if Travis had returned from a business appointment, when she stopped and gaped at a large, dirty gray
mound of fur exploring a bed of marigolds. After a
careful study, she concluded that under the grubby fur
was a dog of rather alarming size.

"I wouldn't do that if I were you," she said in a quiet
voice that had the dog's head jerking up. "Now, don't
be running off. I won't hurt you." The dog hesitated,

eyeing her warily, and she kept the distance between them and continued to speak. "It's just that I've seen Travis's gardener—a terrifying man he is. And one that wouldn't take kindly to anyone digging at his flowers." She crouched down, and they studied each other eye to eye. "Are you lost, then, or just roaming? I can see by your eyes you're hungry, I've been hungry myself a time or two. Wait here," she ordered and stood. "I'll fetch you something."

Entering the kitchen, she commandeered a large hunk of roast beef. The whine of the vacuum cleaner was audible from the living room, and, deciding it would be foolish to disturb Hannah and vowing to apologize to her after the deed was done, Adelia slipped back outside.

"It's prime beef, my lad, and from the looks of you, you've not seen its kind before." She placed the offering on the grass and stepped back a few paces.

He came forward slowly at first, eyes shifting from the beef to his benefactor until either his confidence or his hunger grew and he threw himself on the unexpected meal. She watched him polish off what would have fed three hungry men, finding enormous pleasure in his appetite.

"Well, now, you've made a pig of yourself, and that's the truth, and you don't look a bit ashamed." She grinned and watched the long tail thump in agreement. "Pleased with yourself, are you?" Before she could move, she found herself flat on her back, trapped under a hundred pounds of appreciation, her face being drenched by a large wet tongue. "Get off me, you great hairy brute!" Laughing, she pushed to no avail and tried to turn her face from the moisture. "Surely there's not a rib that's not cracked, and it's God's truth you've not had a bath since the day you were born."

After much pleading and wriggling, she managed to release herself, staggered to her feet, and surveyed the damage. Her shirt and jeans were covered with dirt, her arms smeared with it. She pushed at her disordered hair and stared down at the dog that sat at her feet, his tongue hanging out in adoration.

"We'll both be needing a bath now. Well—" She let out a deep breath, tilted her head, and considered. "You wait here, and I'll see what can be done about you. It might be best if you were cleaned up a bit before I introduce you."

On the way back to the house, she paused on the terrace to brush at the dirt that covered her.

"Dee, what happened? Were you thrown? Are you hurt?" Travis rushed to her, his hands claiming her shoulders, then moving to stroke her face. She shook her head, thrown off balance by the frantic tone of his voice.

"No, I'm not hurt. Travis, you mustn't touch me— you'll get your suit filthy." She tried to take a step away, only to be caught closer.

"The devil with the suit!" His voice was edged with anger as he pressed her against him, one hand cradling her head.

The small intimacy after so many days of impersonal distance swamped her with pleasure, and her arms encircled his waist before she could lecture herself on the wisdom of the action. She felt his lips tarry in her hair, and she thought, with a brief flash of joy, that if she could only have this much of him from time to time, she would be content.

Suddenly, one hand gripped her shoulder while the other tilted her face back, and she saw temper flame in his face. "What in heaven's name have you done to yourself?"

"I haven't done anything to myself," she said with a show of dignity, shaking off his hand. "We've company." She gestured to the lawn.

His eyes moved past her, narrowed, then returned. "Adelia, what in the name of heaven is *that?*"

"It's a dog, Travis, though I wasn't sure myself at first. The poor thing was half starving. That's why"—she paused and braced herself for the confession—"that's why I gave him the roast beef."

"You fed him?" Travis asked in low, even tones.

"Surely you wouldn't begrudge the poor thing a bit of food. I—"

"I don't care a whit about the food, Adelia." He shook her briefly. "Don't you have any more sense than to fool with a strange dog? You could have been bitten."

Straightening, she glared at the censure in his voice. "I know what I'm about, and I was careful. He needed food, so I gave it to him—the same as I'd give it to anyone who needed it. And as for that, he hasn't a thought in his head about biting anyone." Glancing over, she watched the dog's tail begin to thump the ground again. "There"—she pointed triumphantly—"you see."

"I see it appears you've made another conquest. Now," he said, and turned her firmly to face him directly. "Just how did you get in this condition?"

"Oh, well." She looked up at Travis, back to the dog, and back to Travis again. "You see, after he'd finished eating, he was overcome with gratitude, and he—well, he forgot himself for a minute and knocked me down and sort of thanked me in his way. He's a bit dirty—as you can see."

"He knocked you down?" Travis repeated, incredulously.

At his tone, Adelia hurried on. "He's very affectionate, and he didn't mean any harm. Really, Travis, don't be angry with him. See how pretty he is, sitting there now." She glanced over at the dog and saw he was smart enough to blink soulful eyes in Travis's direction. "I told him to wait, and that's just what he's doing. He only wants a bit of affection."

Travis turned back and gave Adelia a long look. "I'm getting the impression you intend to keep him."

"Well, I don't know about keeping him, exactly." She dropped her eyes from him, stared at a spot of dirt on Travis's jacket, and brushed it away.

"What's his name?"

"Finnegan," she responded immediately, then, seeing she had fallen into the trap, looked up frowning.

"Finnegan?" Travis repeated with a sober nod. "How did you come by that?"

"He reminds me of Father Finnegan back in Skibbereen, oversized and clumsy but with much inner dignity."

"I see." He moved over, crouched down, and inspected Finnegan. To Adelia's relief, the dog remembered his manners.

When Travis returned to her, she moistened her lips and launched into her campaign. "I'll take care of him, Travis; he won't be any trouble. I won't let him come in the house and get in Hannah's way."

"There's no need to use your eyes, Adelia." At her bewildered frown, he laughed and tugged her hair. "Lord help the world if you ever realize what you're doing. You're perfectly free to keep him if that's what you want."

"Oh, I do! Thank you, Travis—"

"There are, however, two conditions," he interrupted before she could finish being grateful. "One, that you teach him not to knock you down; he's every bit as big as you are. And two, that he has a bath." He glanced over at Finnegan and shook his head. "Or several baths."

"I think I'm due for one myself." She brushed again without success at the clinging dirt, then lifted her face with a smile. The smile wavered as she found Travis looking down at her strangely.

"You know, Dee, I'm tempted to stuff you in my pocket where I won't have to worry about you."

"I'm small," she agreed, finding it suddenly difficult to breathe, "but I think I'm rather too big for that."

"Your size is intimidating."

She frowned, wondering what he could find intimidating about a bare five feet. His hand wandered through her hair, gently for a moment; then, tousling it with a casual friendliness, he added, "I believe it would be easier if you didn't continually look fifteen instead of twenty-three. . . . I guess I had better change my clothes before I give you a hand bathing that mountain."

A s her marriage approached its third week, Adelia sat in her uncle's hospital room, smiling at him as he spoke with excitement of his discharge scheduled for the following day.

"Anyone would think they'd been torturing you and starving you to death, Uncle Paddy."

"Oh, no, it's a fine place, with good and kind people," he protested. "But a hospital's for the sick and never have I felt better in my life."

"You are better, and it makes me happier than I can say. But"—she paused and gave him a stern look—"you've still got to rest for a while and do as the doctors tell you. You're coming home to stay with Travis and me for a few days, till you can get by on your own."

"Now, Dee, I can't do that," Paddy objected, patting

her hand. "You two should be off on your honeymoon, not worrying about the likes of me."

With a great deal of self-control, she managed not to wince at the word *honeymoon* and went on in calm but firm tones. "You'll be coming back with us, and that's the end of it. I didn't even have to ask—Travis suggested it himself."

Lying back against the pillows, Paddy smiled. "Aye, he would. Travis is a fine man."

"That he is," Adelia agreed with a sigh. She forced a bright smile and continued. "He's fond of you, Uncle Paddy. I knew as soon as I saw the two of you together."

"Aye," he murmured. "Travis and I go back a long way. Just a lad he was when I came to work for his father. Poor motherless child, so solemn and straight he was."

Adelia's mind wandered as she tried to picture Travis as a small boy, wondering if he was tall even then.

"Stuart Grant was a hard man," Paddy went on. "He ran the lad harder than the horses he raised. Trish he left to Hannah, barely showing the girl a passing interest, but the boy he wanted molded in his image. Always giving orders, with never a kind word or a dab of affection.

"I found myself taking the lad in, telling him stories and making games out of the work we did." He grinned, lost in memory. "'Paddy's Shadow,' the hands called him, 'cause he took to following me about whenever his father wasn't there. He worked hard, and he knew the horses even then. A fine, good lad he was, but the old man couldn't see it. Always finding fault. I wondered sometimes when he grew older why he didn't lay the old man out. Goodness knows he was big enough, and the temper was there. But he took the abuse the old man handed him and only looked at him with his eyes so cold." Paddy paused and let out a long breath.

"Travis was away at college when the old man passed on . . . that would be about ten years ago. He stood there looking down at the grave, and I went over and laid my hand on his shoulder. 'I'm sorry about your father, lad,' says I, and he turned and looked down at me. 'He was never my father, Paddy,' says he, just as calm as you please. 'You've been my father since I was ten years old. If you hadn't been there, I'd have left a long time ago and never looked back.'"

The room was suddenly silent. Adelia gripped the hand that lay in hers tighter as Paddy's eyes grew moist with memory. "And now the two of you are together, I couldn't have wished it any better."

"You'll stay with him, Uncle Paddy, always, no matter what? You promise me that?"

He turned to her, surprised by the urgency in her tone. "Of course, little Dee. Where else would I be going?"

CHAPTER 9

The following evening, after Paddy was comfortably settled into his room in the main house, Travis announced plans for a party.

"It's expected after Majesty's win, but with Paddy's heart attack it's had to be postponed." He swirled a glass of after-dinner brandy, his eyes sweeping over her, resting for a moment on her hair shimmering on the shoulders of her Nile blue dress. "Our marriage has, of course, leaked to the press, and it will seem odd we don't have some sort of gathering where you can meet some of my friends and business associates."

"Aye," Adelia agreed, unconsciously nibbling on her lip as she turned to gaze out the window. "And so they can get a look at me."

"That, too," he answered in solemn tones. "Don't worry, Dee: as long as you don't trip over your feet and fall on your face you should get by fairly well."

She whirled around to rage at him that she wasn't exactly a clumsy fool, but his good-natured grin stopped her. "Thank you very much, Master Grant." She smiled back at him. "It's a great comfort you are to me."

She gasped out loud at the length of the list Travis gave her for the projected reception. There couldn't be less than a hundred, she estimated, staring at the paper.

"You've nothing to worry about," he assured her. "Hannah will handle the details. You're only expected to make polite conversation."

The attempt at reassurance hurt her pride. "I'll have you know I'm not a complete cabbagehead, Travis Grant. I'm well capable of helping Hannah, and I won't be making a fool of myself in front of your fancy friends."

"You're the one who said she was afraid of making a fool of herself, not me," Travis reminded her reasonably.

"It's not what I said that matters," she concluded with her own brand of logic. "It's what I'm saying." Tossing her head, she turned and stalked into the kitchen.

Despite her proud claims, Adelia found herself terrified on the evening of the party. There had been no time for nervousness in the days before; she had been too busy with plans and preparations. But now, alone in her room, with only the prospect of dressing ahead of her, she began to feel the first flutter of anxiety.

She chose the green silk gown that Trish had insisted she buy and slipped it carefully over her head. Its classic lines accentuated her softly rounded figure; its deeply scooped neckline revealed a teasing hint of her firm breasts. The silk glowed against the creamy health of her skin. She arranged her hair on top of her head, trying for a more sophisticated style, but gave up in disgust and allowed it to fall loose and full to her shoulders, a fiery auburn waterfall.

Voices were audible in the living room as she descended the stairs. She took several deep breaths before joining Travis and Paddy.

Travis broke off what he had been saying as she entered the room. He rose from his chair. She sought his eyes for approval, but found them strangely veiled and unreadable. She wished that she had chosen one of the other gowns that now hung in the large cherry wardrobe.

"Ah, now, isn't that a beautiful sight, lad?" Paddy said, surveying Adelia with uninhibited pride. "Why, there won't be another woman here tonight will hold a candle to my little Dee. It's a lucky man you are, Travis."

"Uncle Paddy." She smiled and moved to kiss his cheek. "What wonderful blarney. But don't stop—I need it. I have to be honest and say I'm scared witless."

"There's no need for that, Dee." Taking her hand, Travis turned her toward him. "You'll have them eating out of your hand. You look incredible." He smiled at her, his free hand brushing through her hair briefly before he turned away to replenish his drink.

Love me, Travis, her mind shouted suddenly. *I'd give the world and more if you'd only love me half as much as I love you.*

As he turned back, his eyes captured hers. He paused, unreadable emotion flickering over his face. "Dee?" he began, his voice questioning, but before she could speak the doorbell pealed and their guests began to arrive.

It was infinitely easier than Adelia had imagined. After the first wave of guests, she felt her tension dissolve and met the few speculative glances with characteristic boldness. The house was soon filled with people and chatter and laughter and the chink of glasses. It was apparent that Travis was well-liked and respected by his associates, and his choice of bride met with acceptance and approval, if not immediately, then shortly after exposure to Adelia's natural, honest charm.

One sleekly coiffured woman who had cornered Adelia halted Travis as he passed. "Travis, your wife is refreshing and charming and more than likely too good for you." She smiled with the privilege of old friendship. "I believe it would be a treat just to listen to her read the telephone directory. Such a marvelous accent."

"Careful, Carla," Travis admonished, slipping an arm around Adelia's shoulders in the casual way she had missed in the past few weeks. "Dee claims we're the ones with the accent—and for all her sweet looks, her temper is not to be trifled with."

"Travis, darling!" The trio turned, and Adelia caught a glimpse of swirling white as the owner of the voice embraced her husband. "I just got back in town, darling, and heard about your little party. I hope you don't mind."

"Of course not, Margot. It's always a pleasure to see you." He turned, and Adelia noted that he didn't dislodge the red-tipped hand from his arm. "Margot Winters—my wife, Adelia."

Margot turned, and Adelia nearly gasped aloud. She was staring right at the most beautiful woman she had ever seen. Tall and slender, she was elegantly draped in a cool white sheath. Ash-gold hair curled softly around an oval face. Her skin was the color of rich cream. Long-lashed gray eyes, as clear and cool as a mountain lake, looked over and beyond Adelia.

"Why, Travis, she's adorable." The gray eyes focused now on Adelia, making her feel small and inadequate. "But she's little more than a child, barely out of

the schoolroom." The sweet tone was patently patronizing.

"I'm allowed up with the grown-ups now and
again," Adelia said evenly, her chin tilting to meet Margot's gaze. "I hung up my book strap some time back."

"My," Margot observed over Carla's chuckle.
"You're Irish, aren't you?"

"Aye." The quicksilver temper began its swift rise.
"As Paddy's pig. Tell me, Mistress Winters, what are
you?"

"Dee." Trish spoke from behind, laying a hand on
Adelia's arm. "Will you come out here for a minute? I
need you to help me."

Adelia was pulled out on the terrace, and after she
had shut the doors, Trish dissolved into a fit of laughter. "Oh, Dee," she managed between giggles. "How I
would have loved to have left you there and watched
you lay into her! I just didn't think it was quite the right
time. Oh . . ." She wiped at her eyes. "Did you see
Carla? I thought she was going to explode! She kept
choking on her drink and trying to keep a straight face.
I wouldn't have missed that for the world! How Travis
could ever have been involved with that woman is beyond me! She's a cold-blooded snob."

"Travis and Margot Winters?" Adelia asked, attempting to keep her voice casual.

"Oh, yes, I thought you knew." Trish gave a deep
sigh, wiped her eyes again, and grimaced. "I don't really think he was ever serious about her—I give him
more credit than that. She would have given one of
her Tiffany baubles to have him look at her the way
he looks at you." Trish smiled, and Adelia made a val-
iant effort to respond. "They had this big blowup a
few months ago. It seems she resented all the time he
spent with the horses." She gave a snort of disgust and

straightened her skirts. "She wanted him to sit back and
let others do all the work while he spent his time entertaining her. She gave him some kind of ultimatum
and took off for Europe in a cloud of expensive French
perfume." Trish laughed in pure delight. "Her little ploy
failed miserably, and now her nose is out of joint. Instead of pining for her, Travis is happily married to
you." She linked her arm with her sister-in-law's.

"Aye," Adelia murmured. "Now he's married to
me . . ." Her tone was melancholy, and Trish glanced at
her sharply, but Dee refused to meet her eyes.

Paddy moved back to his own house a few days later,
and Adelia missed his presence keenly. He found
Finnegan to be a congenial companion, and the dog di-
vided his time between them. He would accompany
Paddy as he grumbled inside for his afternoon rest, and
Adelia was never quite sure whether Finnegan's motives
were duty or laziness.

Travis made no mention of Margot Winters or Adelia's comments to her, and she found their relationship
drifting away again until she felt more like his ward
than his wife. When they attended social functions,
he treated her with the warm attentiveness expected
of a newly married husband; but once they were alone
again in their own home, he was distant, showing her
only the casual affection he might give to a favored
cousin.

The depression and frustration this caused in her
Adelia hid with apparent success, responding as she
believed he desired and maintaining the same casualness he directed toward her. Rarely did her temper
flare, and she was aware his was under strict control.
At times she imagined they were only polite puppets

pulled on invisible strings. Desperately she wondered how long they could go on.

One afternoon, as July brought summer's throbbing heat to the air, Adelia answered the summons of the bell and found herself confronted with the elegantly clad form of Margot Winters. Her finely penciled brows lifted at Adelia's attire of jeans and shirt. She glided over the threshold without invitation.

"Good afternoon to you, Mistress Winters." Adelia greeted her, determined to act the part of hostess. "Please come in and sit down. Travis is down at the stables, but I'll be glad to send for him."

"That's not necessary, Adelia." Margot strolled into the living room and seated herself in a wingback chair as if she belonged there. "I came to have a little chat with you. Hannah"—she glanced over at the housekeeper, who had entered behind Adelia—"I'll have some tea."

Hannah looked pointedly at Adelia, who merely nodded and moved to join her uninvited guest.

"I shall come straight to the point," Margot began, sitting back and linking her fingers together in an imperious gesture. "I'm sure you're aware that Travis and I were about to be married before we had a slight disagreement a few months ago."

"Is that the truth of it?" Adelia asked with apparently idle interest.

"Yes, it was common knowledge," Margot stated with a regal wave of her hand. "I thought to teach Travis a lesson by going to Europe and giving him time to think things through. He's a very stubborn man." She gave Adelia a small knowing smile. "When I saw the picture of him in the paper kissing this little ragamuffin, I thought nothing of it. The press will blow these things out of proportion. But when I heard he'd actually married some little stablehand"—she shivered delicately—"I knew it was time to come back and set things straight."

"And may the stablehand ask how you mean to do that?"

"When this little interlude is finished, Travis and I can proceed as planned."

"And by interlude I suppose you're meaning my marriage?" Adelia inquired, her voice lowering to an ominous level,

"Well, of course." Slender shoulders moved at the inevitable. "Just look at you. It's obvious Travis only married you to bring me back. You can't possibly hope to hold him for very long. You haven't the breeding or style that's necessary to move in society."

Straightening her spine, Adelia hid her pain with dignity. "I'm telling you this as a fact, Mistress Winters: you had nothing to do with the reason that Travis and I were married. It's true I haven't your elegance or manner of speaking, but there's one thing I have you're lacking. I've Travis's ring on my finger, and you'll be having a good long wait before you can add his name to yours."

Hannah entered bearing a tea tray, and Adelia rose and turned to her. "Mistress Winters won't be staying for tea after all, Hannah. She was just leaving."

"Play the lady of the house while you can," Margot advised, rising and gliding past Adelia's stiff form. "You'll be back in the stables sooner than you think." When the door closed with a sharp bang, Adelia let out a deep breath.

"She's got her nerve coming here and talking that way," an irate Hannah sputtered.

"We'll be paying her no mind." She patted the housekeeper's arm. "And we'll keep this visit between the two of us, Hannah."

"If that's the way you want it, missy," Hannah agreed with obvious reluctance.

"Aye," she replied, staring off into space. "That's the way I want it."

A delia's nerves remained on edge for several days and showed all too plainly in increased temper. The atmosphere in the house went from a near-stagnant calm to volatile motion. Travis greeted her change in attitude with absent tolerance that changed to strained patience.

She paced the living room after dinner one evening while he sat on the sofa and brooded over his brandy.

"I'm going to take Finnegan and go for a walk," she announced suddenly, unable to bear the silence between them any longer.

"Do as you like," he answered with a shrug.

"'Do as you like.'" She whirled and snapped at him, nerves as tight as an overwound watch. "It's sick to death I am of hearing you say that. I will not do as I like. I don't want to do as I like."

"Do you hear what you just said?" he demanded, setting down his brandy and staring at her. "That is the most ridiculous statement I have ever heard."

"It's not ridiculous. It's perfectly clear if you had the sense to understand it."

"What's gotten into you? You make more sense when you mutter in Gaelic."

"Nothing," she returned shortly. "There's not a thing wrong with me."

"Then stop behaving like a shrew. I'm tired of putting up with your foul temper."

"A shrew, am I?" Her color rose.

"Precisely," he agreed with infuriating calm.

"Well, if you're tired of listening to me, I'll keep out of your way." Storming from the room, she flew past an astonished Hannah, out the back door, and into the warm summer night.

She awoke the next morning ashamed, disgusted, and contrite. She had spent an uneasy night struggling with the aftermath of temper and the realization that not only had she been unreasonable, she had made a fool of herself as well. One was as difficult to take as the other.

Travis has done nothing to deserve the way I've been treating him, she decided, pulling on her working uniform of jeans and shirt and hurrying downstairs. She determined to apologize and make a study of being as sweet and mild a wife as any man could want.

Hannah informed her that Travis had breakfasted early and gone out, so Adelia sat down in solitary misery, unable to ease her conscience.

She worked hard in the stables that morning, doing self-imposed penance for her faults. And as morning melted into early afternoon, the manual labor began to erase the depression she carried with her.

"Dee." Travis spoke from outside the tackroom, where she was busily hanging bridles. "Come out here. I want to show you something."

"Travis." She ran after him as he strode away. "Travis." Catching up to him, she tugged on his arm in an attempt to make him slow his pace. "I'm sorry, Travis. I'm sorry for the way I've been behaving, and for raging at you last night when I had no cause to. I know I've been mean and spiteful and no fun to have around, but if you'll forgive me, I'll . . . What are you smiling like that for?"

The smile spread to a grin. "You apologize just as emphatically as you rage. It's fascinating. Now, forget it, half-pint." He ruffled her hair and slipped an arm around her shoulders. "Everyone has their black moods. Look," he said simply and pointed.

She gave a cry of pleasure at the glossy chestnut mare prancing around inside the paddock fence. Moving over, she stood on the first rung of fence and scanned the strong, clean lines. "Oh, Travis, she's beautiful—the most beautiful horse I've ever seen!"

"You say that about all of them."

She smiled at him, then back at the horse with a deep sigh of pleasure. "Aye, and it's always true. Who will you breed her with?"

"That's not up to me. She's yours."

Adelia turned wide, unbelieving eyes to his. "Mine?"

"I had thought to give her to you next month for your birthday, but"—he shrugged and brushed a lock of hair from her face—"I thought your spirits needed a lift, so she's yours a bit early."

She shook her head, the still unfamiliar tears filling her eyes. "But after the way I've been acting, you should have been beating me instead of buying me a present."

"The thought entered my mind last night, but this seemed a better solution."

"Oh, Travis!" She flung herself into his arms without restraint. "No one's ever given me such a grand present, and I don't deserve it." She drew her face from his cheek and pressed her lips to his. His arms tightened around her, the kiss changing from one of gratitude to one of smoldering passion, and she offered herself, lips parting and bones melting. "Travis," she murmured as his face lifted, his cheek brushing hers.

He set her away from him abruptly. "You'd better

get acquainted with your mare, Dee. I'll see you at dinner."

She watched him stride away, biting her lip to prevent herself from calling him back. Finnegan bounded over, and she swallowed the tears of rejection, burying her face in his fur. "I don't have any appeal for him," she told her sympathetic companion. "And I don't know how to go about making him see me as a woman—much less a wife."

CHAPTER 10

Adelia woke to a blinding flash of lightning and a burst of thunder. The room glowed with brief intensity as the sky was broken with spiderwebs of light, and the wind moaned like a man mourning.

Tossing back the covers, she rose from the bed and threw open the French doors leading to her balcony to let the storm enter the room. The hands of the wind pulled at her hair and whipped the soft material of her thin nightgown, molding it against her. Rain fell in torrents like angry tears from the heavens, and she raised her arms wide, laughing in sheer delight at the raging elements.

"Dee?" She turned her head and saw Travis silhouetted in the doorway. "I thought you might be frightened. The electricity's out, and the storm's loud enough to wake the dead."

"Aye," she agreed triumphantly. "It's wonderful!"

"So much for finding you shaking with fear under the covers," he returned with a dry smile and stepped back.

"Oh, Travis, come look!" she cried as another bolt

of lightning illuminated the murky sky and was followed by a deafening roar of thunder.

He watched her slimness outlined against the blackness, the fullness of her hair flying riotously around her bare shoulders. He opened his mouth to speak, but Adelia cried out again.

"Oh, come, just look at it!" Taking a deep breath, he moved to join her. "It's so wild, so strong and powerful and free!" She lifted her face to feel the full force of the wind on her cheeks. "It's angry as the devil and doesn't give a hoot what anyone thinks. Listen to the wind, screaming like a banshee! Oooh, but I love a storm that blows free!"

She turned and found his eyes on her. Lightning flooded the room, and she saw the naked desire darkening his unblinking blue stare. Her smile faded. Her heart pounded in her ears, drowning out the turbulence of the storm as he pulled her against him and crushed her lips in a violent, hungry kiss.

Her arms clutched around his waist as they fused together, and she felt the need in him she had not known existed and knew a moment's delirious pleasure that it was for her. Fire ignited fire. Her response was abandoned and uninhibited. His mouth ravished hers, hard and bruising, and she opened under the pressure like a flower to the sun. His hand slid to her shoulders, and the soft material of her nightgown sighed to the floor. Her hands fumbled with the belt of his robe until no barrier of silk came between them. With a swift, desperate gesture, he lifted her and carried her to the bed.

The passionate violence of the storm paled against the turbulence of their lovemaking. His lips moved over hers slowly, his hands roaming with gentle experience over her trembling body, releasing her desire while he

kept his own in check. When he made her his, she surrendered, drawing her pleasure from the gift she gave.

Later, she slept in the warm circle of his arms, the
deep, peaceful sleep of one who had been lost and
searching and finally found home. . . .

Sunlight streamed warm and loving on Adelia's face,
and she opened her eyes. Travis's face lay close to
hers, and she studied it thoroughly and sighed, her love
nearly bursting her heart. His breathing was slow and
even, the deep blue of his eyes hidden by lowered lids
and lashes which seemed incredibly long and thick
against the strongly masculine face. Her hand lifted and
stroked the dark curls away from his forehead, and she
snuggled closer, murmuring his name.

His eyes opened at her movements and smiled
into hers. "Hello," he said simply as his arm tightened
around her waist. "Do you always look this beautiful
first thing in the morning?"

"I don't know," she answered. "It's the first time
I've ever woken with a man on my pillow." She rolled
on top of him and peered down at his face critically.
"You're not a hard sight on the eyes either." Grinning,
she rubbed a hand over his chin. "Though it's a fact
you're needing a shave."

He tugged the hair that fell streaming from her head
to his shoulders and brought her face down, claiming
her lips. After a moment she lay her head in the curve
of his shoulder, sighing with absolute contentment as
he caressed her back with slow, idle movements. "Travis," she said curiously, "that clock says it's after ten."

He twisted to see for himself and groaned. "That's
what it says."

"But it can't be," Adelia objected, raising herself up

in indignation. "Why, never in my life have I slept as late as that!"

"Well, you did this time." He grinned. "Even you can't argue the day back."

"I'll pretend I didn't see it," she decided and snuggled against his warmth.

"As much as I'd like to do the same, I have an appointment, and I'm already going to be late." He kissed her again, rolling her over, and she clung to him, moving her hands over the rippling muscles of his back. "I've got to go." His lips tarried a moment at the curve of her neck before he disentangled himself. He rose and slipped on his robe, turning back to gaze at her slim form, scantily covered by rumpled sheets. "If you stay there for a couple of hours, I'll be back."

"You could stay now and be a bit later for your appointment," she suggested with a smile as she sat up, clutching the sheet to her breast.

"Don't tempt me." Moving over, he kissed her brow. "I'll be back as soon as I can."

When the door closed behind him, she lay back with a blissful sigh and stretched. *I'm truly his wife now,* she thought, closing her eyes as memories of the previous night ran through her mind. *I'm a married woman, and Travis is my husband. But he never said he loved me.* She sighed and shook her head. *He said he needed me, and that's enough for now. I'll make him love me in time. I'll make our marriage work, and he'll not be thinking of ending it. I'll make him so happy he'll think he's found heaven.*

She jumped from the bed, full of confidence, and danced into the adjoining bathroom to shower.

Later, she paused halfway down the stairs, her face lighting with pleasure as she heard Travis's voice coming from the living room. Before she could begin the

rapid descent she had intended, another voice floated
to her, and she stopped, the smile fading as she recognized Margot Winters's voice raised in exasperation.

"Travis, you know very well I never meant those
things I said before I left. I only went away so that you'd
miss me and come after me."

"Did you expect me to drop everything and run
off to Europe chasing you, Margot?" Adelia heard the
slight amusement in his tone and bit her lip.

"Oh, darling, I know it was foolish." The voice became low and seductive. "I never meant to hurt you. I'm
so terribly sorry. I know you married that little groom
to make me jealous."

"Is that so?" The answer was calm, and Adelia's
hand tightened on the banister at his cool, dispassionate discussion of her.

"Of course, darling, and it worked beautifully. Now
all you have to do is arrange for a quick divorce and give
her a nice little settlement, and we'll get things back to
normal."

"That may be difficult, Margot. Adelia's Catholic;
she'd never divorce me." Her stomach lurched at the
easy remark, and she wrapped her arms around herself
to ward off the sharp, piercing stab of pain.

"Well, then, darling, you'll just have to divorce her."

"On what grounds?" Travis's voice sounded reason-
able.

"For heaven's sake, Travis." The feminine voice rose
in annoyance. "You can arrange something. Give her
some money. She'll do what you want."

Adelia could stand no more. Covering her ears with
her hands, she ran up the carpeted stairs and into her
room.

Oh, 'tis a fool you are, Adelia Cunnane, she berated herself, leaning against her door. *He doesn't*

love you and he never will. Your marriage was just make-believe all along. She dashed away the tears and straightened her shoulders. Now's the time to end it, she decided firmly. Uncle Paddy's strong enough, and I can't go on this way any longer.

She packed only her old clothes and those bought with her own earnings in the well-battered case she had carried from Ireland, then sat at the writing desk and penned notes to her uncle and husband.

Please understand, Uncle Paddy, she pleaded, placing the two envelopes on the smooth surface of the desk. *I can't be going on with this anymore. I can't stay here so close to Travis, not now, not after all that's happened.*

She slipped downstairs and, taking a deep breath, walked outside to await her taxi.

The airport was as busy as it had been on her arrival, throngs of people rushing around her and shaking her confidence. For a moment she felt achingly lost and alone. Sighting the ticket counter, she drew herself up and headed toward it. A hand gripped her arm and spun her around. She dropped her case to the tiled floor with a thud.

"What do you think you're doing?" she began indignantly, stopping openmouthed as she looked up into Travis's furious face.

"That's precisely what I wanted to ask you," he tossed back, his eyes boring into hers with a hard blue light. "Where do you think you're going?"

"To Ireland, back to Skibbereen."

"Are you stupid enough to think I'd let you get on that plane without a word?" he demanded, his grip on her arm increasing.

She winced at his bruising fingers but answered evenly. "I left you a note."

"I saw your note," he hissed between his teeth. "It's a good thing I got back early, or I'd be chasing you across the Atlantic."

"There's no need for you to be chasing me anywhere," Adelia insisted, pulling at her arm as the circulation began to slow down. "You're breaking my arm, Travis Grant. Take your hand off me."

"You're lucky it's not your neck," he muttered, and, lifting her case with his free hand, he began to pull her after him.

"I'm not going with you—I'm going back to Ireland."

"You are coming with me," he corrected. "And you can walk on your own two feet, or I'll cart you out like a sack of Irish potatoes."

"A sack of Irish potatoes, is it?" she spat at him, but as he towered over her, formidable and powerful, she tossed her head and went on calmly. "Aye, I'll walk, Master Grant. There'll be other planes."

Muttering an oath, he strode purposefully out to his waiting car, towing her with him. He opened the door and gave her a none too gentle shove inside. "You've got a lot of explaining to do, Adelia," he said as he started the engine. She opened her mouth to retort, but he cut her off with a deadly look. "Save it until we get home. I have no desire to commit murder publicly."

She remained silent on the drive home, stubbornly staring out the side window. Pulling up in front of the large stone house, Travis got out of the car, slamming his door with such force Adelia was amazed that the glass remained intact. He pulled Adelia out and dragged her inside.

"We're not to be disturbed," he announced to a

gaping Hannah as he hauled Adelia up the staircase. Pushing her into her room, he slammed the door and locked it. "Now, let's hear it."

"I've an earful for you, Travis Grant," she raged. "You great thundering blackguard, I'm sick to death of your shoving me and pushing me and tearing my arms from the sockets. I warn you, you black-hearted son of the devil, you'll not be battering me about any longer unless you've a mind to have a few bruises of your own!"

"If you've finished," he returned evenly, "I'd like to see you use that double-edged tongue of yours for an explanation."

"I've no need to explain a blessed thing to the likes of you." Her eyes glittered bright green in her furious face. "I told you plain in the note: I want nothing from you. I've my pride if nothing else."

"Yes, you and your Irish pride," Travis growled, stepping forward and taking her by the shoulders. "I'd like to strangle you with your pride. What was all that about divorce and annulments?"

"I thought my wording clear enough." She jerked away and backed up. "I said that, as an annulment was no longer possible, I was leaving and you'd be free to divorce me. I wanted none of your money and would pay you back for what I took with me."

"And you expect me to accept that?" he shouted at her, and she backed up another step. "Just calmly read your little note and go from marriage to divorce in one easy step?"

"Don't you shout at me," she snapped back. "It was agreed when we started that this marriage was only for Uncle Paddy, and we'd have an annulment when he was better. Now that can't be, so you'll have to divorce me. I'm not able to do it myself."

"You can talk of annulments and divorce after last night?" he threw back bitterly. "I thought it meant something to you."

"I can speak of it? I can speak of it?" she roared, out of control. "You dare say that to me? The devil take you, Travis Grant, for your hypocrisy! You'd no more than left the bed when you spoke of divorcing me with your fine lady. Give me money to buy me off, will you? You low, sneaking buzzard! I would rather die than touch one penny of your money, you low-lying snake!"

"Dee, is that why you left?" Travis demanded, shaking her as she resorted to Gaelic curses.

"Aye." Her small fists beat uselessly at his chest. "Take your hands off me, you cursed brute. I'll not wait around to be bought off like some cheap fancy lady."

He picked her up bodily, tucking her like a football under his arm, and ignoring the flailing fists, laid her gently on the bed.

"So it's back to bed again, is it? I'll not lie in this bed with the likes of you again. A curse on you, Travis Grant!"

"Be quiet, you little fool." Travis captured her mouth, shutting off the stream of Gaelic, and held it until her furious struggles lost their force. "Did you think I'd let you go after all I've been through to get you?" He cut off her reply with another breathtaking kiss. "Now, you little spitfire, keep your mouth shut and listen. Margot came here this morning without invitation. She brought up the subject of divorce, not I. In the first place— Keep still," he warned as she squirmed beside him, "or I'll have to get tough." He demonstrated by closing his mouth over hers until, for a moment, her struggles lost their force.

"In the first place," he began again, "I had never considered marrying her; any plans in that direction were her own. We had a fairly compatible relationship for a while— Adelia, *hold still*. You're going to hurt yourself." He shifted his weight, took both of her wrists in his hand, and held them over her head. "She got it into her head that I should marry her and give up my work here, with some crazy notion about traveling the world and living in high style. I told her she was out of her mind, and she took off for Europe, telling me it was her or the horses." He grinned down at Adelia's flushed face. "The horses won, hands down. She got it stuck in that small brain of hers that I married you to spite her, and when she came here this morning going on about divorce and settlements, I let her ramble, curious to see how big a fool she'd make of herself."

He took Adelia's chin in his free hand and held her head still. "Now, if you had listened to the entire conversation, you would have heard me tell her that I had no intention of divorcing a wife I loved, now or any time within the next thousand years."

"You said that?" All struggles stopped.

"Or words to that effect. The meaning was clear."

"I—well, you might have told your wife you loved her. It would have saved a great deal of trouble."

"How could I tell her I loved her five minutes after she raged at me, standing there looking like an outraged urchin?" He brushed her curls aside to kiss the creamy skin of her throat. "My first thought was to gentle you so you could stand the sight of me and go from there. Did you really think I took you to Kentucky and New York just for Majesty?" His lips explored her smooth skin. "I didn't dare let you out of my sight; someone might have come along and snatched you away. I decided to wear you down slowly." His mouth moved over her face with slow, lingering kisses. "I thought I was making some headway, but Paddy's heart attack changed everything. I felt the best way to help him was to assure him of your welfare, so I railroaded you into marriage with the promise of an annulment. Of course"—his free hand began fresh explorations—"I never intended to give you one."

"Let go of my hands," she demanded, and he raised his head and shook it.

"Not if I have to keep you here for the next twenty years."

"You thick-brained idiot, couldn't you see how I was dying for loving you? Let go of my hands, blast your eyes, and kiss me."

She pulled his head to hers with her freed hands, and buried her face in the strong column of his neck.

"It appears," he murmured in her scented hair, "we've wasted a great deal of time."

"You seemed so far away. All those weeks you never even touched me. You never even said you loved me last night."

"I didn't dare touch you. I wanted you so much it was driving me mad. If I had told you I love you last night—and how I wanted to!—you might have thought I said it just to keep you in bed."

"I won't think that now, Travis. Let me hear you say it. I've been needing to hear you say it for such a long time."

He obliged her, telling her over and over until his lips sought hers and told her silently.

"Travis," she finally whispered against his ear. "I'm wondering if you could arrange another thunderstorm?"

Sullivan's Woman

CHAPTER 1

Cassidy waited. Mrs. Sommerson tossed a third rejected dress into her arms.

"Simply won't do," the woman muttered and scowled at a midnight-blue linen. After a moment's consideration this, too, was dumped into the pile over Cassidy's arms. Valiantly Cassidy held on to her patience.

After three months as a sales clerk in The Best Boutique, she felt she'd learned patience, but it hadn't been easy. Dutifully she followed the solid bulk of Mrs. Sommerson to another display of dresses. After twenty-seven minutes of standing around like a clothes rack, Cassidy thought, shifting the weight on her arms, her hard-earned patience was sorely strained.

"I'll try these," Mrs. Sommerson finally announced and marched back to the changing room. Mumbling only a little, Cassidy began to replace unsuitable dresses.

She jammed a loose hairpin into her scalp in irritation. Julia Wilson, The Best's owner, was a stickler for neatness. No hair was allowed to tumble over the shoulders of her clerks. Neat, orderly and unimaginative, Cassidy concluded, and wrinkled her nose at the

midnight-blue linen. It was unfortunate that Cassidy
was disorganized, imaginative, and not altogether
neat. Her hair seemed to epitomize her personality.
There were shades from delicate blond to rich brown
melding into a tone like gold in an old painting. It was
long and heavy and protested against the confines
of pins by continuously slipping through them. Like
Cassie herself, it was unruly and stubborn yet soft and
fascinating.

It had been the appeal of Cassidy's slightly unconventional looks that had prompted her hiring. Experience had not been among her qualifications. Julia
Wilson had recognized a potential advertisement for
her merchandise and knew that Cassidy's long, supple
body would set off the bold colors and styles of her
more adventurous line. The face was undoubtedly a
plus, too. Julia hadn't been certain it was a beautiful
face, but she'd known it was striking. Cassidy's features were sharp and angular, undeniably aristocratic.
Her brows arched over long, lidded eyes that seemed
oversized in her narrow face and were a surprising
violet.

Julia had seen Cassidy's face, figure, and her well-
pitched voice as references but had insisted on having
her pin up her hair. With it down around her shoulders,
it lent a distressingly wanton quality to the aristocratic
features. She was pleased with Cassidy's youth, with her
intelligence, and with her energy. Soon after hiring her,
however, Julia had discovered she was not as pliable as
her age had suggested. She had, Julia felt, an unfortunate tendency to forget her place and become overly
friendly with the customers. More than once, she'd
come upon Cassidy as she asked customers impertinent
questions or gave unwarranted advice. From time to
time her smile suggested she was enjoying some pri-

vate joke. And often, far too often, she daydreamed.
Julia had begun to have serious doubts about Cassidy
St. John's suitability.

After returning Mrs. Sommerson's rejected choices
to their proper place, Cassidy took up her post by the
changing room. From inside she could hear the faint
rustle of materials. Idle, her mind did what it invariably
did when given the opportunity. It drifted back to the
manuscript that lay spread over her desk in her apartment. Waiting.

As far back as memory took her, writing had been
her dream. For four years of college she had studied
the craft seriously. At nineteen she'd been left without family and with little money. She had continued to
work her way through college in various odd jobs while
learning the discipline and art of her chosen profession.
Between her education and employment, Cassidy had
been left with meager snatches of free time. Even these
had been set aside for work on her first novel.

To Cassidy writing was not a career but a vocation.
Her entire life had been guided toward it, leaving her
room for few other attachments. People fascinated her,
but there were few with whom she was deeply involved.
She wrote of complex relationships, but her knowledge
of them came almost entirely secondhand. What gave
her work quality and depth was her sharp talent for observation and her surprising depth of emotion. For the
greater part of her life, her emotions had found their
release in her work.

Now, a full year after graduation, she continued
to take odd jobs to pay the rent. Her first manuscript
worked its way from publishing house to publishing
house while her second came slowly to life.

As Mrs. Sommerson opened the door of the changing room, Cassidy's mind was deep into the reworking

of a dramatic scene. Seeing her standing with proper
handmaidenly reserve, Mrs. Sommerson nodded ap-
provingly. She preened ever so slightly.

"This should do nicely. Don't you agree?"

Mrs. Sommerson's choice was a flaming-red silk.
The color, Cassidy noted, accented her florid complexion but was an attractively sharp contrast to her fluffy
black mane of hair. The dress might have been more
appropriate if Mrs. Sommerson had been a few pounds
lighter, but Cassidy saw possibilities.

"You'll draw eyes, Mrs. Sommerson," she announced after a moment's deliberation. With the proper
accessories, she decided, Mrs. Sommerson might very
likely look regal. The silk, however, strained over her
ample hips. A sterner girdle, Cassidy diagnosed, or a
larger dress. "I think we have this in the next size," she
murmured, thinking aloud.

"I beg your pardon?"

Preoccupied, Cassidy failed to note the dangerous
arch of Mrs. Sommerson's brows. "The next size," she
repeated helpfully. "This one's a bit snug through the
hips. The next size up should fit you perfectly."

"This is my size, young woman." Mrs. Sommerson's bosom lifted then fell. It was an awe-inspiring
movement.

Deep into solving the accessory problem, Cassidy
smiled and nodded. "A splashy gold necklace, I should
think." She tapped her fingertip against her bottom lip.
"Just let me find your size."

"This," Mrs. Sommerson stated in a tone that ar-
rested Cassidy's full attention, "*is* my size." Indignation
seethed in every syllable. Recognizing her mistake,
Cassidy felt a sinking sensation in her stomach.

Whoops, she said silently then pulled her scattered wits together. Before she could begin soothing Mrs. Sommerson's ruffled ego, Julia stepped from behind her.

"A stunning choice, Mrs. Sommerson," she stated in her well-modulated contralto. With a noncommittal smile, she glanced from her customer to her clerk then back again. "Is there a problem?"

"This young woman . . ." Mrs. Sommerson heaved another deep breath. "Insists I've made a mistake in my size."

"Oh, no, ma'am," Cassidy protested, but subsided when Julia arched a penciled brow in her direction.

"I'm certain what Miss St. John meant to say was that this particular style is cut a bit oddly. The sizes simply do not run true."

I should've thought of that, Cassidy admitted to herself.

"Well." Mrs. Sommerson sniffed and eyed Cassidy with disapproval. "She might have said so, rather than suggesting that *I* was a larger size. Really, Julia." She turned back to the changing room. "You should train your staff better."

Cassidy's eyes kindled and grew dark at the tone. She watched the seams of the red silk protest against Mrs. Sommerson's generous posterior. The quick glare from Julia had her swallowing retorts.

"I'll fetch the dress myself, Mrs. Sommerson," Julia soothed, slipping her personable smile back into place. "I'm certain it will be perfect for you. Wait for me in my office, Cassidy," she added in an undertone before gliding off.

With a sinking heart, Cassidy watched Julia's retreat. She recognized the tone all too well. Three months, she mused, then sighed. Oh, well. With one backward glance at Mrs. Sommerson, she moved down the narrow hallway and into Julia's small, smartly decorated office.

She surveyed the square, windowless room, then chose a tiny, straight-backed, bronze cushioned chair. It was here, she remembered, I was hired. And it's here I'll be fired. She jammed another rebellious pin into place and scowled. In a few minutes she'll walk in, lift her left brow and sit behind her perfectly beautiful rosewood desk. She'll look at me a moment, gently clear her throat and begin.

"Cassidy, you're a lovely girl, but your heart isn't in your work."

"Mrs. Wilson," Cassidy imagined herself saying, "Mrs. Sommerson can't wear a size fourteen. I was—"

"Of course not." Cassidy pictured Julia interrupting her with a patient smile. "I wouldn't dream of selling her one, but—" here Cassidy envisioned Julia lifting up one slender, rose-tipped finger for emphasis "—we must allow her illusions *and* her vanity. Tact and diplomacy are essential for a salesperson, Cassidy. I'm afraid you've yet to fully develop these qualities. In a shop such as this—" Julia would fold her hand on the desk's surface "—I must be able to depend, without reservation, on my staff. If this were the first incident, of course, I'd make allowances, but . . ." Here Cassidy imagined Julia would pause and give a small sigh. "Just last week you told Miss Teasdale the black crepe made her look like a mourner. This is not the way we sell our merchandise."

"No, Mrs. Wilson." Cassidy decided she would agree with an apologetic air. "But with Miss Teasdale's hair and her complexion—"

"Tact and diplomacy," Julia would reiterate with a

lifted finger. "You might have suggested that a royal-blue would match her eyes or that a rose would set off her skin. The clientele must be pampered while the merchandise moves. Each woman who walks out the door should feel she has acquired something special."

"I understand that, Mrs. Wilson. I hate to see someone buy something unsuitable; that's why—"

"You have a good heart, Cassidy." Julia would smile maternally then drop the ax. "You simply have no talent for selling . . . at least, not the degree of talent I require. I shall, of course, pay you for the rest of the week and give you a good reference. You've been prompt and dependable. Perhaps you might try clerking in a department store."

Cassidy wrinkled her nose at this point in her scenario, then quickly smoothed her features as the door behind her opened. Julia closed it quietly then lifted her left brow and moved to sit behind her rosewood desk. She studied Cassidy a moment then gently cleared her throat.

"Cassidy, you're a lovely girl, but . . ."

Cassidy's shoulders lifted and fell with her sigh.

An hour later, unemployed, she wandered Fisherman's Wharf, enjoying its cheerful shabbiness, its traveling carnival atmosphere. She loved the cornucopia of scents and sound and color. Here there was always a crowd. Here there was life in ever-changing flavors. San Francisco was Cassidy's concept of a perfect city, but Fisherman's Wharf was the end of the rainbow. Make-believe and reality walked hand in hand.

She passed through the emporiums, poking idly through barrels of trinkets, fingering newly imported silk scarfs and soaking up the noise. But the bay drew her. She moved toward it at an easy, meandering pace as the afternoon gave way to evening. The scent of fish dominated the air. Beneath it were the aromas of onions and spice and humanity.

She listened to the vendors hawk their wares and watched as a crab was selected and boiled in a sidewalk cauldron. The wharf was rimmed with restaurants and crammed with stores. Without apology, its ambience was vaguely dilapidated and faintly tawdry. Cassidy adored it. It was old and friendly and content to be itself.

Nibbling on a hot pretzel, she moved through stalls of hanging Chinese turnips, fresh abalone, and live crabs. Wisps of fog began to curl at her feet, and the sun sank lower. She was grateful for her plum-colored quilted jacket as the breeze swept in from the bay.

If nothing else, she thought ruefully, I acquired some nice clothes at a tidy discount. Cassidy frowned and took a generous bite of her pretzel. If it hadn't been for Mrs. Sommerson's hips, I'd still have a job. After all, I did have her best interests at heart. Annoyed, she pulled the pins from her hair then tossed them into a trash can as she passed. Her hair tumbled to her shoulders in long, loose curls. She breathed a sigh of relief.

Rats. She chewed her pretzel aggressively and headed for the watery front yard of Fisherman's Wharf. I needed that job. I really needed that stupid job. Depression threatened as she walked the dock between lines of moored boats. She began a mental accounting of her finances. The rent was due the following week, and she needed another ream of typing paper. According to her shaky calculations, both of these necessities could be met if she didn't put too much emphasis on food for the next few days.

I won't be the first writer to have to tighten her belt in San Francisco, she decided. The four basic food groups are probably overrated anyway. With a shrug she finished off the pretzel. That could be my last full meal for some time. Grinning, she stuck her hands in her pockets and strolled to the rail at the edge of the dock.

Like a gray ghost, the fog rolled in over the bay. It crept closer to land, swallowing up the water along the way. It was thin tonight, full of patches, not the thick mass that often coated the bay and blinded the city. To the west the sun dipped into the sea and shot spears of flame over the rim of the water. Cassidy waited for the last flash of gold. Already her mood was lifting. She was a creature of hope and optimism, of faith and luck. She believed in destiny. It was, she felt, her destiny to write. The sale of articles and occasional short stories to magazines kept the dream alive. For four years of college her life had revolved around perfecting her craft. Jobs kept a roof over her head and meant nothing more. Dating had been permitted only when her schedule allowed and was kept casual. As yet, Cassidy had met no man who interested her seriously enough to make her veer from the straight path she had chosen. There were no curves in her scheme of things. No detours.

The loss of her current job distressed her only temporarily. Even as the evening sky darkened and the lights of the wharf fluttered on, her mood shifted. She was young and resilient.

Something would turn up, she decided as she leaned over the rail. Wavelets slapped gently against the hull of a fishing boat beside her. She had no need for a great deal of money; any job would do. Clerking in a department store might be just right. Perhaps something in home appliances. It would be difficult to step on anyone's vanity while selling a toaster. Pleased with the thought, Cassidy pushed worries out of her head and watched the fog tumble closer. Its fingers reached toward her.

There was a chill in the air now as the breeze picked up. She let it wash over her, tossing her hair and waking up her skin. The sounds and calls from the stands became remote, muffled by the mist. It was nearly dark. She heard a bird call out as it flew overhead and lifted her face to watch it. The first thin light of the moon fell over her. She smiled, dreaming a little. Abruptly she drew in her breath as a hand gripped her shoulder. Before she could make a sound, she'd been turned around and was staring up into a stranger's face.

He was tall, several inches taller than Cassidy, with a shock of black curls around a lean, raw-boned face. Her mind worked quickly to categorize the face, rejecting handsome in favor of dangerous. Perhaps it was her surprise and the creeping fog and darkening sky that caused the adjective to leap into her mind. But she thought, as she looked up at him, that his features were more in tune with the Barbary Coast than Fisherman's Wharf. His eyes were a deep, intense blue under black, winged brows, and his forehead was high under the falling black curls. His nose was long and straight, his mouth full, and his chin faintly cleft. It was a compelling, hard-hitting face with no softening features. He had a rangy build accentuated by snug jeans and a black pullover. After her initial shock passed, Cassidy gripped her purse tight and squared her shoulders.

"I've only got ten dollars," she told him, keeping her chin fearlessly lifted. "And I need it at least as badly as you."

"Be quiet," he ordered shortly and narrowed his eyes. They were oddly intent on her face, searching, probing in a manner that made her shiver. When he cupped her chin in his hand, Cassidy's courage slipped away again. Without speaking, he turned her head from one side to the other, all the while studying her with absolute concentration. His eyes were hypnotic. She watched him, speechless, as his brows lowered in a frown. There was speculation in the look. She tried to jerk away.

"Be still, will you?" he demanded. His deep voice sounded annoyed, and his fingers were very firm.

Cassidy swallowed. "Now listen," she said with apparent calm. "I've a black belt in karate and will certainly break both your arms if you try to molest me." As she spoke she glanced past his shoulder and was dismayed to see the lights of the restaurants behind them had dimmed in the fog. They were alone. "I can break a two-by-four in half with my bare hand," she added when his expression failed to register terror and respect. She noted that the fingers on her chin were strong, and that despite his rangy build his shoulders were broad. "And I can scream very loudly," she continued. "You'd better go away."

"Perfect," he murmured and ran his thumb along her jawline. Cassidy's heart thudded with alarm. "Absolutely perfect. Yes, you'll do." All at once the intensity cleared from his eyes, and he smiled. The transformation was so rapid, so startling, Cassidy simply stared. "Why would you want to do that?"

"Do what?" Cassidy asked, astonished by his metamorphosis.

"Break a two-by-four in half with your bare hand."

"Do *what*?" Her own bogus claim was forgotten. Confused, she frowned at him. "Oh, well, it's—it's for practice, I suppose. You have to think right through the board, I believe, so that—" She stopped, realizing she was standing on a deserted dock in the fog holding an absurd conversation with a maniac who still had her chin in his hand. "You'd really better let me go and be on your way before I have to do something drastic."

"You're exactly what I've been looking for," he told her but made no attempt to act on her suggestion.

"Well, I'm sorry. I'm not interested. I have a husband who's a linebacker for the 49ers. He's six feet five, two hundred and sixty-three pounds and *very* jealous. He'll be along any minute. Now let me go and you can have the blasted ten dollars."

"What the devil are you babbling about?" His brows lowered again. With the fog swirling thinly at his back, he looked fierce. Abruptly, one black brow flew up to disappear beneath the careless curls. "Do you think I'm going to mug you?" A flash of irritation crossed his face. "My dear child, I've no designs on your ten dollars or on your honor. I'm going to paint you, not ravish you."

"Paint me?" Cassidy was intrigued. "Are you an artist? You don't look like one." She considered his dashing, buccaneer's features. "What sort of an artist are you?"

"An excellent one," he replied easily and tilted her face a tad higher. A splash of moonlight found it. "I'm famous, talented, and temperamental." The charming smile was back on his face, and the cadence was Irish. Cassidy responded to both.

"I'm desperately impressed," she said. He was obviously a lunatic but an appealing one. She forgot to be afraid.

"Of course you are," he agreed and turned her head to left profile. "It's only to be expected." He freed her chin at last, but the tingle of his fingers remained on her skin. "I've a houseboat just outside the city. We'll go there and I can start sketching you tonight."

Cassidy's eyes lit with wary amusement. "Aren't you supposed to offer to show me sketches, or is this a variation on an old theme?" She no longer considered him dangerous, merely persistent.

He sighed, and she watched the quick annoyance flash over his face. "The woman has a one-track mind. Listen . . . what is your name?"

"Cassidy," she answered automatically. "Cassidy St. John."

"Oh, no, half Irish, half English. We'll have trouble there." He stuck his hands into his pockets. His eyes seemed determined to know every inch of her face. "Cassidy, I have no need for your ten dollars, and no plans to tamper with your virtue. What I want is your face. I've a sketch pad and so forth on my houseboat."

"I wouldn't go on Michelangelo's boat if he handed me that line." Cassidy relaxed the grip on her purse and pushed her hair from her shoulders. Though he made a swift sound of exasperation, she grinned.

"All right." She sensed the impatience in his stance as he glanced behind him. "We'll get a cup of coffee in a well-lit, crowded restaurant. Will that suit you? If I try anything improper, you can break the table in half with your famous bare hand and draw attention."

Cassidy's lips trembled into a fresh grin. "I think I could agree to that." Before she could say anything else, he had her hand in his and was pulling her toward the cluster of restaurants. She felt an odd intimacy in the gesture along with a sense of his absolute control and determination. He was a man, she decided, who wouldn't take no for an answer. He walked quickly. She wondered if he were perpetually in a hurry. His stride was smooth, loose-limbed.

He pulled her into a small, rather dingy café and found a booth. The moment they were seated he again fixed her with his intent stare. His eyes, she noted, were even more blue than they had seemed in the dim light. Their color was intensified by his thick black lashes and bronze-toned skin. Cassidy met him stare for stare as she wondered what sort of man lived behind that incredible shade of blue. It was the waitress who broke her attention.

"What'll ya have?"

"Oh . . . coffee," she said when her companion made no move to speak or cease his staring. "Two coffees." When the waitress clomped away, Cassidy turned back to him. "Why do you stare at me like that?" she demanded. It annoyed her that her nerves responded to the look. "It's very rude," she pointed out. "And very distracting."

"The light's dreadful in here, but it's some improvement over the fog. Don't frown," he ordered. "It gives you a line right here." Before she could move he had lifted a finger and traced it down between her brows. "You have a remarkable face. I can't decide whether the eyes are an advantage or a drawback. One tends to disbelieve violet."

As Cassidy attempted to digest this, the waitress returned with their coffee. Glancing up, he plucked the pencil from her pocket and gave her one of his lightning smiles. "I need this for a few minutes. Drink your coffee. Relax," he directed with a careless gesture of his hand. "This won't hurt a bit."

Cassidy obeyed as he began to sketch on the paper placemat in front of him. "Do you have a job we'll need to work around or does your fictitious husband support you with his football prowess?"

"How do you know he's fictitious?" Cassidy countered and forced her eyes away from the planes of his face.

"The same way I know you'd have a great deal of trouble with a two-by-four." He continued to sketch. "Do you have a job?"

"I was fired this afternoon," she muttered into her coffee.

"That simplifies matters. Don't frown, I'm not a patient man. I'll pay you the standard sitting fee." He glanced up as Cassidy's brows lifted. "What I have in mind should take no more than two months, if all goes well. Don't look so shocked, Cassidy, my intentions were pure and honorable from the beginning. It was only your lurid imagination—"

"My imagination is not that lurid," she tossed back indignantly. She shifted in her seat as she felt her cheeks warm. "When people come looming up out of the fog and seizing other people—"

"Looming?" he interrupted and stopped sketching long enough to give her a dry look. "I don't believe I did any looming or seizing tonight."

"It seemed a great deal like looming and seizing from my perspective," she grumbled before she sipped her coffee. Her eyes dropped to the sketch he made. She set down the cup, her eyes widening with surprised admiration. "That's wonderful!"

In a few bold strokes he had captured her. She saw not just the shape of her own hair, but an expression she recognized as essentially her own. "It's really wonderful," she repeated as he began another sketch. "You really *are* talented. I thought you were bragging."

"I'm unflinchingly honest," he murmured as his borrowed pencil moved across the placemat.

Recognizing the quality of his work, Cassidy became more enthusiastic. Her mind raced ahead. Steady

employment for two months would be a godsend. By
the end of that time she should have heard from the publishing house that had her manuscript under consideration. Two months without having to sell toasters! She
would have her evenings free to work on her new plot.
The benefits began to mount and multiply. Destiny
must have sent Mrs. Sommerson in search of a dress
that afternoon.

"Do you really want me to sit for you?"

"You're precisely what I need." His manner suggested that the matter was already settled. The second sketch was nearly completed. His coffee cooled,
untouched. "I want you to start in the morning. Nine
should be early enough."

"Yes, but—"

"Keep your hair down, and don't pile on layers
of makeup, you'll just have to wash it off. You might
smudge up your eyes a bit, but little else."

"I haven't said I'd—"

"You'll need the address, I suppose," he continued,
ignoring her protests. "Do you know the city well?"

"I was born here," she told him with a superior sniff.
"But I—"

"Well then, you shouldn't have any trouble finding
my studio." He scrawled an address on the bottom of
the placemat. Abruptly he lifted his eyes and captured
hers again.

They stared at each other amid the clatter of cutlery
and chatter of voices. What Cassidy felt in that brief
moment she could not define, but she knew she had
never experienced it before. Then, as quickly as it had
occurred, it passed. He rose, and she was left feeling
as if she had run a very long race in a very short time.

"Nine o'clock," he said simply; then as an afterthought he dropped a bill on the table for the coffee. He left without another word.

Reaching over, Cassidy picked up the placemat with the sketches and the address. For a moment she studied her face as he had seen it. Was her chin really shaped that way? she wondered and lifted her thumb and finger to trace it. She remembered his hand holding it in precisely the same fashion. With a shrug she dropped her hand then carefully folded the placemat. It wouldn't do any harm to go to his studio in the morning, she decided as she slipped the paper into her purse. She could get a look at things and then make up her mind if she wanted to sit for him or not. If she had any doubts, all she had to do was say no and walk out. Cassidy remembered his careless dominance and frowned. All I have to do, she repeated to herself sternly, is to say no and walk out. With this thought she rose and strolled out of the café.

CHAPTER 2

The morning was brilliantly clear, with a warmth promising more before afternoon. Cassidy dressed casually, not certain what was *de rigueur* for a prospective artist's model. Jeans and a full-sleeved white blouse seemed appropriate. As instructed she had left her hair loose, and her makeup was light enough to appear nonexistent. She had yet to decide if she would sit for the strange, intriguing man she had met in the fog, but she was curious enough to keep the appointment.

With the address safely copied onto her own notepad and tucked in her purse, Cassidy grabbed a cable car that would take her downtown. The scribbled address had surprised her, as she had recognized the exclusiveness of the area. Somehow she'd expected her artist to have his studio near her own apartment in North Beach. There the atmosphere was informal and enduringly bohemian. Traditionally, clutches of writers and artists and musicians inhabited that section of the city and maintained its flavor. She wondered if perhaps he had a patron who had set him up in an expensive studio. He hadn't fit her conception of an artist. At least, she corrected herself, until she had seen his hands. They were, Cassidy recalled, perhaps the most beautiful hands she had ever seen, long and narrow with lean, tapering fingers. The bones had been close to the surface. Sensitive hands. And strong, she added, remembering the feel of his fingers on her skin.

His face remained clear in her mind, and she brooded over its image for several moments. Something about it tugged at a vague memory, but she couldn't bring her recollection into focus. It was a distinctive face, unique in its raw appeal. She thought if she were an artist, it would be a face she would be compelled to paint. There were good bones there and shadows and secrets, dominated by the terrifying blue of his eyes.

The trolley's bells clanged and snapped Cassidy out of her reverie. Stupid, she thought and lifted her face to the breeze. I didn't even get his name, and I'm obsessed with his face. He's supposed to be obsessed with mine, not the other way around. She jumped from the trolley and stepped onto the sidewalk. She scanned the street numbers looking for the address. I was right, she mused, about the quality of the neighborhood.

Still, like all of the city, it was a fascinating mixture of the exotic and the cosmopolitan, the romantic and the practical. San Francisco's dual personality was as prevalent here as it was in Chinatown or on Telegraph Hill. There remained a blending of the antique and the revolutionary. Cassidy could hear the clang of the old-fashioned trolley as she looked up at a radically new steel-and-glass skyscraper.

The day was fine and warm, and her body enjoyed

it while her mind drifted back to the plot that sat on her desk at home. She brought her attention back to the present when she reached the number corresponding to the address in her purse. She stood frowning.

The Gallery. Cassidy scanned the number on the door for confirmation, and her frown deepened. She'd browsed through The Gallery only a few months before, and she remembered quite well when it had opened five years ago. Since its opening it had gained an enviable reputation as a showcase for the finest art in the country. A showing at The Gallery could make a fledgling artist's career or enhance that of a veteran. Collectors and connoisseurs were known to gather there to buy or to admire, to criticize or simply to be seen. Like much of the city it was a combination of the elegant and the unconventional. The architecture of the building was simple and unpretentious, while inside was a treasure trove of paintings and sculpture. Cassidy was also aware that one of The Gallery's biggest draws was its owner, Colin Sullivan. She searched her memory for what she had read of him, then began to put the bits and pieces into order.

An Irish immigrant, he had lived in America for more than fifteen years; his career had taken off when he had been barely twenty. Oil was his usual medium, and a unique use of shading and light his trademark. He had a reputation for impatience and brilliance. He would be just past thirty now and unmarried, though there had been several women linked romantically with him. There had been a princess once, and a prima ballerina. His paintings sold for exorbitant sums, and he rarely took commissions. He painted to please himself and painted well. As she stood in the warmth of the morning sunlight piecing together her tidbits of gossip and information, Cassidy recalled why the face of her artist had jarred a memory. She'd seen his picture in the newspaper when The Gallery had opened five years before. Colin Sullivan.

She let out a long breath then lifted her hands to either side of her head to push at her hair. Colin Sullivan wanted to paint her. He had once flatly refused to do a portrait of one of Hollywood's reigning queens, but he wanted to paint Cassidy St. John, an unemployed writer whose greatest triumph to date was a short story printed in a woman's magazine. All at once she remembered that she'd thought he'd been a mugger, that she had said absurd things to him, that she had told him with innocent audacity that his sketches were good. In annoyance and humiliation she chewed on her lip.

He might have introduced himself, she thought with a frown, instead of sneaking up behind me and grabbing me. I behaved quite naturally under the circumstances. I've nothing to be embarrassed about. Besides, she reminded herself, he told me to come. He's the one who arranged the entire thing. I'm only here to see if I want to take the job. Cassidy shifted her purse on her shoulder, wished briefly she had worn something more dignified or more exotic and moved to the front door of The Gallery. It was locked.

She pushed against the door again then concluded with a sigh that it was too early for The Gallery to be open. Perhaps there was a back entrance. He had spoken of a studio; surely it would have its own outside door. With this in mind Cassidy strolled around the side of the building and tried a side door, which refused to budge. Undaunted, she continued around the square brick building to its rear. When another door proved uncooperative, she turned her attention to a set of wooden steps leading to a second level.

Craning her neck, she squinted against the sun and

scanned the ring of windows. The glass tossed back the light. If I were an artist with a studio, she reflected, it would definitely be up there. She began to climb the L-shaped staircase. The treads were open and steep. Faced with another door at the top, she started to test the knob, hesitated and opted to knock. Loudly. She glanced back over her shoulder and discovered the ground was surprisingly far below. A tiny sound of alarm escaped her when the door swung open.

"You're late," Colin stated with a frown of impatience and took her hand, pulling her inside before she could respond. Her senses were immediately assailed with the scents of turpentine and oils. He looked no less formidable in broad daylight than he had in the murky fog. In precisely the same manner he had employed the night before, he caught her chin in his hand.

"Mr. Sullivan . . ." Cassidy began, flustered.

"Ssh!" He tilted her head to the left, narrowed his eyes and stared. "Yes, it's even better in decent light. Come over here, I want some proper sketches."

"Mr. Sullivan," Cassidy tried again as he yanked her across a high, airy room lined with canvases and cluttered with equipment. "I'd like to know a little more about all this before I commit myself."

"Sit here," he commanded and pushed her down on a stool. "Don't slouch," he added as he turned away.

"Mr. Sullivan! Would you please listen to me?"

"Presently," he replied as he picked up a wide pad and a pencil. "For now be quiet."

Totally at a loss, Cassidy sighed gustily and folded her hands. It would be simpler, she decided, to let him get his sketches out of his system. She allowed her eyes to wander and search the room.

It was large, barnlike, with wide windows and a

skylight that pleased her enormously. The expanses
of glass let in all the available sunlight. The floor was
wood and bare, except for splatters of paint, and the
walls were a neutral cream. Unframed canvases were
stacked helter-skelter, facing the walls. Easels were
propped here and there, and a large table was scattered
with paints and brushes and rags and bottles. There
was a couch at the far end of the room, sitting there as
if added in afterthought. Three wooden chairs were
placed at odd intervals as if pushed aside by an impatient hand and left wherever they landed. There were
two other stools, two inside doors, and a large goose
necked high-intensity lamp.

"Look out the window," Colin ordered abruptly. "I
want a profile."

She obeyed. The vague annoyance she felt slipped
away as she spotted a sparrow building a nest in the
crook of an oak. The bird moved busily, carrying wisps
of this and that in her beak. Patient and tenacious, she
swooped and searched and built, then swooped again.
Her wings caught the sun. Enchanted, Cassidy watched
her. A quiet smile touched her lips and warmed her eyes.

"What do you see?" Colin moved to her, and her absorption was so deep she neither jolted nor turned.

"That bird there." She pointed as the sparrow made
another quick dive. "Look how determined she is to finish that nest. The whole thing built from bits of string
and grass and whatever other treasures sparrows find.
We need bricks and concrete and prefabricated walls,
but that little bird can build a perfectly adequate home
out of next to nothing, without hands, without tools,
without a union representative. Marvelous, don't you
think?" Cassidy turned her head and smiled. He was
closer than she had imagined, his face near hers in order

for him to follow her line of vision. As she turned, he shifted his eyes from the window and caught hers. She felt a sudden jolt, as if she had stood too quickly and lost her inner balance.

"You might be even more perfect than I had originally thought," Colin said. He brushed her hair behind one shoulder.

She suddenly remembered her resolve to be businesslike. "Mr. Sullivan—"

"Colin," he interrupted. He continued to arrange her hair. "Or just Sullivan, if you like."

"Colin, then," she said patiently. "I had no idea who you were last night. It didn't occur to me until I was standing outside The Gallery." She shifted, faintly disturbed that he remained standing so close. "Of course, I'm flattered that you want to paint me, but I'd like to know what's expected of me, and—"

"You're expected to hold a pose for twenty minutes without fidgeting," he began while he pushed her hair forward again then back over her other shoulder. His fingers brushed Cassidy's neck and caused her to frown. He appeared not to notice. "You're expected to follow instructions and keep quiet unless I tell you otherwise. You're expected to be on time and not to babble about leaving early so you can meet your boyfriend."

"I was on time," Cassidy retorted and tossed her head so that his arrangement of her hair flew into confusion. "You didn't tell me to come to the back, and I wandered around until I found the right door."

"Bright, too," he said dryly. "Your eyes darken dramatically when your Irish is up. Who named you Cassidy?"

"It's my mother's family name," she said shortly. She opened her mouth to speak again.

"I knew some Cassidys in Ireland," he commented as he lifted her hands to examine them.

"I don't know any of my mother's family," Cassidy murmured, disconcerted by the feel of his hands on hers. "She died when I was born."

"I see." Colin turned her palms up. "Your hands are very narrow-boned. And your father?"

"His family was from Devon. He died four years ago. I don't see what this has to do with anything."

"It has to do with everything." He lifted his eyes from her hands but kept them in his. "You get your eyes and hair from your mother's family, and your skin and bone structure from your father's. It's a face of contradictions you have, Cassidy St. John, and precisely what I need. Your hair must have a dozen varying shades and it looks as though you've just taken your head from a pillow. You're wise not to attempt to discipline it. Your eyes go just past Celtic-blue into violet and add a touch of the exotic with the shape of them. They tend to dream. But your bones are all English aristocracy. Your mouth tips the balance again, promising a passion the cool British complexion denies. Pure skin, just a hint of rose under the ivory. You haven't walked through life without having to scale a few walls, yet there's a definite aura of the ingenue around you. The painting I want to do must have certain elements. I need very specific qualities in my model. You have them." He paused and inclined his head. "Does that satisfy your curiosity?"

She was staring at him, transfixed, trying to see herself as he described. Did her heritage so heavily influence her looks? "I'm not at all certain that it does," Cassidy murmured. She sighed, then her eyes found him again. "But I'm vain enough to want Colin Sullivan to paint me and destitute enough to need the job." She smiled. "Shall I be immortal when you've finished? I've always wanted to be."

Colin laughed, and the sound was warm and free in the big room. He squeezed her hands, then surprisingly brought them to his lips. "You'll do me, Cass."

Cassidy's fumbling reply was interrupted as the studio door swung open.

"Colin, I need to—" The woman who swirled into the room halted abruptly and fixed sharp eyes on Cassidy. "Sorry," she said as her gaze drifted to their joined hands. "I didn't know you were occupied."

"No matter, Gail," Colin returned easily. "You know I lock the door when I'm working seriously. This is Cassidy St. John, who'll be sitting for me. Cassidy, Gail Kingsley, a very talented artist who manages The Gallery."

Gail Kingsley was striking. She was tall and thin as a reed with a long, triangular face set off by a spiky cap of vivid red hair. Everything about her was vital and compelling. Her eyes were piercingly green and darkly accented, her mouth was wide and slashed in uncompromising scarlet. Gold hoops poked through the spikes of vibrant hair at her ears. Her dress was flowing, without a definite line, a chaotic mix of greens washed over silk. The effect was bold and breathtaking. She moved forward, and her entire body seemed charged with nervous energy. Even her movements were quick and sharp, her eyes probing as they rested on Cassidy's face. There was something in the look that made Cassidy instantly uncomfortable. It was a purposeful intrusion while it remained completely impersonal.

"Good bones," Gail commented in a dismissing tone. "But the coloring's rather dull, don't you think?"

Cassidy spoke with annoyed directness. "We can't all be redheads."

"True enough," Colin said and, lifting a brow at Cassidy, turned to Gail. "What was it you needed? I want to get back to work."

There is a certain aura around people who have been intimate, Cassidy thought. It shows in a look, a gesture, a tone of voice. In the moment Gail's eyes left Cassidy to meet Colin's, she knew they were, or had been, lovers. Cassidy felt a vague sense of disappointment. Uncomfortable, she tried vainly to pull her hands from Colin's. She received an absentminded frown.

"It's Higgin's *Portrait of a Girl*. We've been offered five thousand, but Higgin won't accept unless you approve. I'd like to have it firmed up today."

"Who made the offer?"

"Charles Dupres."

"Tell Higgin to take it. Dupres won't haggle and he's fair. Anything else?" There was a simple dismissal in the words. Cassidy watched Gail's eyes flare.

"Nothing that can't wait. I'll go give Higgin a call."

"Fine." Colin turned back to Cassidy before Gail was halfway across the room. He was frowning at her hair as he pushed it back from her face. Over his shoulder, Cassidy watched Gail's glance dart back when she reached the door. Gail shut it firmly behind her. Colin stepped away and scanned Cassidy from head to toe.

"It won't do," he announced and scowled. "It won't do at all."

Confused by his statement, shaken by what she had recognized in Gail's eyes, Cassidy stared at him then ran her fingers through her hair. "What won't?"

"That business you have on." He made a gesture

with his hand, a quick flick of the wrist, which encompassed her blouse and jeans and sandals.

Cassidy looked down and ran her palms over her hips. "You didn't specify how I should dress, and in any case I hadn't decided to sit for you." She shrugged her shoulders, annoyed with herself for feeling compelled to justify her attire. "You might have given me some details instead of scrawling down the address and bounding off."

"I want something smooth and flowing—no waist, no interruptions." He ignored Cassidy's comments. "Ivory, not white. Something long and sleek." He took her waist in his hands, which threw her into speechless shock. "You haven't any hips to speak of, and the waist of a child. I want a high neck so we won't worry about the lack of cleavage."

Blushing furiously, Cassidy slipped down from the stool and pushed him away. "It's my body, you know. I don't care for your observations on it or your—your hands on it, either. My cleavage or the lack of it has nothing to do with you."

"Don't be a child," he said briskly and set her back on the stool. "At the moment, your body only interests me artistically. If that changes, you'll know quickly enough."

"Now just a minute, Sullivan." Cassidy slipped off the stool again, tossing back her head as she prepared to put him neatly in his place.

"Spectacular." He grabbed a handful of her hair to keep her face lifted to his. "Temper becomes you, Cass, but it's not the mood I'm looking for. Another time, perhaps." The corners of his mouth lifted as his fingers moved to massage her neck. His smile settled lazily over his face, and though Cassidy suspected the calculation, it was no less effective. She was conscious of his fingers on her skin. The essential physicality of the sensation was novel and intrigued her into silence. This was something new to be explored. His voice lowered into a caress no less potent than the hand on her skin. The faint lilt of Ireland intensified. "It's an illusion I'm looking for, and a reality. A wish. Can you be a wish for me, Cass?"

In that moment, with her face inches from his, their bodies just touching, the warmth of his fingers on her skin, Cassidy felt she could be anything he asked. Nothing was impossible. This was where his power over women lay, she realized: in the quick charm, the piratical features, the light hint of an old country in his speech. Added to this was an undiluted sexuality he turned on at will and an impatience in the set of his shoulders. She knew he was aware of his power and used it shamelessly. Even this was somehow attractive. She felt herself submitting to it, drawn toward it while her emotions overshadowed her intellect. She wondered what his mouth would feel like on hers, and if the kiss would be as exciting as she imagined. Would she lose or find herself? Would she simply experience? As a defense against her own thoughts, she placed her hands on his chest and pushed herself to safety.

"You're not an easy man, are you, Colin?" Cassidy took a deep breath to steady her limbs.

"Not a bit." There was careless agreement in his answer. She defined what flicked over his face as something between annoyance and curiosity. "How old are you, Cassidy?"

"Twenty-three," she answered, meeting his eyes levelly. "Why?"

He shrugged, stuck his hands in his pockets then

paced the room. "I'll need to know all there is to know about you before I'm done. What you are will creep into the portrait, and I'll have to work with it. I've got to find the blasted dress quickly—I want to start. The time's right." There was an urgency in his movements that contrasted sharply with the man who had seduced her with his voice only moments before. Who was Colin Sullivan? Cassidy wondered. Though she knew finding out would be dangerous, she felt compelled to learn.

"I think I know one that might do," she hazarded while his mood swirled around the room. "It's more oyster than ivory, actually, but it's simple and straight with a high neck. It's also horribly expensive. It's silk, you see—"

"Where is it?" Colin demanded and stopped his pacing directly in front of her. "Never mind," he continued even as she opened her mouth to tell him. "Let's go have a look."

He had her by the hand and had passed through the back door before she could say another word. Cassidy took care to go along peacefully down the stairs, not wishing to risk a broken neck. "Which way?" he demanded as he marched her to the front of the building.

"It's just a few blocks that way," she said and pointed to the left. "But, Colin—" Before she could finish her thought, she was being piloted at full speed down the sidewalk. "Colin, I think you should know . . . Good grief, I should've worn my track shoes. Would you slow down?"

"You've got long legs," he told her and continued without slackening his pace. Making a brief sound of disgust, Cassidy trotted to keep up. "I think you should know the dress is in the shop I was fired from yesterday."

"A dress shop?" This appeared to interest him enough to slow him down while he glanced at her. With a gesture of absent familiarity, he tucked her hair behind her ear. "What were you doing working in a dress shop?"

Cassidy sent him a withering stare. "I was earning a living, Sullivan. Some of us are required to do so in order to eat."

"Don't be nasty, Cass," he advised mildly. "You're not a professional dress clerk."

"Which is precisely why I was fired." Amused by her own ineptitude, she grinned. "I'm also not a professional waitress, which is why I was fired from Jim's Bar and Grill. I objected to having certain parts of my anatomy pinched and dumped a bowl of coleslaw on a paying customer. I won't go into my brief career as a switchboard operator. It's a sad, pitiful story, and it's such a lovely day." She tossed back her head to smile at Colin and found him watching her.

"If you're not a professional clerk or waitress or switchboard operator, what are you, Cass?"

"A struggling writer who seems singularly inept at holding a proper job since college."

"A writer." He nodded as he looked down at her. "What do you write?"

"Unpublished novels," she told him and smiled again. "And an occasional article on the effects of perfume on the modern man. I have to keep my hand in."

"And are you any good?" Colin skirted another pedestrian without taking his eyes from Cassidy.

"I'm positively brimming with fresh, undiscovered talent." She tossed her hair behind her shoulders then pointed. "There we are, The Best Boutique. I wonder what Julia will have to say about this. She'll probably think you're keeping me." She bit her lip to suppress a giggle then slid her glance back to his. "Have you any smoldering looks up your sleeve, Colin?" Mischief danced in her eyes as she paused outside the front door of the shop. "You could send me a few and give Julia something to talk about for weeks." She swung through the door, her lovely face flushed with laughter.

True to form, Julia greeted Colin with scrupulous politeness and only the faintest glimmer of curiosity. There was a speculative glance for her former clerk, then recognition of Colin widened her eyes. She lifted a brow at Cassidy's request for the oyster silk dress then proceeded to wait on them personally.

In the changing room Cassidy stripped off her jeans and marveled at the irony of life. Little more than twenty-four hours before, she had been standing outside that very room with discarded dresses heaped over her arms . . . without a thought of Colin Sullivan in her head. Now he seemed to dominate both her thoughts and her actions. The thin, cool silk was slipping over her head because he wished it. Her heart beat just a fraction quicker because he waited to see the results. Cassidy fastened the zipper, held her breath and turned. Her reflection stared back at her with undisguised awe.

The dress fell from a severely high neck in a straight line, softened by the fragility of the material. Her arms and shoulders gleamed under the thin transparency of its full sleeves. Her hair glowed with life against the delicacy of color. Cassidy let out her breath slowly. It was a wish of a dress, as romantic as the material, as practical as its line. In it she not only looked both elegant and vulnerable but felt it. With taut nerves she moistened her lips and stepped from the changing room.

Colin was charming Julia into blushes. The incongruity of flirtatious color in the cool, composed face turned Cassidy's nerves into amusement. There was the devil of a smile in Colin's eyes as he lifted Julia's hand and brushed his lips over her knuckles. Cassidy schooled her features to sobriety. A hint of a smile lurked on her lips.

"Colin."

He turned as she called his name. The smile that lit his face and brightened his eyes faded then died. Releasing Julia's hand, he took a few steps closer but kept half the room between them. Cassidy, who had been about to grin and spin a circle for inspection, stood still, hypnotized by his eyes.

Very slowly, his eyes left her face to travel down the length of her then back again. Cassidy's cheeks grew warm with the flurry of her emotions. How could he make her feel so vitalized then so enervated with just a look? She wanted to speak, to break her own trance, but the words were jumbled and uncooperative. She found she could only repeat his name.

"Colin?" There was the faintest hint of invitation in the word, a question even she did not understand.

Something flashed in his eyes and was gone. The intense concentration was inexplicably replaced by irritation. When he spoke it was brisk and dismissive.

"That will do very well. Have it packed up and bring it with you tomorrow. We'll start then."

Cassidy's mind raced with a hundred questions and a hundred demands. His tone stiffened her pride, however, and hers was cool when she spoke. "Is that all?"

"That's all." Temper hovered in his voice. "Nine o'clock tomorrow. Don't be late."

Cassidy took a deep breath and let it out carefully. In that moment she was certain she despised him. They

watched each other for another minute while the air
crackled with tension and something more volatile.
Then she turned her back on him and glided into the
changing room.

CHAPTER 3

Cassidy spent most of the night lecturing herself. By morning she felt she had herself firmly in hand. There had been absolutely no reason for her to be annoyed with Colin. His brisk, impersonal attitude over the dress was only to be expected. As she rode the trolley across town, she shifted the dress box into her other arm and determined to preserve a cool, professional distance from him.

He's simply my employer. He's an artist, obviously a temperamental one. She added the modifier with a sniff. Deftly she jumped from the cable car to finish the trip on foot. *He's a man who sees something in my face he wants to paint. He has no personal feelings for me, nor I for him. How could I? I barely know Colin Sullivan. What I felt yesterday was simply the overflow of his personality. It's very strong, very magnetic. I only imagined that there was an immediate affinity between us. Things don't happen that way, not that fast. All there is between us is the bond between artist and subject. I was writing scenes again.*

Cassidy paused at the base of the stairs that led to

Colin's studio. Still, he might have thanked me for finding the dress he was looking for, she thought. Never
mind. She made an involuntary gesture with her hand
as she climbed the steps. He's so self-absorbed he probably forgot I suggested the shop in the first place. With
a quick toss of her head, Cassidy knocked, prepared to
be brisk and professional in her new employ. Her resolve
wavered a bit when Gail Kingsley opened the door.

"Hello," she said and smiled despite the cool assess-
ment in Gail's eyes. For an answer Gail made a sweeping arm gesture into the room that would have seemed
overdone on anyone else. Flamboyance suited her.

Gail was just as striking today in a shocking-pink
jumpsuit no other redhead would have had the courage
to wear. Colin was nowhere in sight. Cassidy was torn
between admiration for the redhead's style and disappointment that Colin hadn't answered the door. She felt
juvenile and ragged in jeans and a pullover.

"Am I too early?"

Gail placed her hands on her narrow hips and
walked around Cassidy slowly. "No, Colin's tied up.
He'll be along. Is that curl in your hair natural or have
you a perm?"

"It's natural," Cassidy replied evenly.

"And the color?"

"Mine, too." Gail's bold perfume dominated the
scents of paint. When she came back to stand in front
of her, Cassidy met her eyes levelly. "Why?"

"Just curious, dear heart. Just curious." Gail flashed
a quick, dazzling smile that snapped on and off like a
light. It was momentarily blinding, then all trace of it
vanished. "Colin's quite taken with your face. He seems
to be drifting into a romantic period. I've always avoided
that sort of technique." She narrowed her eyes until she
seemed to be examining the pores of Cassidy's skin.

"Want to count my teeth?" Cassidy invited.

"Don't be snide." Gail touched a scarlet-tipped finger to her lips. "Colin and I often share models. I want to see if I can use you for anything."

"I'm not a box lunch, Miss Kingsley," retorted Cassidy with feeling. "I don't care to be shared."

"A good model should be flexible," Gail reproved, stretching her slender arms to the ceiling in one long, luxurious movement. "I hope you don't make a fool of yourself the way the last one did."

"The last one?" Cassidy responded then immediately wanted to bite off her tongue.

"She fell desperately in love with Colin." Gail gave her quick light-switch smile again. Her sharp, rapid gestures skittered down Cassidy's nerves. She was a cat looking for something to stalk. "Worse, she imagined Colin was in love with her. It was really quite pathetic. A lovely little thing—milky skin, dark eyes. Naturally Colin was beastly to her in the end. He tends to be when someone tries to pin him down. There's nothing worse than having someone mooning and sighing over you, is there?"

"I wouldn't know," Cassidy returned in mild tones. "But you needn't worry that I'll be mooning and sighing over Colin. He needs my face, I need a job." She paused a moment. Perhaps, she thought, it's best to be clear from the start. "You won't have any trouble from me, Gail. I'm too busy to orchestrate a romance with Colin."

Gail stopped her pacing long enough to fix her with a speculative frown. The frown vanished, and she moved swiftly to the door. "That simplifies matters, doesn't it? You can change through there." She flung out an arm to her left and was gone.

Cassidy took time to inhale deeply. She shook her

head. Artists, she decided, were all as mad as hatters. Shrugging off Gail's behavior, she moved to the door indicated and found a small dressing room. Closeting herself inside, Cassidy began to change. As before, the gown made her feel different. Perhaps, she thought as she pulled a brush through her hair, it's the sensation of real silk against my skin, or the elegant simplicity of the line and color. Or is it because it's the image of what Colin wants me to be?

Whatever the reason, Cassidy couldn't deny that she felt heightened when she wore the gown—more alive, more aware, more a woman. After giving herself one last quick glance in the mirror, she opened the door and stepped into the studio.

"Oh, you're here," she said foolishly when she saw Colin scowling at a blank canvas. She had only a side view of him, and he didn't turn at her entrance. His hands were stuffed in his pockets, and his weight was distributed evenly on both legs. There was an impression of sharp vitality held in check—waiting, straining a bit for release. He was dressed casually, as she was now accustomed to seeing him, and the clothes seemed to suit his rangy, loose-limbed build. His face was in a black study: brows lowered, eyes narrowed, mouth unsmiling. The thought crossed Cassidy's mind that he was unscrupulously attractive and would be a terrifying man to care for. She remained where she was, certain he had not even heard her speak.

"I'm going to start on canvas straight away," he said. Still he did not turn to acknowledge her. "There're violets on the table." With one shoulder he made a vague gesture. "They match your eyes."

Cassidy looked over and saw the small nosegay tossed amid the artistic rubble. Her face lit with instant pleasure. "Oh, they're lovely!" Moving to the table, she took them then buried her face in their delicate petals. The fragrance was subtle and sweet. Touched and charmed, Cassidy lifted her smile to thank him.

"I want a spot of color against the dress," Colin murmured. His preoccupation was obvious and complete. He did not glance at her or change expression.

Pleasure shattered, Cassidy stared down at the tiny flowers and sighed. It's my fault, she thought ruefully. He bought them for the painting, not for me. It was ridiculous to think otherwise. Why in the world should he buy me flowers? With a shake of her head and a wry smile, she moved over to join him. "Do you see me there already?" she asked. "On the empty canvas?"

He turned then and looked at her, but the frown of his concentration remained. He lifted the hand that held the flowers. "Yes, they'll do. Stand over here, I want the light from this window."

As he propelled her across the room, Cassidy twisted her head to look up at him. "Good morning, Colin," she said in the bright, cheerful voice of a kindergarten instructor.

He lifted a brow as he stopped by the window. "Manners are the least of my concerns when I'm working."

"I'm awfully glad you cleared that up," Cassidy replied, smiling broadly.

"I've also been known to devour young, smart-tongued wenches for breakfast."

"Wenches!" Cassidy's smile became a delighted grin. "How wonderfully anachronistic. It sounds lovely when you say it, too. I do wish you'd said lusty young wenches, though. I've always loved that phrase."

"The description doesn't fit you." Colin lifted her chin with one finger and brushed her hair over her shoulder with his other hand.

"Oh." Cassidy felt vaguely insulted.

"Once I've set the pose, don't fidget. I just might throw an easel at you if you do." While he spoke, he moved her face and body with his hands. His touch was as impersonal as a physician's. I might as well be a still-life arrangement, Cassidy thought. By his eyes, she saw that his mind had gone beyond her and into his art. She recognized his expression of absolute concentration from her own work. She, too, had a tendency to block out her surroundings and step into her own mind.

At length he stood back and studied her in silence. It was a natural pose and simple. She stood straight, with the nosegay cupped in both hands and held just below her right hip. Her arms were relaxed, barely bent at the elbows. He had left her hair tumbled free, without design, over both shoulders. "Lift your chin a fraction higher." He held up a hand to stop the movement. "There. Be still and don't talk until I tell you."

Cassidy obeyed, moving only her eyes to watch him as he strode behind the easel again. He lifted a piece of charcoal. Minutes passed in utter silence as she watched the movements of his arms and shoulders and felt the probing power of his eyes. They returned again and again to her face. She knew he could look into her eyes and see directly into her soul, learning more perhaps than she knew herself. The sensation made her not nervous so much as curious. What would he see? How would he express it?

"All right," Colin said abruptly. "You can talk for the moment, but don't move the pose. Tell me about those unpublished novels of yours."

He continued to work with such obsessed concentration that Cassidy assumed he had invited her to talk only to keep her relaxed. She doubted seriously if her words made more than a surface impression. If he heard them at all, he would forget them moments later.

"There's only one actually, or one and a half. I'm working on a second novel while the first bounces from rejection slip to rejection slip." She started to shrug but caught herself in time. "It's about a woman's coming of age, the choices she makes, the mistakes. It's rather sentimental, I suppose. I like to think she makes the right choices in the end. Do you know it's very difficult to talk without your hands? I had no idea mine were so necessary to my vocabulary."

"It's your Gaelic blood." Colin frowned deeply at the canvas then lifted his eyes to hers. By the movement of his shoulders she knew he continued to work. "Will you let me read your manuscript?"

Surprised, Cassidy stared a moment before gathering her wits. "Well, yes, if you'd like. I—"

"Good," he interrupted and slashed another line on the canvas. "Bring it with you tomorrow. Be quiet now," he commanded before Cassidy could speak again. "I'm going to work the face."

Silence reigned until he put down the charcoal and shook his head. "It's not right." He scowled at Cassidy then paced. Unsure, she held the pose and her tongue. "You're not giving me the right mood. Do you know what I want?" he demanded. There was impatience and a hint of temper in his voice. She opened her mouth then closed it again, seeing the question had been rhetorical. "I want more than an illusion. I want passion. You've passion in you, Cassidy, more, by heaven, than I need for this painting." He turned to face her again, and she felt the room vibrate with his tension. Her heart began to quicken in response. "I want a promise. I want a

woman who invites a lover. I want expectation and the
freshness that springs from innocence. Untouched but
not untouchable. It's that you have to give me. That's
the essence of it." In his frustration, the cadence of his
native land became more obvious. The fire of his talent
flickered in his eyes. Fascinated, Cassidy watched him,
not speaking even when he stopped directly in front of
her. "There would be a softness in your eyes and just
a trace of heat. There would be a giving in the set of
your mouth that comes from having just been kissed,
from waiting to be kissed again. Like this."

His mouth took hers quickly, stunningly. He framed
her face with his hands, thumbs brushing her cheeks
while he took the kiss into trembling intimacy with
terrifying speed. His lips were warm and soft and experienced. His tongue plundered without warning.
Somewhere deep within her came an answer. Passion,
long overlooked, smoldered then kindled then licked
tentatively into flame. She tasted the flavor of power. As
quickly as his mouth had taken, it liberated.

Though she was unaware of it, her expression was
exactly what he'd demanded of her—expectant, inviting, innocent. Fleetingly he dropped his gaze to her
mouth; then, taking his time, he removed his hands
from her face. Impatience flickered in his eyes before
he turned and strode to his easel.

Cassidy tried to steady her spinning brain. Reason
told her the kiss had meant nothing, a means to an end,
but her heart thudded in contradiction. In a few brief
seconds he had stirred up a hunger she hadn't been
aware of having, had stirred up desires she hadn't been
aware she had. It was more a revelation, she thought be-
musedly, than a kiss. Forcing her breathing to slow,
she tried to keep the quick encounter in perspective.

She was a grown woman. Kisses were more common than handshakes. It was her treacherous imagination that had turned it into something else. *Only my imagination,* she decided as she calmed, and his utter effrontery. He'd taken her totally by surprise. He'd kissed her when he'd had no right to do so, and in a way that had been both proprietary and intimate. No man had ever been permitted either of the privileges, and his seizure of them had left her shaken. Cassidy could justify her reaction to Colin by intellectually dissecting the scene, its cause and results. She turned her emotions over to her mind and plotted the scene. She examined motivations. Still, something lingered inside her that could not quite be rationalized or explained away. Disturbed, she tried to ignore it.

"We'll stop now," Colin stated abruptly and put aside the charcoal. He glanced up as he cleaned his hands on a paint rag. She thought perhaps he saw Cassidy St. John again for the first time since he had set the pose. "Relax."

When Cassidy obeyed, she was surprised to find her muscles stiff. "How long have I been standing there?" she demanded as she arched her back. "A good bit more than twenty minutes."

Colin shrugged, his eyes back on the canvas. "Perhaps. It's moving nicely. Do you want coffee?"

Cassidy scowled at his casual dismissal of the time. "Twenty minutes is quite long enough to stand in one position. I'll bring a kitchen timer with me from now on, and yes, I want coffee."

He ignored the first two-thirds of her statement and headed for the door. "I'll fix some."

"Am I allowed to look?" She gestured toward the canvas as he drew back the bolt.

"No."

She made a sound of disgust. "What about the others?" Her gesture took in the canvases against the wall. "Are they a secret, too?"

"Help yourself. Just stay away from the one I'm working on." Colin disappeared, presumably to fetch the promised coffee.

Making a face at the empty doorway, Cassidy set down the nosegay and wandered toward the neglected canvases. They were stacked here and tilted there, without order or design. Some were small while others were large enough to require some effort on her part to turn them around. Within moments, whatever minor irritation she'd felt was eclipsed by admiration for his talent. She saw why Colin Sullivan was considered a master of color and light. Moreover she saw the sensitivity she had detected in his hands and the strength she had felt there. There was insight and honesty in his portraits, vitality in his city scenes and landscapes. A play of shadows, a splatter of light, and the paintings breathed his mood. She wondered if he painted what he saw or what he felt, then understood it was a marriage of both. She decided that he saw more than the average mortal was entitled to see. His gift was as much in his perception as in his hands. The paintings moved her almost as deeply as the man had.

Carefully she turned another canvas. The subject was beautiful. The woman's undraped body lounged negligently on the couch that now sat empty at the far end of the studio. There was a lazy smile on her face and a careless confidence in the attitude of her naked limbs. From the milky skin and dark eyes, Cassidy recognized the model Gail had spoken of that morning.

"A lovely creature, isn't she?" Colin asked from behind. Cassidy started.

"Yes." She turned and accepted the proffered mug. "I've never seen a more beautiful woman."

Colin's brow arched as he moved his shoulders. "Of a type, she's nearly perfect, and her body is exquisite."

Cassidy frowned into her coffee and tried to pretend the stab of irritation didn't exist.

"She has a basic sexuality and is comfortable with it."

"Yes." Sipping her coffee, Cassidy spoke mildly. "You've captured it remarkably well."

Her tone betrayed her. Colin grinned. "Ah, Cass, it's an open book you are and surely the most delightful creature I've met in years." The thickened brogue rolled easily off his tongue. Better women than she, Cassidy was certain, had fallen for the Gaelic charm.

She tossed her head, but the glare she had intended to flash at him turned of its own volition into a smile. "I can't keep up with you, Sullivan." She studied him over the rim of her mug. Sunlight shot through her hair and shadowed the silk of the dress. "Why did you settle in San Francisco?" she asked.

Colin straddled one of the abandoned wooden chairs, keeping his eyes on her. She wondered if he saw her as a person now or still as a subject. "It's a cross section of the world. I like the contrasts and its sordid history."

"And that it trades on that sordid history rather than apologizing for it," Cassidy concluded with an agreeing nod. "But don't you miss Ireland?"

"I go back now and then." He lifted his coffee and drank deeply. "It feeds me, like a mother's breast. Here I find passion, there I find peace. The soul requires both." He glanced up at her again and searched her face. The violet of her eyes had darkened. Her expression revealed her thoughts. They were all on him. Colin turned away from the innocent candor of her eyes. "Finish your coffee. I want to perfect the preliminary outline today. I'll start in oil tomorrow."

The morning passed almost completely in silence while she took advantage of Colin's absorption to study him. She had read of the dark devil looks and fiery blue eyes of the volatile black Irish, and now she found them even more compelling in the flesh. She wondered at the strange quirk in her own personality that caused her to find moodiness appealing.

With only the barest effort she could feel the swift excitement of his lips on hers. Warmed, she drifted with the sensation. For a moment she imagined what it would be like to be held by him in earnest. Though her experience with men had been limited, her instincts told her Colin Sullivan was dangerous. He interested her too much. His dominance challenged her, his physicality attracted her, his moodiness intrigued her.

Gail Kingsley's scathing comment about Cassidy's predecessor came back to her. She had a quick mental picture of the redhead's demanding beauty and the model's sultry allure. Cassidy St. John, she mused, is at neither end of the spectrum. She isn't strikingly vivid nor steamily sexy. Feminine extremes apparently appeal to Colin both as an artist and as a man. She caught herself, annoyed with the train of her own thoughts. It would not do to get involved or form any personal attachments with a man like Colin Sullivan. Don't get too close, she cautioned herself. Don't open any doors. *Don't get hurt.* The last warning came from nowhere and surprised her.

"Relax."

Cassidy focused on Colin and found him staring

down at the canvas. His attention was concentrated on what only he could see. "Go change," he directed without glancing up. Cassidy's thoughts darkened at his tone. Rude, she decided, was a mild sort of word for describing Sullivan the artist. Controlling her temper, Cassidy went back to the dressing room.

My worries are groundless, she told herself and closed the door smartly. No one could possibly get close enough to that man to be hurt.

A few moments later Cassidy emerged from the dressing room in her own clothes. Colin stood, facing the window, his hands jammed into his pockets, his eyes narrowed on some view of his own.

"I've left the dress hanging in the other room," Cassidy said coldly. "I'll just be off, since you seem to be done." She snatched up her purse from the chair. Even as she swung it over her shoulder and turned for the door, Colin took her hand in his.

"You've that line between your brows again, Cass." He lifted a finger to trace it. "Smooth it out and I'll buy you some lunch before you go."

The line deepened. "Don't use that patronizing tone on me, Sullivan. I'm not an empty-headed art groupie to be patted and babied into smiles."

His brow lifted a fraction. "Quite right. Then again, there's no need to go off in a tiff."

"I'm not in a tiff," Cassidy insisted as she tried to jerk out of his hold. "I'm simply having a perfectly normal reaction to rudeness. Let go of my hand."

"When I'm through with it," he replied evenly. "You should mind your temper, Cass my love. It does alluring things to your face, and I'm not one for resisting what appeals to me."

"It's abundantly clear the only appeal I have for you is on that canvas over there." Cassidy wriggled her hand in an attempt to free it. With a quick flick of the wrist, Colin tumbled her into his chest. Mutinous and glowing, her face lifted to his. "Just what do you think you're doing?"

"You challenge me to prove you wrong." There was amusement in his eyes now and something else that made her heart beat erratically.

"I don't challenge you to anything," she corrected with a furious toss of her head. Her hair swung and lifted with the movement then settled into its own appealing disarray.

"Oh, but you do." His free hand tangled in her hair and found the base of her neck. "You threw down the gauntlet the night I found you in the fog. I think it's time I picked it up."

"You're being ridiculous." Cassidy spoke quickly. She realized her temper had carried her into territory she would have been wise to avoid. As she began to speak again, he caught her bottom lip between his teeth. The movement was sudden, the pressure light, the effect devastating.

Though she made a tiny sound of confused protest, her fingers clutched at his shirt instead of pushing him away. The tip of his tongue traced her lip as if experimenting with its flavor. When he released it, she stood still. Her eyes locked with his.

"This time when I kiss you, Cass, it's to pleasure myself," he said as his mouth lowered to take hers. Knowing he would meet no resistance, he circled her waist to mold her against him. Cassidy responded as if she'd been waiting for the moment all of her life. Her body seemed to know his already and fitted its soft, subtle curves to his firm, taut lines. Her hands traveled from his neck to tangle in his hair, while her mouth grew more mobile under his. For one brief instant, he crushed her to him with staggering force, ravishing her conquered mouth. Just as swiftly, her lips were freed. Her breath came out in a quick rush as she gripped him for balance. He held her close, keeping their bodies as one, his eyes boring into hers. Only the sound of their mixed breathing disturbed the silence.

The weakness Cassidy felt was a shock to her. Her knees trembled beneath her, and she shook her head in a quick attempt to deny what he had awakened. Something deep and secret was struggling for release. The strength of it alarmed and fascinated her. Still, her fear outweighed her curiosity. Instinct warned her it was not yet time. Even as she found the will to draw away, Colin pulled her closer.

"No, Colin, I can't." She swallowed as her hands pushed against his chest. She watched his eyes darken as his lips lingered just over hers.

"I can," he murmured, then crushed her mouth. She swirled back into the storm.

Nothing in her experience had ever prepared her for the new demands of her own body. With innocent allure, she moaned against his mouth. She felt his lips move against hers as he murmured something. Then he plundered, pulling her down into a world of heat and darkness. A quickening fear rose with her passion. When he released her mouth, her breath came in short gasps. Her eyes clouded with desire and confusion.

"Please, Colin, let me go. I think I'm frightened."

He was capable of taking her, she knew, and of making her glad that he had. His eyes were blazing blue, and she kept hers locked on them. To let her eyes drift to his mouth would have been her downfall. The fingers at her neck tightened, then relaxed and dropped away. Seizing the moment, Cassidy stepped back. The narrowness of her escape shook her, and she dragged her hand through her hair.

Colin watched her, then folded his arms across his chest. "I wonder if you had more difficulty fighting yourself or me."

"So do I," Cassidy replied with impulsive candor.

He tilted his head at her response and studied her. "You're an honest one, Cassidy. Mind how honest you are with me—I'd have few qualms about taking advantage."

"No, I'm sure you wouldn't." After blowing out a long breath, Cassidy straightened her shoulders. "I don't suppose that could have been avoided forever," she began practically. "But now that it hasn't been, and it's done, it shouldn't happen again." Her brow furrowed as Colin tossed back his head and roared with laughter. "Did I say something funny?"

"Cass, you're unique." Before she could respond, he had moved to her and had taken her shoulders in his hands. He kneaded them quickly in a friendly manner. "That streak of British practicality will always war with the passionate Celt."

"You're romanticizing," she claimed and lifted her chin.

"The door's been opened, Cassidy." She frowned because his words reminded her of her earlier thoughts. "Better for you perhaps if we'd kept it locked." He shook her once, rapidly. "Yes, it's done. The door won't stay closed now. It'll happen again." He released her then stepped back, but their eyes remained joined. "Go on now, while I'm remembering you were frightened."

The strong temptation to step toward him alarmed her. In defense against it, she turned swiftly for the door.

"Nine o'clock," he said, and she turned with her hand on the knob.

He stood in the room's center, his thumbs hooked in his front pockets. The sun fell through the skylight, silhouetting his dark attraction. It occurred to Cassidy that if she were wise, she would walk out and never come back.

"Not a coward, are you, Cass?" he taunted softly, as if stealing her thoughts from her brain.

Cassidy tossed her head and snapped her spine straight. "Nine o'clock," she stated coolly then slammed the door behind her.

CHAPTER 4

As the days passed Cassidy found herself more at ease in the role of artist's model. As for Colin himself, she felt it would be a rare thing for anyone to remain relaxed with him. His temperament was mercurial, with a wide range of degrees. Fury came easily to him, but Cassidy learned humor did as well. As she began to uncover different layers of the man, he became more fascinating.

She justified her concentrated study of Colin Sullivan as a writer's privilege. It was a personality like his—varied, unpredictable, bold—that she needed as grist for her profession. There was nothing between them, she told herself regularly, but an artistic exchange. She reminded herself that he hadn't touched her again, except to set the pose, since the first day he had begun work on the canvas. The stormy kiss was a vivid memory, but only that . . . a memory.

Sitting at her typewriter in her apartment, Cassidy told herself she was fortunate—fortunate to have a job that kept the wolf from the door, and fortunate that Colin Sullivan was absorbed in his work. Cassidy was honest enough to admit she was more than mildly attracted to him. It was much better, she mused, that he was capable of pouring himself into his work to the extent that he barely noticed she was flesh and blood. *Unless I move the pose.* She frowned at the reflection of her desk lamp in the window.

Being attracted to him is perfectly natural, she decided. I'm not behaving like my predecessor with the milky skin and falling in love with him. I'm much too sensible. *Don't be so smug,* a voice whispered inside her head. Cassidy's frown became a scowl. I *am* sensible. I won't make a fool of myself over Colin Sullivan. He has his art and his Gail Kingsley. I have my work. Cassidy glanced down at the blank sheet of paper in her typewriter and sighed. But he keeps interfering with it. No more, she vowed then shifted in her seat until she was comfortably settled. I'm going to finish this chapter tonight without another thought of Sullivan.

At once the keys on her typewriter began to clatter with the movement of her thoughts. Once begun, she became totally involved, lost in the characters of her own devising. The love scene developed on her pages as she unconsciously called on her own feelings for her words. The scene moved with the same lightning speed as had the embrace with Colin. Now Cassidy was in control, urging her characters toward each other, propelling their destinies. It was as she wanted, as she planned, and she never noticed the influence of the man she had vowed to think no more about. The scene was nearly finished when a knock sounded on her door. She swore in annoyance.

"Who is it?" she called out and stopped typing in midsentence. She found it simpler to pick up her thoughts when returning to them that way.

"Hey, Cassidy." Jeff Mullans stuck his friendly, red-bearded face through her door. "Got a minute?"

Because he was her neighbor and she was fond of him, Cassidy pushed away the urge to sigh and smiled instead. "Sure."

He eased himself, a guitar, and a six-pack of beer through the door. "Can I put some stuff in your fridge? Mine's busted again. It's like the Mojave Desert in there."

"Go ahead." Cassidy spun her chair until she faced him, then quirked her brow. "I see you brought all your valuables. I didn't know your six-string needed refrigeration."

"Just the six-pack," he countered with a grin as he marched back into her tiny kitchen. "And you're the only one in the building I'd trust with it. Wow, Cassidy, don't you believe in real food? All that's in here's a quart of juice, two carrots, and half a stick of oleo."

"Is nothing sacred?"

"Come next door and I'll fix you up with a decent meal." Jeff came back into the room holding only his guitar. "I got tacos and stale doughnuts. Jelly-filled."

"It sounds marvelous, but I really have to finish this chapter."

Jeff's fingers pawed at his beard. "Don't know what you're missing. Heard anything from New York?" After glancing at the papers scattered over her desk, he settled cross-legged on the floor. He cradled his guitar in his lap.

"There seems to be a conspiracy of silence on the East Coast." Cassidy sighed, shrugged and tucked up her feet. "It's early days yet, I know, but patience isn't my strong suit."

"You'll make it, Cassidy, you've got something." He began to strum idly as he spoke. His music was simple and soothing. "Something that makes the people you write about important. If your novel is as good as that magazine story, you're on your way."

Cassidy smiled, touched by the easy sincerity of the compliment. "You wouldn't like to apply for a job as an editor in a New York publishing house, would you?"

"You don't need me, babe." He grinned and shook back his red hair. "Besides, I'm an up-and-coming songwriter and star performer."

"I've heard that." Cassidy leaned back in her chair. It occurred to her suddenly that Colin might like to paint Jeff Mullans. He'd be the perfect subject for him—the blinding red hair and beard, the soft contrast of gray eyes, the loving way the long hands caressed the guitar as he sat on her wicker rug. Yes, Colin would paint him precisely like this, she decided, in faded, frayed jeans with a polished guitar on his lap.

"Cassidy?"

"Sorry, I took a side trip. Have you got any gigs lined up?"

"Two next week. What about your gig with the artist?" Jeff tightened his bass string fractionally, tested it then continued to play. "I've seen his stuff . . . some of it, anyway. It's incredible." He tilted his head when he smiled at her. "How does it feel to be put on canvas by one of the new masters?"

"It's an odd feeling, Jeff. I've tried to pin it down, but . . ." She trailed off and brought her knees up, resting her heels on the edge of the chair. "I'm never certain it's me he's seeing when he's working. I'm not certain I'll see myself in the finished portrait." She frowned then shrugged it away. "Maybe he's only using part of me, the way I use parts of people I've met in characterizations."

"What's he like?" Jeff asked, watching her eyes drift

with her thought. The glow of her desk lamp threw an aura around her head.

"He's fascinating," she murmured, all but forgetting she was speaking aloud. "He looks like a pirate, all dashing and dangerous with the most incredible blue eyes I've ever seen. And his hands are beautiful. There's no other word for them; they're perfectly beautiful."

Her voice softened, and her eyes began to dream. "He exudes a thoughtless sort of sensuality. It seems more obvious when he's working. I suppose it's because he's being driven by his own power then, and is somehow separate from the rest of us. He tells me to talk, and I talk about whatever comes into my head." She moved her shoulders then rested her chin on her knees. "But I don't know if he hears me. He has a dreadful temper, and when he rages his speech slips back to Ireland. It's almost worth the storm to hear it. He's outrageously selfish and unbearably arrogant and utterly charming. Each time I'm with him I find a bit more, uncover another layer, and yet I doubt I'd really know him if I had years to learn."

There was silence for a moment, with only Jeff's music. "You're really hung up on him," he observed.

Cassidy snapped back with a jolt. Her violet eyes widened in surprise as she straightened in the chair. "Why, no, of course not. I'm simply . . . simply . . ." *Simply what, Cassidy?* she demanded of herself. "Simply interested in what makes him the way he is," she answered and hugged her knees. "That's all."

"Okay, babe, you know best." Jeff stood in an easy, fluid motion, the guitar merely an extension of his arm. "Just watch out." He smiled, leaned over, and cupped her chin. "He might be a great artist, but if the gossip columns are to be believed, he's very much a man, too. You're a fine-looking lady, and you might as well be fresh from the farm."

"I'd hardly call four years at Berkeley fresh from the farm," Cassidy countered.

"Only someone utterly naive could evade every pass I make and still make me like her." Jeff closed the distance and gave her a gentle invitation of a kiss. It was as pleasant and as soothing as his music. Cassidy's heartbeat stayed steady. "No dice, huh?" he asked when he lifted his head. "Think of the rent we could save if we moved in together."

Cassidy tugged on his beard. "You're only lusting after my refrigerator."

"A lot you know," he scoffed and headed for the door. "I'm going home to write something painfully sad and poignant."

"Good grief, I'm always inspiring someone these days."

"Don't get cocky," Jeff advised then closed the door behind him.

Cassidy's smile faded as she stared off into space. Hung up on, she repeated mentally. What a silly phrase. In any case, I'm not hung up on Colin. Can't a woman express an interest in a man without someone reading more into it? Thoughtfully she ran her fingertip over her bottom lip and brought back the feel of Jeff's kiss. Easy, undisturbing, painless. What sort of chemistry made one man's kiss pleasant and another's exhilarating? The smart woman would go for the pleasant, Cassidy decided, knowing Jeff would be basically kind and gentle. Only an idiot would want a man who was bound to bring hurt and heartache.

With a quick shake of her head she swung back

to her typewriter and began to work. Her fingers had barely begun to transfer her thoughts when a knock sounded again. Cassidy rolled her eyes to the ceiling.

"You can't possibly be finished writing a painfully sad and poignant song," she called out and continued to type. "And the beer certainly isn't cold yet."

"I can't argue with either of those statements."

Cassidy spun her chair quickly and stared at Colin. He stood in her opened doorway, negligently leaning against the jamb and watching her. There was light amusement on his face and male appreciation in his eyes as they roamed over her skin. It was scantily covered in brief shorts and a T-shirt that had shrunk in the basement laundry. His lazy survey brought out a blush before she found her tongue.

"What are you doing here?"

"Enjoying the view," he answered and stepped inside. He closed the door at his back then lifted a brow. "Don't you know better than to keep your door unlatched?"

"I'm always losing my key and locking myself out, so I . . ." Cassidy stopped because she realized how ridiculous she sounded. One day, she promised herself, I'll learn to think before I speak. "There isn't anything in here worth stealing," she said.

Colin shook his head. "How wrong you are. Wear your key around your neck, Cass, but keep your door locked." Her brain formed an indignant retort, but before she could vocalize it he spoke again. "Who did you think I was when I knocked?"

"A songwriter with a faulty refrigerator. How did you know where I lived?"

"Your address is on your manuscript." He gestured with the thick envelope before setting it down.

Cassidy glanced at the familiar bundle with some

surprise. She had assumed Colin had forgotten her manuscript as soon as she'd given it to him. Suddenly it
occurred to her why she hadn't asked him before if he
had read it, or what he'd thought of it. His criticism
would be infinitely harder to bear than an impersonal
rejection slip from a faceless editor. Abruptly nervous,
she looked up at him. Any critique she was expecting
wasn't forthcoming.

Colin wandered the room, toying with an arrangement of dried flowers, examining a snapshot in a silver
frame, peering out of the window at her view of the city.

"Can I get you something?" she asked automatically
then remembered Jeff's inventory of her refrigerator.
She bit her lip. "Coffee," she added quickly, knowing
she could provide it as long as he took it black.

Colin turned from the window and began to wander again. "You have a proper eye for color, Cass," he
told her. "And an enviable way of making a home from
an apartment. I've always found them soulless devices,
lacking in privacy and character." He lifted a small mirror framed with sea shells. "Fisherman's Wharf," he
concluded and glanced at her. "It must be a particular
haunt of yours."

"Yes, I suppose. I love the city in general and that
part of it in particular." She smiled as she thought of it.
"There's so much life there. The boats are all crammed
in beside each other, and I like to imagine where they've
been or where they're going." As soon as the words
were spoken Cassidy felt foolish. They sounded romantic when she had been taking great pains to prove to
Colin she was not. He smiled at her, and her embarrassment became something more dangerous. "I'll make
coffee," she said quickly and started to rise.

"No, don't bother." Colin laid a hand on her shoulder to keep her seated then glanced at her desk. It was

cluttered with papers and notes and reference books. "I'm interrupting your work. Intolerable."

"It seems to be the popular thing to do tonight." Cassidy shook off her discomfort and smiled as he continued to pace the room. "It's all right because I was nearly done, otherwise I suppose I'd behave as rudely as you do when you're interrupted." She enjoyed the look he gave her, the ironical lift of his brow, the light tilt of a smile on his mouth.

"And how rudely is that?"

"Abominably. Please sit, Colin. These floors are thin, you'll wear them through." She gestured to a chair, but he perched on the edge of her desk.

"I finished your book tonight."

"Yes, I thought perhaps that's why you brought the manuscript back." She spoke calmly enough, but when he made no response, she moaned in frustration. "Please, Colin, I'm no good with torture. I'd confess everything I knew before they stuck the first bamboo shoot under my fingernail. I'm a marshmallow. No, wait!" She held up both hands as he started to speak. She rose and then took a quick turn around the room. "If you hated it, I'll only be devastated for a short time. I'm certain I'll learn to function again . . . well, nearly certain. I want you to be frank. I don't want any platitudes or cushioned letdowns." She pushed her mane of hair back with both hands, letting her fingers linger on her temples a moment. "And for heaven's sake, don't tell me it was interesting. That's the worst. The absolute worst!"

"Are you finished?" he asked mildly.

Cassidy blew out a long breath, tugged her hand through her hair and nodded. "Yes, I think so."

"Come here, Cass." She obeyed instantly because his voice was quiet and gentle. Their eyes were level, and he took her hands in his. "I haven't mentioned the book until now because I wanted to read it when I wouldn't be interrupted. I thought it best not to talk about it until I finished." His thumbs ran absently over the back of her hands. "You have something rare, Cass, something elusive. Talent. It's not something they taught you at Berkeley, it's something you were born with. Your college years polished it, perhaps, disciplined it, but you provided the raw material."

Cassidy released her breath. Astonishing, she thought, that the opinion of a man known barely a week should have such weight. Jeff's opinion had pleased her; Colin's had left her speechless.

"I don't know what to say." She shook her head helplessly. "That sounds trite, I know, but it's true." Her eyes drifted past him to the disorder of papers on her desk. "Sometimes you just want to chuck it all. It just isn't worth the pain, the struggle."

"And you would choose to be a writer," Colin said.

"No, I never had any choice." She brought her eyes back to his. The violet glowed almost black in the shadowed light. "If anything, it picked me. Did you choose to be an artist, Colin?"

He studied her a moment, then shook his head. "No." He turned her hands, palms up, and looked at them with lowered brows. "There are things that come to us whether we ask for them or not. Do you believe in destiny, Cass?"

She moistened her lips, finding them suddenly dry, then swallowed. "Yes." The single syllable was little more than a breath.

"Of course, I was certain you did." He lifted his eyes and locked them on hers. Cassidy's heartbeat jumped skittishly. "Do you think it's our destiny to be lovers, Cassidy?" Her mouth opened but no words came out. She shook her head in mute denial. "You're a poor liar," he observed; then, cupping her chin in his palm, he moved his lips to hers. In direct contrast to the ease and pleasantness of Jeff's kiss, this brought a pain that seemed to vibrate in every cell of her body. Defensively Cassidy jerked her head back.

"Don't!"

"Why?" he countered, and his voice was soft. "A kiss is a simple thing, a meeting of lips."

"No, it's not simple," Cassidy protested, feeling herself being pulled to him by his eyes only. "You take more."

He kissed one cheek, then the other, barely touching her skin. Cassidy's eyelids fluttered down. "Only as much as you'll give me, Cass. That much and no more." His lips moved over hers, teasing, persuading, until her blood thundered in her brain. His fingers were gentle on her face. "You taste of things I'd forgotten," he murmured. "Fresh, young things. Kiss me, Cass, I've a need for you."

With a moan, half despair, half wonder, she answered his need.

The flames that leapt between them were intense and wild. Her brain sent out quick, desperate protests and was ignored. A hunger for him drove her; her mouth became urgent and searching as his hands began to explore her soft curves. The fear she felt only added to her excitement, the exquisite terror of losing control. She was overwhelmed by a primitive need, an ageless necessity. When their lips parted and met again, hers ached for the joining.

Abruptly he tore his mouth from hers and buried it against her neck. Cassidy shuddered from the onslaught even as she tilted back her head to offer him more. With his teeth he brought her skin alive with delicious pain. His hands found their way under her shirt, running up her rib cage. With his thumbs he stroked the sides of her breast while she strained against him.

Her joints went fluid, leaving her helpless but for his support. For a moment, when their lips met again, there was nothing she had that was not his. The offer was complete and unconditional. Slowly, with his hands on her shoulders, Colin drew her away. Her lashes fluttered up then down, before she found the strength to open her eyes. His expression was dark and forbidding. Briefly his hands tightened.

"It seems you were right," he began in a voice thick with desire. "A kiss isn't a simple thing. I want you, Cass, and you'd best know nothing in heaven or hell will keep me from taking you when I've a mind to." His hands relaxed, the grip becoming a caress. "When the painting's finished, we'll have no choice but to meet our destinies."

"No." Frightened, disturbed by feelings that were too intense, Cassidy pulled out of his arms. She dragged a trembling hand through her hair, and her breath came quickly. "No, Colin, I won't be the latest in your string of lovers. I won't! I think more of myself than that. That's something you'd best understand." She stepped away from him, her shoulders straightening with inherent pride.

Colin's eyes narrowed. She could see his temper rising. "It should be an interesting contest." He took a step forward and grabbed a handful of her hair. With a quick jerk he brought her face to his, then gave her a hard, brief kiss. Cassidy's breath trembled out, but she kept her eyes steady. "Time will tell, Cass my love. Now it's late, nearly midnight, and I'd best be on my way." Lifting her hand, he brushed her fingers with his lips. "Sinning is much more appealing after midnight."

With another careless smile, he turned for the door.
Reaching it, he pushed the latch so that it would engage
when he shut it. "Find your keys," he ordered and was
gone.

CHAPTER 5

Another week passed without any clash between Colin and Cassidy. She had returned to his studio the day after his visit to her apartment determined to resist him. She'd spoken the truth when she'd told him she wouldn't be one of his lovers.

All her life she had waited for a relationship with depth and permanence. Her own ideals and her dedication to her studies had kept her aloof from men, and her aloofness had prolonged her naiveté. She'd grown up with only a father and had never closely witnessed the commitment of a man and a woman to each other. She had watched her father enjoy several light relationships as she'd grown up, but none of the women in his life had become important to him. Watching him drift through life with only his work, Cassidy had vowed she would find someone one day to share hers.

She didn't consider her vow romantic, but as necessary to her soul as food was to her body. Until she found what she searched for, she would wait. Before Colin there had never been any temptation to do otherwise. Still, when she returned to his studio, she was prepared to stand firm against him. Her preparation proved unnecessary.

Colin spoke to her only briefly, and when he set the pose, his touch was impersonal. But there seemed to be some surge of emotion just under the surface of his face, something that just stirred the air. Whether it was temper or passion or excitement, Cassidy had no way of knowing. She knew only she was vitally aware of it . . . and of him.

They passed the days with only what needed to be said, and long gaps of silence filled the sessions. By the end of the week Cassidy's nerves were stretched taut. She wondered if Colin felt the tension, or if it was simply within her. He seemed intent only on the painting.

The sun fell over Cassidy warmly, but her muscles were growing stiff from holding the pose. Colin stood behind his easel, and she watched his brush move from palette to canvas. He could work for hours without a moment's rest. Cassidy tried to imagine how he had painted her.

Will I hang in The Gallery or face the wall in a corner up here until he decides what to do with me? she thought. Will I be sold for some astronomical price and hang in a manor house in England? What will he title me? *Woman in White. Woman with Violets.* She tried to imagine being discussed and pondered over by an art class in a university. A century from now, will someone see me in some dusty gallery and wonder who I was or what I was thinking when he painted me?

The idea gave Cassidy an odd feeling, one she was not certain wholly pleased her. How much of her soul could Colin see, and how much would be revealed with oil and canvas? Would she, in essence, be as naked as the model who'd lounged on the couch?

Colin swore roundly, snapping her attention back to him. Her eyes widened as he slammed down his palette.

"You've moved the pose." He stalked toward her as her mouth opened to form an apology. "Hold still, blast you," he ordered curtly, adjusting her shoulders with impatient hands. His brows were lowered in annoyance. "I won't tolerate fidgeting."

Cassidy's mouth snapped shut on her apology. Swift and heated, her temper rose. With one quick jerk she pulled out of his hands. "Don't you speak to me that way, Sullivan." She threw her nosegay on the windowsill and glared at him. "I was not fidgeting, and if I were, it would be because I'm human, not a—a robot or a dime-store dummy." She tossed her head, effectively destroying his arrangement of her hair. "I'm sure it's difficult to understand a mere mortal when one is so lofty and godlike, but we can't all be perfect."

"Your opinions are neither requested nor desired." Colin's voice was as cold as his eyes were heated. "The only thing I require from a model is that she hold still." He took her shoulders again, firmly. "Keep your temper to yourself when I'm working."

"Go paint a tree, then," she invited furiously. "It won't give you any back talk." Cassidy turned to stalk to the dressing room, but Colin grabbed her arm and spun her around. His face was alive with temper.

"No one walks away from me."

"Is that so?" Cassidy lifted her chin, infuriated with his arrogance. "Watch this." She turned her back on him only to be whirled around again before she had taken two steps. "Let go of me," she ordered as blood surged angrily under her skin. Nerves that had been stretched for a week strained to the breaking point. "I've nothing more to say, and I'm through holding your blasted pose for the day."

His grip on her arm tightened. "Very well, but there's more between us than painting and talking, isn't there?" He bit off the words as he dragged her against him.

Cassidy's heart jumped to her throat when she felt the violence of his fingers against her skin. She saw that temper ruled him now, a temper sharp enough to cut through any protest she could make. He was a man of passion, and she was aware that his darker side could carry them both past the turning point. In a desperate attempt to hold him off, Cassidy arched away from him. Even as she made the move, his mouth crushed hers. She tasted his fury.

Her sounds of protest were muffled, her arms pinioned by his. In her throat, her heart thudded with the knowledge that she was totally at his mercy. His lips were bruising, unyielding, as his tongue penetrated her mouth. The kiss became as intimate as it was savage. When she tried to turn her face from his, he gripped her hair tightly and held her still. His mouth was hard and hot and ruthless. Behind her closed lids, a dull red mist swirled. For the first time in her life, Cassidy feared she would faint. Her protests became slighter. Colin took more.

He was pulling her too deep too quickly, down dark corridors, beyond the border of thought and into sensation. There was no gentleness on the journey, only hard, uncompromising demand. Unable to fight him any longer, Cassidy went limp. She made no struggle when his hand moved to unfasten the dress. Her body was consumed by fire, instinctively responding to his touch. The knock on the studio door vibrated like a cannon through the room. Ignoring it, Colin continued to ravish her mouth.

"Colin." Dimly Cassidy heard Gail Kingsley's voice and the sound of another knock. "There's someone here to see you."

With a savage oath, Colin tore his mouth from Cassidy's. He released her abruptly, and freed of support she staggered and fell against him. Cursing again, he took her arms and held her away, but his words halted as he studied her wide, frightened eyes.

Her mouth was trembling, swollen by his demands. Her breath sobbed in and out of her lungs as she clung to him for balance.

"Colin, don't be nasty." Gail's voice sounded with practiced patience through the door. "You must be pretty well finished by now."

"All right, blast it!" he called out brusquely to Gail but kept his eyes on Cassidy. Leading her by the arm, he walked to the dressing room. Inside he turned her again to face him. In silence she looked up, struggling to balance her system and discipline her breathing. The need to weep was tearing at her.

An expression came and went in Colin's eyes. "Change," he said in a quiet voice. He seemed to hesitate, as if to say more, then he turned away. When he shut the door, Cassidy turned to face the wall.

She let the trembling run its course. Several minutes passed before the voices in the studio penetrated.

There was Gail's quick, nervous tone and Colin's, calm now, without any trace of the temper of passion that had dominated it before. An unfamiliar voice mixed with theirs. It was light and male with an Italian accent. Cassidy concentrated on the voices rather than the words. Turning, she stared at her own reflection. What she saw left her stunned.

Color had not yet returned to her cheeks, leaving them nearly as white as the dress she wore. Her eyes were haunted. It was the look of utter vulnerability that disturbed her the most; the look of a woman accepting defeat.

No. No, I won't. She pressed her palm over the face in the glass. *He'll win nothing that way, and we both know it.* Quickly she stripped out of the dress and began to pull on her clothes. The straight, uncompromising lines of her khakis and button-down shirt made her appear less frail, and she began a careful repair of her face. The conversation in the outer room started to penetrate her thoughts. The first moments of eavesdropping were unconscious.

"An interesting use of color, Colin. You seem to be working toward a rather dreamlike effect." Hearing Gail's comment, Cassidy realized they were discussing the painting. She frowned as she applied blusher to her cheeks. *He lets her look at it,* she thought resentfully. *Why not me?* "It seems almost sentimental. That should be a surprise to the art world."

"Sentimental, yes." The Italian voice cut in while Cassidy now eavesdropped shamelessly. "But there is passion in this play of color here, and a rather cool practicality in the line of the dress. I'm intrigued, Colin—I can't figure out your intention."

"I have more than one," Cassidy heard him answer in his dry, ironic tone.

"How well I know." The Italian chuckled then made a sound of curiosity. "You have not begun the face."

"No." Cassidy recognized the dismissal in the word, but the Italian ignored it.

"She interests me . . . and you, too, it appears. She would be beautiful, of course, and young enough to suit the dress and the violets. Still, she must have something more." Cassidy waited for Colin's reply, but none came. The Italian continued, undaunted. "Will you keep her hidden, my friend?"

"Yes, Colin, where is Cassidy?" Gail's question held an undertone of amusement that made Cassidy's eyes narrow. "You know she'd adore meeting Vince." She gave a light laugh. "She is rather a sweet-looking thing. Don't tell me we ran her off?"

Thoroughly annoyed with the condescending description, Cassidy turned and opened the door. "Not at all," she said and gave the trio by the easel a brilliant smile. "And of course I'd adore meeting Vince." She saw Gail's eyes glitter with a quick fury then shifted her gaze to Colin. His face told her nothing, and again her gaze shifted.

The man beside Colin was nearly a head shorter, but his lean build and proud carriage gave the illusion of height. His hair was as dark as Colin's, but straight, and his eyes were darkly brown against the olive of his skin. He had smooth, handsome features, and when he smiled, he was all but irresistible.

"Ah, *bella*." The compliment was a sigh before he crossed the room to take both of Cassidy's hands in his. "*Bellisima*. But of course, she is perfection. Where did you find her, Colin?" he demanded as his eyes caressed her face. "I will go and set up camp there until I find a prize of my own."

Cassidy laughed, amused by his undisguised flirtation. "In the fog," she told him when Colin remained silent. "I thought he was a mugger."

"Ah, my angel, he is much worse than that." Vince turned to Colin with a grin but retained Cassidy's hand. "He is a black Irish dog whose paintings I buy because I have nothing better to do with my money."

Colin lifted a brow as he moved to join them.

"Vince, Cassidy St. John. Cass, Vincente Clemenza, the duke of Maracanti."

At the introduction Cassidy's eyes grew wide. "Ah, now you have impressed her with my title." Vince's teeth flashed into a grin. "How accommodating of you." With perfect charm he lifted both of Cassidy's hands to his lips. "My pleasure, *signorina*. Will you marry me?"

"I've always thought I'd make a spectacular duchess. Do I curtsy?" she asked, smiling at him over their joined hands. "I'm not certain I know how."

"Vince normally requires that one kneel and kiss his ring." At the comment, Cassidy let her eyes drift to Colin. His gaze was dark and brooding on her face. Fractionally, she lifted her chin. Though he said nothing, she sensed his acknowledgment of the gesture.

"You exaggerate, my friend." Vince released Cassidy's hands then laid his own on Colin's shoulder. "As never before, I envy you your gift. You will give me first claim on the portrait."

Colin's eyes remained fixed on Cassidy's face. "There's been a prior claim."

"Indeed." Vince shrugged. The movement was at once elegant and foreign. "I shall have to outbid my competition." There was an inflection in his tone of a man used to having his own way. Hearing it Cassidy wondered how he and Colin dealt together with such apparent amiability.

"Vince wanted to see *Janeen*," Gail cut in and moved across the room to a stack of canvases.

"If you'll excuse me, then," Cassidy began, but Vince scooped up her hand again.

"No, *madonna,* stay. Come peruse the master's work with me." Without waiting for her assent he urged her across the room.

Gail took a canvas then propped it on an easel. It was the portrait of the nude with the milky skin. Cassidy glanced up to see Gail smiling.

"Cassidy's predecessor," she announced then stepped back to stand with Colin. Cassidy recognized the proprietary nature of the gesture. She turned her attention back to the portrait without looking at Colin.

"An exquisite animal," Vince murmured. "One would say a woman without boundaries. There is quite an attractive wickedness about her." He turned his head to smile at Cassidy. "What do you think?"

"It's magnificent," she replied immediately. "She makes me uncomfortable, and yet I envy her confidence in her own sexuality. I think she would intimidate most men . . . and enjoy it."

"Your model appears to be an astute judge of character." Vince rubbed his thumb absently over Cassidy's knuckles. "Yes, I want it. And the Faylor Gail showed me downstairs. He shows promise. Now, madonna . . ." He turned to face Cassidy again. His eyes were dark and appreciative. "You will have dinner with me tonight? The city is a lonely place without a beautiful woman."

Cassidy smiled, but before she could speak Colin laid a hand on her shoulder. "The paintings are yours, Vince. My model isn't."

"Ah." Vince's one syllable was ripe with meaning. Cassidy's eyes narrowed with fury. Smoothly Colin turned to take the painting from the easel.

"Have someone package this and the Faylor for Vince," he told Gail as he handed her the canvas. "I'll be down shortly and we'll discuss terms."

Without a word Gail crossed the studio and swung through the door. Vince watched her with a thoughtful eye then turned back to Cassidy.

"*Arrivederci,* Cassidy St. John." He kissed her hand

then sighed with regret. "It seems I must find my own dream in the fog. I will expect a bargain price to soothe my crushing disappointment, my friend." He shot a look at Colin as he moved to the door. "If you are ever in Italy, madonna . . ." With a final smile he left them.

Trembling with rage, Cassidy turned on Colin the moment the door closed. "How *dare* you?" Now she had no need of blusher to bring color to her cheeks. "How dare you imply such a thing?"

"I merely told Vince he could have the paintings but not my current model," Colin countered. Carelessly he moved across the room and covered Cassidy's portrait. "Any implication was purely coincidental."

"Oh, no!" Cassidy followed him, propelled by fury. "That was no coincidence. You knew precisely what you were doing. I won't tolerate that sort of interference from you, Sullivan." She took a finger and poked him in the chest. "I'm perfectly free to see whomever I choose, whenever I choose, and I won't have you implying otherwise."

Colin hooked his hands in his pockets. For a moment he studied her face in silence. When he spoke, it was with perfect calm. "You're very young and remarkably naive. Vince is an old friend and a good one. He's also a charming rake, if you'll forgive the archaic term. He has no scruples with women."

"And you do?" Cassidy retorted in an instant of blind heat. She saw Colin stiffen, saw his eyes flare and the muscles in his face tense. For the first time she witnessed his calculated control of his temper.

"Your point, Cass," he said softly. "Well taken." His hands stayed in his pockets as he watched her. "Don't come back until Thursday," he told her and turned to walk to the door. "I need a day or two."

Cassidy stood alone in the empty studio. I may have scored a point, she thought wretchedly, but this victory isn't sweet. She was drained, physically as well as emotionally. She returned to the dressing room for her purse. Colin wasn't the only one who needed a day or two.

"Oh, what luck, I've caught you." Gail swept into the studio just as Cassidy emerged from the dressing room. "I thought we might have a little chat." Gail shot her a quick, flashing smile and leaned back against the closed door. "Just us two," she added.

Cassidy sighed with undisguised weariness. "Not now," she said and shifted her purse to her shoulder. "I've had enough temperament for one day."

"I'll make it brief, then, and you can be on your way." Gail spoke pleasantly enough, but Cassidy felt the antagonism just below the surface.

It's best not to argue, Cassidy decided. It's best to hear her out, agree with everything she says, and go quietly. That's the sensible thing to do.

She gave her what she hoped was an inoffensive smile. "All right, go ahead, then."

Gail took a quick, sweeping survey. "I'm afraid perhaps I haven't made myself clear . . . about myself and Colin." Her voice was patient—teacher to student. Cassidy ignored a surge of annoyance and nodded.

"Colin and I have been together for quite some time. We meet a certain need in each other. Over the years he's had his share of flirtations, which I'm quite capable of overlooking. In many cases these relationships were intensified for the press." She shrugged a gauze-covered shoulder. "Colin's romantic image helps maintain the mystique of the artist. I'll sanction anything when it helps his career. I understand him."

As if unable to remain still for more than short spurts, Gail began to roam the room.

"I'm afraid I don't see why you're telling me this," Cassidy began. The last thing she needed to hear at the moment was how experienced Colin Sullivan was with women.

"Let's you and I understand each other, too." Gail stopped pacing and faced Cassidy again. Her eyes were hard and cold. "As long as Colin's doing this painting, I have to tolerate you. I know better than to interfere with his work. But if you get in my way . . ." She wrapped her fingers around the strap of Cassidy's purse. "I can find ways of removing people who get in my way."

"I'm sure you can," Cassidy returned evenly. "I'm afraid you'll find I don't remove easily." She pried Gail's fingers from her strap. "Your relationship with Colin is your own affair. I've no intention of interfering with it. Not," she added as a satisfied smile tilted the corner of Gail's mouth, "because you threaten me. You don't intimidate me, Gail. Actually, I feel rather sorry for you."

Cassidy ignored Gail's harsh intake of breath and continued. "Your lack of confidence where Colin is concerned is pathetic. I'm no threat to you. A blind man could see he's only interested in what he puts on that canvas over there." She flung out a hand and pointed to the covered portrait. "I interest him as a *thing*, not as a person." She felt a quick slash of pain as her own statement came home to her. She continued to speak, though the words rushed out in desperation. "I won't interfere with you because I'm not in love with Colin, and I have no intention of ever being in love with him."

Whirling, she darted through the back door of the studio, slamming it at her back. Only after she had gulped in enough air to steady her nerves did Cassidy realize she had lied.

CHAPTER 6

For the next two days Cassidy buried herself in her work. She was determined to give herself a time of peace, a time of rest for her emotions. She knew she needed to cut herself off from Colin to accomplish it. The disruption of their day-to-day contact wasn't enough. She knew she needed to block him from her mind. In addition, Cassidy forced herself not to consider the knowledge that had come to her after the scene with Gail. She wouldn't think of being in love with Colin or of the circumstances that made her love impossible. For two days she would pretend she'd never met him.

Cassidy wrote frantically. All her fears and pain and passion were expressed in her words. She worked late into the night, until she could be certain there would be no dreams to haunt her. When she slept, she slept deeply, exhausted by her own drive. More than once she forgot to eat.

On the second day it began to rain. There was a solid gray wall outside Cassidy's window of which she remained totally unaware. Below, pedestrians scrambled about under umbrellas.

Cassidy's concentration was so complete that when a hand touched her shoulder, she screamed.

"Wow, Cassidy, I'm sorry." Jeff tried to look apologetic but grinned instead. "I knocked and called you twice. You were totally absorbed."

Cassidy held a hand against her heart as if to keep it in place. She took two deep breaths. "It's all right. We all need to be terrified now and again. It keeps the blood moving. Is it your refrigerator?"

Jeff grimaced as he ran a finger down her nose. "Is that where you think my heart is? In your refrigerator? Cassidy, I'm a sensitive guy, my mother'll tell you." Cassidy smiled, leaning back in her chair.

"I've got that gig in the coffeehouse down the street tonight. Come with me."

"Oh, Jeff, I'd love to, but—" She began to make her excuses with a gesture at the papers on her desk. Jeff cut her off.

"Listen, you've been chained to this machine for two days. When are you coming up for air?"

She shrugged and poked a finger at her dictionary. "I've got to go back to the studio tomorrow, and—"

"All the more reason for a break tonight. You're pushing yourself, babe. Take a rest." Jeff watched her face carefully and pressed his advantage. "I could use a friendly face in the audience, you know. We rising stars are very insecure." He grinned through his beard.

Cassidy sighed then smiled. "All right, but I can't stay late."

"I play from eight to eleven," he told her then ruffled her hair. "You can be home and tucked into bed before midnight."

"Okay, I'll be there at eight." Cassidy glanced down at her watch, frowned then tapped its face with

her fingertips. "What time is it? My watch stopped at
two-fifteen."

"A.M. or P.M.?" Jeff asked dryly. He shook his
head. "It's after seven. Hey." He gave her a shrewd look.
"Have you eaten?"

Cassidy cast her mind back and recalled an apple
at noon. "No, not really."

With a snort of disgust Jeff hauled her to her feet.
"Come on with me now, and I'll spring for a quick ham-
burger."

Cassidy pushed her hair back out of her face. "Golly,
I haven't had such a generous offer for a long time."

"Just get a coat," Jeff retorted, stalking to her door.
"In case you haven't noticed, it's pouring outside."

Cassidy glanced out her window. "So it is," she
agreed. She pulled a yellow slicker out of the closet and
dragged it on. "Can I have a cheeseburger?" she asked
Jeff as she breezed past him.

"Women. Never satisfied." He closed the door behind them.

The rain didn't bother Cassidy. It was refreshing
after her hibernation. The hurried cheeseburger and soft
drink were a banquet after the scant meals of the past
two days. The smoky, crowded coffeehouse gave her a
taste of humanity that she relished after her solitude.

Seated near the back, she drank thick café au lait
and listened to Jeff's soothing, introspective music. The
evening had grown late when she realized she had relaxed her guard. Colin had slipped over her barrier without her being aware. He stood clearly in her mind's
eye. Once he had breached her defenses, Cassidy knew
it was useless to attempt to force him out again. She
closed her eyes a moment, then opened them, accepting the inevitable. She could not avoid thinking of him
forever.

Colin Sullivan was a brilliant artist. He was a confident man who twisted life to suit himself. He had wit and charm and sensitivity. He was selfish and arrogant and totally dedicated to his work. He was thoughtless and domineering and capable of violence.

And I love him completely.

Cassidy trembled with a sigh, then stared into her coffee. I'm an idiot, a romantic fool who knew the pitfalls then fell into one anyway. I see he has a lover, I understand he sees me as important only as a subject for his painting. I'm aware he would make love to me without his heart ever being touched. I know there've been dozens of women in his life, and none of them have lasted.

No, not even Gail, she mused, for all her claims. She's just another woman who's touched the corners of his life. Colin's never made a commitment to a woman. Knowing all this, and wanting a healthy, one-to-one relationship with a man, I fall in love with him. Brilliant.

It's insane. He'll trample me. So what do I do? Slowly Cassidy lifted her coffee and sipped. She drifted away from her surroundings.

I have to finish the portrait; I gave my word. It would be impossible to be in the studio together day after day and not speak. I'm not capable of feuding in any case. Her elbows were propped on the table, the cup held between her hands, but her eyes were staring over the rim and into the distance.

Fighting with him is too dangerous because it brings the emotions to the surface. I don't know how deeply inside me he's capable of seeing. I won't humiliate myself or embarrass him with the fact that I've been stupid enough to fall in love with him. The only thing to do is to behave naturally. Hold the pose for him, talk when he asks me to talk and be friendly. The painting seems to be moving well; it should be finished in a few more weeks. Surely I can behave properly for that amount of time. And when it's finished . . .

Her thoughts trailed off into darkness. And when the painting's finished, what? I pick up the pieces, she answered. For a moment her eyes were lost and sad. When the painting's finished and Colin drops out of my life, the universe will still function. What a small thing one person's happiness is, she reflected. What a tiny, finite slice of the whole.

With a sigh Cassidy shook off her thoughts and finished the coffee. Setting down the cup she let herself be stroked by Jeff's quiet music.

Cassidy pulled her jacket closer as she stood outside the studio door and searched her bag for the key Colin had given her.

Blasted key, she grumbled silently as she groped for it. She blew her hair from her eyes then pulled out a notepad, three pencils and a linty sourball.

"How did that get in there?" she mumbled. Her eyes flew up when Colin opened the door. "Oh. Hello."

He inclined his head at the greeting then dropped his eyes to her laden hands. "Looking for something?"

Cassidy followed his gaze. Embarrassed, she dumped everything back into her bag and fumbled for poise. "No, I . . . nothing. I didn't think you'd be here so early." She shifted her purse back to her shoulder.

"It appears it's fortunate I am. Have you lost your key, Cass?" There was a smile on his face that made her feel foolish and scatter-brained.

"No, I haven't lost it," she muttered. "I just can't find it." She walked past him into the studio. Her shoulder barely brushed his chest and she felt a jolt of heat. It wasn't going to be as easy as she'd thought. "I'll change," she said briefly then went directly to the dressing room.

When she emerged, Colin was setting his palette and gave her not so much as a glance. His ignoring of her brought a wave of relief. There, you see, she told herself, there's nothing to worry about.

"I'm going to do some work on the face today," Colin stated, still mixing paints. His use of the imper- sonal pronoun was further proof his thoughts were not on Cassidy St. John. She denied the existence of the ache in her chest. Keeping silent, she waited until he was finished then stood obligingly while he set the pose. She would, she determined, give him absolutely no trouble. But when he cupped her chin in his hand, she stiffened and jerked away.

Colin's eyes heated. "I need to see the shape of your face through my hands." He set the pose again with meticulous care, barely making contact. "It's not enough to see it with my eyes. Do you understand?"

She nodded, feeling foolish. Colin waited a moment then took her chin again, but lightly, with just his fin- gertips. Cassidy forced herself to remain still. "Relax, Cassidy, I need you relaxed." The patient tone of the order surprised her into obeying. He murmured his ap- proval as his fingers trailed over her skin.

To Cassidy it was an agony of delight. His touch was gentle, though he frowned in concentration. She won- dered if he could feel the heat rising to her skin. Colin traced her jawline and ran his fingers over her cheek- bones. Cassidy focused on bringing air in and out of her lungs at an even pace. She tried to tell herself that his touch was as impersonal as a doctor's, but when his hand lingered on her cheek, she brought her eyes warily to his.

"Hold steady," he commanded briskly, then turned

to go to his easel. "Look at me," he ordered as he picked up his palette and brush.

Cassidy obeyed, trying to put her mind on anything but the man who painted her. Even as her eyes met his, she realized it was hopeless. She could not look at him and not see him. She could not be with him and not be aware of him. She could not block him out of her mind with any more success than she could block him out of her heart.

Would it be wrong, she wondered, to let myself dream a little? Would it be wrong to look for some pieces of happiness in the time I have left with him? Unhappiness will come soon enough. Can't I just enjoy being near him and pay the price after he's gone? It seemed a small thing.

Cassidy watched him work, memorizing every part of him. There would come a time, she knew, when she would want the memories. She studied the dark fullness of the hair falling on his forehead and curling over his collar. She studied the black arched brows which were capable of expressing so many moods. The planes of his face fascinated her. His eyes lifted again and again to her face as he painted. There was a fierce concentration in them, an urgency that intensified an already impossible blue.

She couldn't see his hands, but she envisioned them, long and narrow and beautiful. She could feel them learning her face, seeing what perhaps she herself would never see, understanding what she might never understand. If one has to fall foolishly in love, she decided, there couldn't be a more perfect man.

They worked for hours, taking short breaks for Cassidy to stretch her muscles. Colin was always impatient to begin again. She sensed his mood, his excitement, and knew something exceptional was being created.

The studio was alive with it. Eagerness, anticipation, tingled in the air.

"The eyes," he muttered and set down his palette. Quickly he stalked over to her. "Come, I need to see you closer." He pulled her to just behind the easel. "The eyes can be the soul of a portrait."

Colin took her by the shoulders, and his face was barely an inch from hers. The smell of paint and turpentine was sharp in her nostrils. Cassidy knew she would never smell them again without thinking of him.

"Look at me, Cass. Straight on."

She obeyed, though the look of his eyes nearly undid her. It was deep, intruding, reaching past what was offered and seeking the whole. Reflected in his eyes, she saw herself.

I'm a prisoner there, she thought. His. Their breaths mingled, and her lips parted, inviting his to close the minute distance. Something flickered and nearly caught flame. Abruptly he stepped back to his canvas.

Cassidy spoke without thinking. "What did you see?"

"Secrets," Colin murmured as he painted. "Dreams. No, don't look away, Cass, it's your dreams I need."

Helplessly Cassidy brought her eyes back. It was far too late for resistance. Setting down his palette and brush, Colin frowned at the canvas for several long moments, then he stepped toward Cassidy and smiled.

"It's perfect. You gave me what I needed."

Cassidy felt a tiny thrill of alarm. "Is it finished?"

"No, but nearly." He lifted her hands and kissed them one at a time. "Soon."

"Soon," she repeated and thought it an ugly word. Quickly she shoved back depression. "Then it must be going well."

"Yes, it's going well."

"But you're not going to let me see it yet."

"I'm superstitious." He gave her hands a gentle squeeze. "Humor me."

"You let Gail see it." Unable to prevent herself, Cassidy let resentment slip into her tone.

"Gail's an artist," Colin pointed out. He released her hands then patted her cheek. "Not the model."

With a sigh of defeat Cassidy turned to wander the room. "You must have painted her . . . at one time or other," she commented. "She's so striking, so vital."

"She can't hold a pose for five minutes," Colin said. He began to clean his brushes at the worktable.

Smiling, Cassidy leaned on the windowsill. "Do you have a hard time with your seascapes?" she asked him. "Or do you simply command the water and clouds to stop fidgeting? I believe you could do it." She stretched then lifted the weight of her hair from her neck. With an expansive sigh, she let it fall again to tumble as it chose. The sun shimmered through its shades.

When she turned her head to smile at Colin again, she found him watching her, the brush he was cleaning held idly in one hand. Something pulled at her, urging her to go to him. Instead, she walked to the other end of the room.

"The first painting of yours I ever saw was an Irish landscape." Cassidy kept her back to him and tried to speak naturally. "It was a small, exquisite work bathed in evening light. I liked it because it helped me imagine my mother. Isn't that odd?" She turned back to him as the thought eclipsed her nerves. "I have several pictures of her, but that painting made her seem real. She rarely seems real to me." Her voice softened with the words; then, suddenly, she smiled at him. "Are your parents alive, Colin?"

His eyes held hers for a moment. "Yes." He went back to cleaning his brushes. "Back in Ireland."

"They must miss you."

"Perhaps. They've six other children. I don't imagine they find much time to be lonely."

"Six!" Cassidy exclaimed. Her lips curved at the thought. "Your mother must be remarkable."

Colin looked over again, flashing a grin. "She had a razor strap that could catch three of us at one time."

"No doubt you deserved it."

"No doubt." He scrutinized the sable of his brush. "But I recall wishing a time or two her aim hadn't been so keen."

"My father lectured," Cassidy remembered, taking a long breath in and out. "I'd often wish he'd whack me a time or two and be done with it. Lectures are a great deal more painful, I think, than a razor strap."

"Like Professor Easterman's at Berkeley?" Colin asked with a grin. Cassidy blinked at him.

"How did you know about him?"

"You told me yourself, Cass my love. Last week, I think it was. Or perhaps the week before."

"I never thought you were listening," she murmured. Cassidy tried to remember all she had rambled about since the sittings had begun. Her teeth began to worry her bottom lip. "I can't think of half the things I talked about."

"That's all right, I do . . . well enough." After wiping his hands on a rag, Colin turned back to her. She was frowning, displeased. "You've got those lines between your brows again, Cass," he said lightly and smiled when she smoothed them out. "Well now, I've made you miss lunch, and that's a crime when you're already thin enough to slip under the door. Shall I poison

you with whatever's in the kitchen, or will you settle
for coffee?"

"I think I'll pass on both those gracious invitations."
She swung around and glided toward the dressing room.
"I'll take my chances at home. I have a neighbor who
hoards stale doughnuts."

Cassidy closed the door behind her and smiled. That
wasn't so bad, she told her reflection. The ground was
only shaky a couple of times. Now that the worst of it's
over, the rest of the sittings should be easy.

Humming lightly, she began to strip out of the
gown. Everything's going to be all right. After all, I'm
a grown woman. I can handle myself.

After she had slipped out of the dress, Cassidy held
it aloft to shake out the folds. When the door opened,
her humming turned to a shriek. In a quick jerk she
pressed the dress against her naked skin and held on
with both hands.

"What about dinner?" Colin asked and leaned
against the open door.

"Colin!"

"Yes?" he asked in a pleasant tone.

"Colin, go away. I'm not dressed." She hugged the
dress close and hoped she was somewhat covered.

"Yes, so I see, but you haven't answered my question."

Cassidy made an anxious sound and swallowed.
"What question?"

"What about dinner?" he repeated. His eyes
skimmed over her bare shoulders.

"What about dinner?" she demanded.

"You can't eat stale doughnuts for dinner, Cass. It's
not healthy." He smiled at the incredulity on her face.
She shifted the dress a bit higher.

"He keeps tacos as well," she said primly. "Now, would you mind shutting the door on your way out?"

"Tacos? Oh, no, that won't do." Colin shook his head and ignored her request. "I'll have to feed you myself."

Cassidy began to demand her privacy again then stopped. For a moment she studied him thoughtfully. "Colin, are you asking me for a date?"

"A date?" he repeated. For a moment he said nothing as he appeared to consider the matter. One brow arched as he studied her. "It certainly seems that way."

"To dinner?" Cassidy asked cautiously.

"To dinner."

"What time?"

"Seven."

"Seven," she repeated with a nod as she shut her ears on her practical side. "Now, close the door so I can get dressed."

"Certainly." A wicked gleam shot into his eyes, making her clutch the dress with both hands. She took one wary step in retreat. "By the way, Cass, you'd never've been a successful general."

"What?"

"You forgot to cover your flank," he told her as he shut the door behind him.

Twisting her head, Cassidy caught the full rear length of herself in the mirror.

CHAPTER 7

As Cassidy dressed that evening she blessed her short skip into the boutique business. The wisteria crepe de chine was worth all the hours she had practiced patience. It was a thin, dreamlike dress with floating lines. Her shoulders were left bare as the bodice was caught with elastic just above her breasts. The material nipped in at the waist then fell fully to the knees. She slipped on the cap-sleeved matching jacket and tied it loosely at the waist. The color was good for her eyes, she decided, bringing out the uniqueness of their shade. This was a night she didn't want to feel ordinary.

You shouldn't even be going. Cassidy brought the brush through her hair violently in response to the nagging voice. I don't care. I am going. *You'll get hurt.* I'll be hurt in any case. Moving quickly, she fastened small gold lover's knots to her ears. Doesn't everyone deserve one special moment? Aren't I entitled to a glimpse of real happiness? I'll have my one evening with him without that blasted painting between us. I'll have my moment when he's looking at me, seeing me, and not whatever it is he sees when we're in the studio.

She lifted her scent and sprayed a cloud as delicate as the wisteria. I won't think about tomorrow, only tonight. The painting's almost finished and then it'll be over. I have to have something. One evening isn't too much to ask. I'll pay the price later, but I'm going to have it. After tossing her hair behind her shoulders, Cassidy glanced at her watch.

"Oh, good grief, it's already seven!" Frantically she began to search for her key. She was on her hands and knees, peering under the convertible sofa that doubled as her bed, when the knock came. "Yes, yes, yes, just a minute," she called out crossly and stretched out for something shiny in the dark beneath the sofa.

She pulled it out with an "Aha!" of triumph, then sighed when she saw a quarter and not a key in her fingers.

"I said I'd buy," Colin told her, and Cassidy's head shot up. He stood inside her door, looking curiously at the woman on her hands and knees. Cassidy straightened up, blew her hair from her eyes and studied him.

He wore a slimly tailored black suit. Its perfect cut accentuated the width of his shoulders and leanness of his build. His shirt was a splash of white in contrast and opened at the throat. Cassidy concluded Colin Sullivan would never restrict himself with a tie. She leaned back on her heels.

"I've never seen you in a suit before," she commented. The lamplight fell softly on her upturned face. "But you don't look too conventional. I'm glad."

"You're an amazing creature, Cassidy." He held out a hand to help her up, touching the other to her hair as she rose.

Standing, she tilted her head back and smiled at him. "Do you think so?"

A smile was his answer as he stepped back, keeping her hand in his. "You look lovely." The survey he made was quick and thorough. "Perfectly lovely." Taking her other hand, he turned it palm up and revealed the quarter. "Cab fare?" he asked. "It won't take you far."

Cassidy frowned down at her own hand. "I thought it was my key."

"Of course." Colin took the quarter and examined it critically. "It looks remarkably like one."

"It did in the dark under the sofa," Cassidy retorted then resumed her search. "It has to be here somewhere," she muttered as she shuffled through papers on her desk. "I've looked everywhere, positively everywhere."

"Where's the bedroom?" Colin asked, watching her shake out the pages of a dictionary.

"This *is* the bedroom," Cassidy informed him and poked through the leaves of a fern. "And the living room, and the study and the parlor. I like things all in one place, it saves steps." She found an eraser under a pile of notebooks and scowled at it. "I looked all over for this yesterday." With a long sigh she set it down.

"All right, just a minute," she said to the room in general as she leaned back on the desk. "I'll get it." Her eyes closed as she rubbed the tip of her finger over the bridge of her nose. "Last time I had it, I'd been to the market. I came in," she said, pointing to the door, "and I took the bag into the kitchen. I put a can of juice into the freezer, and . . ." Her eyes widened before she scrambled into the next room.

When she came back, she bounced the key from palm to palm. "It's cold," she explained and flushed under Colin's amused glance. "I must have been thinking of something else when I left it in there." Picking up a small gold bag, Cassidy dropped the frozen key inside. "That should do it." She moved to the door and engaged the lock. Gravely, Colin walked to her then cupped her face in his hands.

"Cass."

"Yes?"

"You don't have any shoes on."

"Oh." She lifted her shoulders then let them fall. "I suppose I'll need them."

He kissed her forehead and let her go. "It's best to be prepared for anything." A grin accompanied the gesture of his arm. "They seem to be by your desk."

In silence, Cassidy walked to the desk and slipped into her shoes. Her eyes were smiling as she returned to Colin. "Well, have I forgotten anything else?"

He took her hand, interlocking their fingers. "No."

"Do you like organized people particularly, Colin?" She tilted her head with the question.

"Not particularly."

"Good. Shall we go?"

Cassidy's first surprise of the evening was the Ferrari that sat by the curb. It was red and sleek and flashy. "That must be yours," she murmured, taking her eyes from bumper to bumper then back again. "Or my neighbor has suddenly inherited a fortune."

"One of Vince's bribes." Colin opened the door on the passenger side. "For this I did a portrait of his niece. A remarkably plain creature with an overbite. Shall I put the top up?"

"No, don't." Cassidy settled into the seat as she watched him round the hood. Cinderella never had a pumpkin like this, she thought and smiled. "I thought you didn't paint anyone unless you were particularly interested in the subject."

"Vince is one of the few people I have difficulty refusing." The Ferrari roared into life. Excitement vibrated under Cassidy's feet.

"Did you know you can buy a three-bedroom brick rambler in New Jersey for what this car costs? With a carport and five spreading junipers."

Colin grinned and swung away from the curb. "I'd make a lousy neighbor."

Colin drove expertly through the city. They skirted Golden Gate Park and avoided the labyrinthine stretches of freeway. They took side roads, narrow roads, and he maneuvered through traffic with smooth skill.

Cassidy could smell the varied scents from the sidewalk flower vendors and hear the brassy clang of the trolley bell. Tilting her head back, she could see the peak of a slender skyscraper. "Where're we going?" she asked but cared little as the breeze fluttered over her cheeks. It was enough to be with him.

"To eat," Colin returned. "I'm starving."

Cassidy turned to face him. "For an Irishman, you're not exactly talkative. Look." She sat up and pointed. "The fog's coming in."

It loomed over the bay, swallowing the bridge with surprising speed. As Cassidy watched, only the pinnacles of the Golden Gate speared the tumbling cloud.

"There'll be foghorns tonight," she murmured then looked at Colin again. "They make such a lonely sound. It always makes me sad, though I never know why."

"What sound makes you happy?" He glanced over to her, and she brushed wisps of flying hair from her face.

"Popping corn," she answered instantly then laughed at herself.

Leaning her head back, Cassidy looked up at the sky. It was piercingly blue. How many cities could have tumbling fog and blue skies? she wondered. When Colin pulled to the curb, her gaze traveled down until it encountered the huge expanse of the hotel. Her lips parted in surprise as she recognized the area. Nob Hill. She had paid no attention to their direction.

Her door was opened by a uniformed doorman who offered his hand to help her alight. She waited while Colin passed him a bill then joined her.

"Do you like seafood?" He took her hand and moved toward the entrance.

"Why, yes, I—"

"Good. They have rather exceptional seafood here."

"So I've heard," Cassidy murmured.

In a few steps she walked from a world she knew into one she had only read of.

The restaurant was huge and sumptuous. High, iridescent glass ceilings crowned a room dripping with chandeliers. The carpet was rich, the tables many and elegantly white clothed. The maître d' was immediately attentive, and as Colin called him by name Cassidy realized the artist was no stranger there.

The secluded corner table set them apart from the vastness of the restaurant yet left Cassidy with a full view of the splendor. Jeff's cheeseburger seemed light-years away. Having gawked as much as she deemed proper, Cassidy turned to Colin.

"It seems I'm going to do better than tacos after all."

"I'm a man of my word," he informed her. "That's why I give it as seldom as possible. Wine?" he asked and smiled at her in his masterfully charming fashion. "You don't look the cocktail type."

"Oh?" Her head tilted. "Why not?"

"Too much innocence in those big violet eyes." He brushed her hair behind her shoulder. "It almost makes me consider doing something bourgeois like cutting the wine with water."

A black-coated waiter stood respectfully at Colin's elbow. "A bottle of Château Haut-Brion blanc," he ordered, keeping his eyes on Cassidy. With a slight bow the waiter drifted backward and away. She watched him then took another long look around the room, trying to absorb every detail. "I noticed by your desk that you've been working. Is it going well?"

Cassidy studied Colin with some surprise. Perhaps he saw more than she assumed he did. "Yes, actually, I think it is. I'm having one of those periods when everything falls into place. They don't last long, but they're productive. Does it work like that with painting?"

"Yes. Times when everything seems to flow without effort, and times when you scrape the canvas down again and again." He smiled at her, and his long fingers traced her wrist. "Somewhat like you tearing up pages, I imagine."

The waiter returned with their wine, and the ritual of opening and tasting began. Gratefully, Cassidy remained silent. The pulse in her wrist had leapt at Colin's casual touch, and she used the time to quiet its skittish rhythm. When her glass was filled, she was able to lift it with complete composure. The wine was lightly chilled and exquisite.

"To your taste?" Colin asked as he watched her sip.

Cassidy's eyes smiled into his. "It could become a habit."

"Tell me what you're writing about." He, too, lifted his glass, but his free hand covered hers.

"It's about two people and their life together and apart from each other."

"A love story?"

"Yes, a complex one." She frowned a moment at their joined hands then brought her eyes to Colin's again. The flame of the candle threw gold among the violet. She reminded herself to enjoy the moment, not to think of tomorrow. A smile lifted her lips as she touched the glass to them. "They both seem to be volatile characters and get away from me sometimes. There's a fierce determination in them both to stand separate, yet they're drawn together. I'd like to think love allows them to remain separate in some aspects."

"Love makes its own rules, depending on who's playing." His finger trailed over her knuckles then down to her nails before they traveled back. The simple gesture quickened her heartbeat. "Will they have a happy ending?"

Cassidy allowed herself to absorb the pure blue of his eyes. "Perhaps they will," she murmured. "Their destinies are in my hands."

Watching her, Colin brought her hand to his lips. "And for tonight, Cass," he said softly, "is yours in mine?"

Her eyes were dark and steady on his. "For tonight."

He smiled then, with the flash of the pirate. Lifting his glass, he toasted her. "To the long evening ahead."

It was a luxuriously lengthy meal. Wine sparkled in crystal. Even after endless courses, they lingered long over coffee. Cassidy savored each moment. If she was to have only one evening with the man she loved, she would relish each morsel of time. Perhaps by the force of her own will, she could slow the hands of the clock.

The candle flickered low when they rose from the table. Her hand slipped into his. Just as they reached

the lobby Cassidy heard Colin's name called. Looking up, she saw a round, balding man in an impec-
cably cut suit coming toward them. He had a full smile
and an extended hand. On reaching Colin, he pumped
it enthusiastically while his other thumped on Colin's
shoulder. Cassidy saw a large diamond flash from the
ring on his hand.

"Sullivan, you rascal, it's good to see you."

"Jack." An easy grin spread over Colin's face.
"How've you been?"

"Getting by, getting by. Have a little job in town."
His eyes drifted to Cassidy and lingered.

"Cass, this is Jack Swanson, a perfect reprobate.
Jack, Cassidy St. John, a perfect treasure."

Cassidy was torn between pleasure at Colin's description and astonishment as she put Swanson's face
and name together. Over the past twenty-five years he
had produced some of the finest motion pictures in
the industry. As he took her hand and squeezed it, she
struggled to conceal her feelings.

"Reprobate?" Swanson snorted and kept possession
of Cassidy's hand. "You can't believe half the things
this Irishman says. I'm a pillar of the community."

"There's a plaque in his den that says so," Colin
added.

"Never did have an ounce of respect. Still . . ."
Swanson's eyes roamed over Cassidy's face. There was
appreciation in the look. "His taste is flawless. Not an
actress, are you?"

"Not unless you count being a mushroom in the
fourth-grade pageant." Cassidy smiled.

Swanson chuckled and nodded. "I've dealt with actresses who had lesser credits."

"Cassidy's a writer," Colin put in. He draped an
arm around her shoulders, running his hand lightly

down her arm. "You warned me to stay away from actresses."

"Since when have you listened to my sage advice?" Swanson scoffed. He pursed his lips as he studied Cassidy. Appreciation became speculation. "A writer. What sort of writer are you?"

"Why, a brilliant one, of course," she told him. "Without a scrap of ego or temperament."

Swanson patted her hand. "I've a late meeting or I'd steal you away from this young scamp now. We'll have dinner before I leave town." He cast an eye at Colin. "You can bring him along if you like." With another slap for Colin's shoulder, he lumbered away.

"Quite a character, isn't he?" Colin asked as he steered Cassidy toward the door again.

"Marvelous." It occurred to her that since meeting Colin, she had held hands with an Italian duke and one of Hollywood's reigning monarchs.

They stepped outside into the soft light of evening. The sun was gone, but some of its light still lingered. Cassidy slipped into the Ferrari with a contented sigh. She watched the first star flicker into life. With surprise she noted that Colin was headed away from the direction of her apartment.

"Where are we going?"

"There's this little place I know." He turned a corner and eased into traffic. "I thought you'd enjoy it." He shot her a glance and a smile. "Not tired, are you?"

Cassidy's lips curved. "No, I'm not tired."

The nightclub was dimly lit and smoky. Tables were small and crowded together. Jeans sat next to elegant evening dresses and splashy designer outfits. Brassy music blared from a band near a postage-stamp dance floor. Couples swayed together as they moved to the beat.

Colin escorted Cassidy to a dark table at the side of the room. His name was called now and again, but he only made a gesture of acknowledgment and continued until they were seated.

"This is wonderful! I'm certain it's a front for gun running or jewel smuggling," Cassidy exclaimed.

Colin laughed, taking both her hands. "You'd like that, would you?"

"Of course." She grinned, and her eyes lit with mischief.

A waitress had pushed her way over to them and stood, impatient, with her weight on one hip. "The lady needs champagne," Colin told her.

"Who doesn't," she mumbled and shoved her way back through the tables.

Cassidy laughed with unbridled delight. "No deferential bows for Mr. Sullivan in here," she commented.

"It's all a matter of atmosphere. I'm rather fond of sassy waitresses in the right setting. And," he added softly, turning her hand over and kissing the inside of her wrist, "crowded tables that require very close contact. Poor lighting," he continued, pressing his lips to her palm. "Where I can enjoy the taste of your skin in relative privacy." With a slight movement of his head, he kissed the sensitive skin behind her ear.

"Colin," she said breathlessly and lifted her hand to his lips in defense. He merely took it in his and kissed her fingers.

The bottle of champagne came down on the table with a bang. Colin pulled out a bill and handed it to the waitress. Shoving it in her pocket, she stalked away.

"Annoyingly speedy service tonight," he murmured as he opened the bottle. The pop was drowned out by the loud horns of the band. Cassidy accepted the wine and took a long, slow sip in the hope of stabilizing her pulse.

They drank champagne in quiet companionship, watching the raucous nightlife revolve around them. Cassidy's mood grew mellow and dreamy. Reality and make-believe became too difficult to separate. When Colin stood and took her hand, she rose to go with him to the dance floor.

The music had turned low and bluesy. He slipped both arms around her waist, and in response she lifted hers to circle his neck. Their bodies came together. The air was thick with smoke and clashing perfumes. Other couples were little more than shadows in the dim light. Their movement was only a slow swaying with their bodies pressed close.

Cassidy tilted back her head to look at him. Their eyes joined, their lips tarried less than a whisper apart. She felt a quick surge of desire. If they had been on an island without a trace of humanity, she could not have felt more alone with him. The music ended on a haunted bass note.

Silently Colin took her hand and led her from the crowd.

The moon was a white slice. Cooler air blew some of the heat from Cassidy's blood and some of the clouds from her brain. The Ferrari climbed a hill then descended. Cassidy smiled to herself. There was nothing in the evening she would have changed. No regrets.

Fog curled in twisting fingers on the road ahead. As she glanced to the side Cassidy saw the solid mass of clouds over the bay below them. Again she turned to Colin.

"To my houseboat," he told her before she could form the question. "I have something for you."

Warning lights flashed on and off in her brain. The bittersweet taste of danger was in her mouth. Cassidy looked out on the fog-choked bay and told herself she should ask Colin to take her home. But the night isn't over, she reminded herself. I promised myself tonight.

Fog swirled more thickly as they drove toward sea level. Now and again, from somewhere deep in the mist, came the low warning horns. She'd lost all sense of time when Colin stopped the car. Once again she was in a make-believe world. This one had drifting mists and the sigh of lapping water. Colin led her toward a shrouded shape. The high, maniacal call of a loon speared the silence. A narrow rope bridge swayed lightly under her feet as they crossed it. A breeze blew aside a curtain of fog, and the houseboat jumped into the opening.

"Oh, Colin." She stopped to stare at it with delight and surprise. "It's wonderful."

She saw a wide structure of aged wood in two levels with a high deck on the bow. Fog misted over again as they approached.

Inside Cassidy shook the dampness from her hair as Colin switched on a light. They walked down two steps and into the living room. It was a large square room with a low, inviting couch and tables scattered for convenience. To the right another short set of stairs led to the galley.

"How marvelous to live on the water." Cassidy spun to Colin and smiled.

"On a clear night the city's all prisms and crystals. In the fog it's brooding and wrapped in mystery." He came to her and, with a habitual gesture, brushed her hair behind her shoulder. His fingers lingered. "Your hair's damp," he murmured. "Do you know how many shades of gold and brown I used to paint your hair? It changes in every light, daring someone to define its color." Colin frowned suddenly and dropped his hand. "You should have a brandy to ward off the chill."

He turned away and walked to a cabinet. Cassidy watched him pour brandy into snifters while she dealt with the effect the intimate tone of his voice and the touch of his hand had had on her.

After accepting the brandy she turned to wander around the room. On a far wall was a painting of the bay at sunrise. The sky was molten with color, reds and golds at their most intense. There was a feeling of frenzied motion and brilliance. Even before she looked for the signature, Cassidy knew it was a Kingsley.

"She's immensely talented," Colin commented from behind.

"Yes," Cassidy agreed with sincerity. The painting gripped her. "It makes the start of a day demand your attention. A sunrise like this would be exciting, but I don't think I could begin each morning with such violence, however beautiful."

"Are you speaking of the painting or of the artist?"

Realizing his question had followed her thoughts, Cassidy shrugged and stepped away. "Strange," she began again. "One would think an artist would cover his walls with paintings. You have relatively few." She began to examine his collection, moving slowly from one to the next. Abruptly she stopped, staring at a small canvas. It was the Irish landscape she had told him of that morning.

"I wondered if you'd remember it." He stood behind her again, but this time his hands came to her shoulders. There was something casually possessive in the gesture.

"Yes, of course I do."

"I was twenty when I painted that. On my first trip back to Ireland."

"How odd that I should have spoken of it just this morning," Cassidy murmured.

"Destiny, Cass," Colin claimed and kissed the top of her head. Stepping around her, he took the canvas from the wall. "I want you to have it."

Cassidy's eyes flew to his. "No, Colin, I couldn't." Distress and amazement mingled in her voice.

"No?" His brow arched under his fall of hair. "You appeared to like it."

"Oh, Colin, you know I do. It's beautiful, it's wonderful." Her distress deepened, reflecting clearly on her face. "I can't just take one of your paintings."

"You're not taking it, I'm giving it to you," he countered. "That's one of the privileges of the artist."

"Colin." Her eyes went back to the painting then lifted to his. "You wouldn't have kept it all this time if it hadn't meant something special to you. You'd have sold it."

"Some things you don't sell. Some things you give." He held the small canvas out to her. "Please."

Tears thickened in her throat. "I've never heard you say 'please' before."

"I save it for special occasions."

Cassidy looked back at him. He had given her more than the painting; it was a bond—between herself and a woman she had never known. Her smile came slowly. "Thank you."

Colin traced her lips with a fingertip. "This is one of the loveliest things about you," he murmured. "Come," he said abruptly. "Sit down and drink your brandy." He took the canvas and set it aside, then led Cassidy to the sofa.

"Do you paint here, too?" she asked as she sipped her brandy.

"Sometimes."

"I remember the night I met you, your wanting me to come back here for sketches."

"And you threatened me with a husband in a football helmet."

"It was the best I could think up on the spur of the moment." She turned her head to grin at him and found his face dangerously close. His fingers tangled in her hair before she could ease away. Slowly he leaned closer until his lips brushed her cheek. Feather light, the kiss moved to her other cheek, lingering over her lips without touching. Still, she could taste the kiss on them.

"Colin," Cassidy whispered. She put a hand to his chest as his lips moved to her temple. She knew the warmth she felt was not from the brandy.

"Cassidy." He trailed his mouth down to her jawline then drew away. His eyes were grave as he looked down at her, his hand light on her shoulder. "The last time I kissed you, I hurt you. I regret that."

"Please, Colin." Cassidy shook her head to halt his words. "We were both angry."

"You've already forgiven me, because it's your nature to do so. But I remember the look on your face." He ran his hand down her arm until it linked with hers. "I want to kiss you again, Cass, the way you should be kissed." He took his hand and gently circled her neck. "But I need you to tell me it's what you want."

It would be so easy to refuse. She had only to form the word "no," and she knew he'd let her go. But she was as truly his prisoner now as if she were chained to him. "Yes," she said and closed her eyes. "Yes."

His mouth touched hers lightly, and her lips parted. His kisses were soft and gentle, lingering before one

ended and another began. She felt him slip the light
jacket from her shoulders and enjoyed the warmth of
his hands on her skin. Slowly the kisses grew deeper.
Her arms found their way around him. The languor that
spread through her went far beyond the effects of the
wine. Her limbs were pliant, her mind clouded as her
senses grew sharper.

When their lips parted, Colin loosened his hold.
"Cass."

With a sigh she snuggled against him, brushing his
neck with a kiss. She ran a hand experimentally up the
silk of his shirt. "Yes?" she murmured, lifting her face
to his. Her eyes were slumberous, her lips a temptation. Colin swore under his breath before he crushed his
mouth to hers.

Cassidy's response was instantaneous. Her passion
went from languid to flaming in the space of a heartbeat. Blood pounded thickly in her brain as she found
herself falling backward onto the cushions of the sofa.
Colin's body was taut. His hands caressed the bare skin
of her shoulders as the kiss deepened. At the base of
her throat he found more pleasure, and his mouth lingered there as her pulse beat wildly beneath it.

The elastic of her bodice slid down at his insistence,
freeing her breasts to his searching hands. Unbridled,
her passion raced through her, bringing a moan that
spoke of longing and delight. His mouth trailed down
through the valley between her breasts, devouring her
heated skin. His fingers brushed over the peak of her
breasts, exploring, learning, until his mouth replaced
them. Cassidy gave a shuddering moan as he brought
his lips back to hers, accepting the fierce, final urgency
that flared before he ended the kiss. Her eyes opened
to meet the dark fire of his.

Seeing the tumble of his hair over his brow, she

lifted a hand to push it back. She murmured his name. Colin caught her hand in his as she took it to his cheek. Carefully he drew the bodice of her dress into place then pulled her with him to a sitting position.

"I make few noble gestures, Cassidy." His voice was husky, and under her palm she could feel the rapid beat of his heart. "This is one of them." Rising, he drew her to her feet then draped her jacket over her shoulders. "I'll take you home."

"Colin," she began, knowing only that she wanted to be his.

"No, don't say anything." He dropped his hands from her shoulders and put them in his pockets. "You put your destiny in my hands for tonight. I'll take you home. Next time the decision will be in your hands."

CHAPTER 8

The sun was high and bright. Cassidy watched it spear through her window as she lay in bed. It fell in a patch on the floor and shimmered. Her eyes drifted to the painting that hung to her left. It had hung there for only two days, but she knew every minute detail of the canvas. She knew the very texture of the brush strokes. Sighing, she stared up at the ceiling.

She remembered every moment of her evening with Colin, from the instant she had looked up from her hands and knees by her couch to the brief good-bye at the door.

When she had returned to the studio the morning after their date, Colin had fallen into his work pattern with apparent ease. Whatever had been between them, Cassidy decided, had been for that night. For him, it was over. For me, she thought, studying the painting again, it's forever.

I should be grateful to him for taking me home when he did. If I had stayed . . . If I had stayed, she repeated after a long breath, I would have become one of his lovers. And then he would have picked up his life exactly where he left off, and I would be even more alone than I am now. As it is, I have one exceptional evening to remember. Wine and candlelight and music.

"Romantic fool," she muttered abruptly then rolled over and punched her pillow.

"Cassidy." The knock sounded as a brief concession before Jeff burst through the door. "Hey, Cassidy." He stopped and gave her a look of disgust. "Still in bed? It's eleven o'clock."

Cassidy pulled the sheet up to her chin and scrambled to sit up. "Yes, I'm still in bed. I worked till three-thirty." She frowned past him. "I thought I'd remembered to lock that door."

"Uh-uh." Jeff hurried over and plopped on the bed while she flushed with embarrassed amusement.

"Make yourself at home," she said with a grand gesture of her free arm. "Don't mind me."

"Take a look at this! You got yourself in the paper."

"What?" Cassidy glanced down at the newspaper Jeff had clutched in his hand. "What are you talking about?"

"I splurged on a Sunday paper," he began then his lips spread in a grin. He touched her nose with a fingertip. "And who do I see when I take a look at the society section, but my friend and neighbor, Cassidy St. John."

"You're making that up," Cassidy accused and tossed back her sleep-tumbled hair. "What would I be doing on the society page?"

"Dancing with Colin Sullivan," Jeff informed her as he waved the paper under her nose.

Cassidy grabbed his wrist to stop the movement, then her mouth fell open in astonishment. She stared, unbelievingly, at the picture. In two quick moves she had dropped the sheet and grabbed the paper from Jeff's hand. "Let me see that."

"Help yourself," he said amiably. He settled back on one elbow to watch myriad expressions cross her face. The flush sleep had put into her cheeks grew deeper. "Seems you were seen together in some hot spot. A picture gets snapped, and they add a bit of interesting speculation of who Sullivan's latest flame is." He pulled on his beard and chuckled. "Little do they know she's sitting right here in a number fifty-three football jersey that looks a lot better on her than it would on a right tackle." He chuckled again then peered down at the newspaper. "You look real good in there, too."

"This is all—all drivel!" Cassidy slammed down the paper then scrambled to her knees. Pushing Jeff aside she stepped over him to the floor. "Did you read that story?" she demanded and kicked a stray tennis shoe into a corner. "How dare they imply such things?"

Jeff sat back up, watching her spin around the room. "Hey, Cassidy, it's just a story, nothing to get all worked up about. Besides . . ." He picked up the discarded paper and smoothed it out. "They're really pretty complimentary where you're concerned. Listen, they call you a . . ." He paused while he searched down the phrase. "Oh, yeah, here it is. A 'nubile young beauty.' Sounds pretty good."

Cassidy made a low sound in her throat then kicked the mate to the tennis shoe into an opposing corner. "That's just like a man," she stormed back at him. Turning away, she pulled open a drawer and yanked out a pair of cutoffs; then, spinning around, she waved them at him. "Toss out a few compliments and it makes everything all right." Cassidy dove back into the drawer and came up with a crimson scoop-necked T-shirt. "Well, it's not, it's absolutely not." She pushed her hair out of her face and drew in a deep breath. "Can I keep that?" she asked in more controlled tones.

"Sure." Warily, Jeff rose and handed her the paper. He cleared his throat. "Well, I guess I'll just go read the rest of the paper," he told her, but she was already scowling down at the picture again. Taking advantage of her preoccupation, he slipped out the door.

L ess than an hour later Cassidy was stalking down the pier toward Colin's houseboat. Gripped in her hand was the folded page of the Sunday paper. Filled with righteous indignation, she crossed the narrow swaying bridge then pounded on the door. There was silence and the lapping of waves. She glanced around then scowled at the Ferrari.

"Oh, you're home all right, Sullivan," she muttered darkly, then pounded again.

"What the devil are you banging about?" Colin's voice boomed over her head. Cassidy backed away from the door, looked up and was blinded by the sun. Furious, she flung up a hand to shade her eyes.

She saw him leaning over the rail of the top deck. He was bare-chested, his cutoffs a slight concession to modesty. He held a paint brush tipped in blue in his hand.

"I've got to talk to you!" Cassidy shouted and waved the paper at him.

"All right then, come up, but stop that idiotic banging." He disappeared from the rail before she could speak again. Cassidy walked toward the bow until she spotted a steep set of stairs. After climbing them, she stood on the upper deck with her hands on her hips. She scowled at his back.

He was on a three-legged stool in front of a canvas, painting with sure, rapid strokes. Glancing over, she saw the sailboats he was recreating. They skimmed over the bay with spinnakers billowing in a riot of color.

"Well, what brings you rapping at my door, Cass?" His voice was muffled as he held the stem of a brush between his teeth like a pirate's saber. Another glided over the canvas. Cassidy stomped over and fearlessly waved the paper in front of his face.

"This!"

With surprising calm, Colin put down both of his brushes, cast her a raised-brow look, then took the paper from her. "It's a good likeness," he said after a moment.

"Colin!"

"Ssh. I'm reading." He lapsed into silence, eyes on the paper, while Cassidy ground her teeth and stalked around the deck. Once he laughed outright but held up a hand when she started to speak. She shut her mouth on something like a growl and turned her back on him. "Well," he said at length. "That was highly entertaining."

Cassidy whirled around. "Entertaining? *Entertaining?!* Is that all you have to say about this—this trash?"

Colin shrugged. "It could be better written, I suppose. Do you want coffee?"

"Did you *read* that?" she demanded and stormed forward until she stood in front of him. The wind tugged at her hair, and she pushed it back, annoyed. "Did you read the things it said, the things . . ." Cassidy sputtered to a halt, stomped her foot in frustration then gave him a firm rap on the chest with her fist. "I am not your latest flame, Sullivan."

"Ah."

Her eyes kindled. "Don't you use that significant 'ah' on me. I am *not* your latest flame, or your flame of any sort, and I resent the term. I resent all the little insinuations and innuendos in that article. I resent the unstated fact that you and I are lovers." She tossed back her head. "What sort of logic is it that because we dance together, we have to be lovers?"

"You have to admit the idea is appealing." He chuckled at her smoldering glare. The breeze rolling in from the bay continued to blow her hair around her face. Absently Colin brushed it back then laid a hand on her shoulder. "Would you like to sue the paper?"

She heard the soft amusement in his voice and stuck her hands in her pockets. "I want a retraction," she said stubbornly.

"For what?" he countered. "For snapping a picture? For writing a bit of gossip? My dear child, the picture's enough all by itself." He held it out, drawing her eyes to it. "These two people appear to be totally absorbed in each other."

Cassidy turned away and walked to the rail. She knew it had been the picture that had set her off. Their bodies were close, her arms around his neck, their eyes locked. The dark, smoky nightclub was a backdrop. No words were needed to complete the picture. She remembered the moment, the feeling that had rushed through her, the utter intimacy they had shared.

The picture was an invasion of her private self, and she hated it. She detested the chatty little column beside it that linked her so casually with Colin. Without even having learned her name, they had titled her his woman, his woman of the moment . . . until the next one. Cassidy frowned out at the water, watching the gulls swoop.

"I don't like it," she muttered. "I don't like being splashed in print for speculation over cornflakes and coffee. I don't like being made into something I'm not by someone's lively imagination. And I don't like being described as a . . ."

"'Nubile young beauty'?" Colin provided.

"I see nothing funny in that grand little phrase. It makes me feel absurd." She folded her arms over her chest. "It's not a compliment, whatever you and Jeff might think."

"Who the devil is Jeff?"

"He thought the article was just peachy," she continued, working up to a high temper again. "He sat on my bed this morning, telling me I should be flattered, that I should—"

"Perhaps," Colin interrupted and walked to her, "you'd tell me who Jeff is and why he was in your bed this morning?"

"Not in, *on*," Cassidy corrected impatiently. "And stick to the point, Sullivan."

"I'd like this matter cleared up first." He took a final step toward her then captured her chin. His fingers were surprisingly firm. "In fact, I insist."

"Will you stop it?" she demanded and jerked away. "How can I get anywhere when you're constantly badgering and belittling me."

"Badgering and belittling?" Colin repeated, then tossed back his head and roared with laughter. "Now *that's* a grand little phrase. Now, about Jeff."

"Oh, leave him out of it, would you?" Cassidy blew out a frustrated breath, making a wide sweep with her arms. Her eyes began to glitter again. "He brought me the article this morning, that's all. I'm telling you, Colin, I won't be lumped in with all your former and future flames. And I won't be used to sustain the romantic mystique of the artist."

His brows drew together. "Now what precisely is the meaning of that last sentence, for those of us who missed the first installment?"

"I think it's clear, a simple declarative sentence in the first person. I mean it, Colin."

"Yes." He studied her curiously. "I can see you do."

They watched each other in silence. She was painfully aware of the lean attraction of his build, of the bronzed skin left bare but for low-slung cutoffs. Thrown off balance by her own thoughts, Cassidy turned away again and leaned over the rail. For a moment she listened to the gentle slap of water against the wood of the boat. Her shoulders moved with her sigh.

"I'm basically a simple person, Colin. I've never been out of the state and scarcely been more than a hundred miles from the city. I don't have a fascinating background. I'm not a woman of mystery." Composed again, she turned back to him. The breeze picked up her hair and tossed it behind her. "I don't like being misrepresented." She lifted her hands a moment then dropped them to her sides. "I'm not the sort of woman they made me seem in that paper."

Colin folded the paper then tucked it in his back pocket before he crossed to her. "You are infinitely more fascinating than the sort of woman they made you seem in that paper."

Cassidy shook her head. "I wasn't fishing for a compliment."

"A simple statement of fact." He kissed her before she could decide whether to accept or evade him. "Feel better now?"

Cassidy frowned at him. "I'm not a child having a temper tantrum."

His brow lifted. "A nubile young beauty, then."

Cassidy narrowed her eyes at him then glanced down at herself. "I'm nubile enough, I should think."

"And certainly young."

Bringing her eyes back up, she gave him a provocative look. "Don't you think I'm beautiful?"

"No."

"Oh."

Colin laughed then captured her face with his hands. "That face," he said as his eyes roamed over her, "has superb bones, exquisite skin. There's strength and frailty and vivacity, and you're totally unaware of it. A unique, expressive face. *Beautiful* is far too ordinary a word."

Color warmed Cassidy's cheeks. She wondered why, after so many close examinations, her blood still churned when he studied her face. "A charming way to make up for an insult," she said lightly. "It must be the Irish in you."

"I've a much better way."

The kiss was so quickly insistent, Cassidy had no time for thought, only response. A sound of pleasure escaped her as she moved her hands up the taut, bare skin of his chest. She felt the heat of the sun and her own instant need. Her mouth became avid. Desire swirled through her blood, causing her to demand rather than surrender. The passion he released in her ruled her, changing submission to aggression. She felt Colin's arms tighten around her and heard his low moan of approval.

"Cassidy," he murmured as his lips roamed over her face. "You bewitch me."

With a curiosity of their own, her hands explored the long line of his torso, the wiry muscles of his arms and back. His heart hammered against hers as she touched him. Here was a whole new world, and her mouth searched his ravenously as she tested it.

"Oh, dear, I seem to be interrupting."

Startled, Cassidy pulled her mouth from Colin's but was unable to break his hold. Twisting her head, she stared at Gail Kingsley. She stood just at the top of the stairs, one hand poised on the railing. An emerald silk scarf rippled at her throat and trailed in the breeze.

"That seems obvious enough," Colin returned evenly. Flushing to the roots of her hair, Cassidy wriggled for freedom.

"I do apologize, Colin darling. I had no idea you had company. So rare for you on a Sunday, after all." She gave him a smile that established her knowledge of his habits. "I needed to pick up those Rothchild canvases, you remember? And we do have one or two things to discuss. I'll just wait downstairs." She crossed the deck as she spoke and opened a door that led inside. "Shall I make coffee for three?" she added, then disappeared without waiting for an answer.

Cassidy twisted her head back to Colin, pressing her hands against his chest. "Let me go," she demanded between her teeth. "Let me go this minute."

"Why? You seemed happy enough to be held a moment ago."

She threw back her head as she shoved against him. The muscles she had just tested made her movements useless. "A moment ago I was blinded by animal lust. I see perfectly now."

"Animal lust?" Colin repeated. He grinned widely in appreciation. "How interesting. Does it come over you often?"

"Don't you grin at me, Sullivan. Don't you dare!"

Colin released her without sobering his features. "At times it's difficult not to."

"I won't have you holding me while Gail stands

there with her superior little smile." With a sniff, she brushed at her T-shirt and shorts.

"Why, Cass, are you jealous?" His grin grew yet wider. "How flattering."

Her head snapped up, her breathing grew rapid. "Why you smug, insufferable—"

"You were perfectly willing to suffer me when you were blinded by animal lust."

A sound of temper came low in her throat. Tested past her limit, Cassidy took an enthusiastic swing at him that carried her in a complete circle. He dodged it, catching her neatly by the waist.

"Women are supposed to slap," he instructed. "Not punch."

"I never read the rules," she snapped then jerked away. Cassidy turned, intending to leave in the same manner she had arrived. Colin caught her hand and spun her back until she collided with his chest. He smiled then kissed the tip of her nose.

"What's your hurry?"

"There's an old Irish saying," she told him as she pushed away again. "Three's a crowd."

He chuckled, patting her cheek. "Cass, don't be a fool."

She rolled her eyes to the sky and prayed for willpower. Screaming wouldn't solve anything. She took several deep breaths. "Oh, go . . . go paint your spinnakers," she suggested and stalked down the steps to the lower deck.

"Sure and it's a fine-looking woman you are, Cassidy St. John," Colin called after her in an exaggerated brogue. She glanced back over her shoulder with eyes blazing. He leaned companionably over the rail. "And it's the truth it's no more hardship watching your temper walking away than it is watching it coming ahead.

Next time I'll be wanting to paint you in a pose that shows your more charming end."

"When pigs fly," she called back and doubled her pace. His laughter raced after her.

CHAPTER 9

Cassidy knew the painting was nearly finished. She had the frantic, hollow sensation of one living on borrowed time. Though she sensed the end would be almost a relief, a release from the tension of waiting, she tried to hold it off by sheer force of will. As she held the pose, she sensed Colin was perfecting, polishing, rather than creating fresh. His quick impatience had relaxed.

He made no mention of her Sunday visit, and she was grateful. In retrospect, with her temper at a reasoning degree, she knew she had overreacted. She was also forced to admit that she had made a fool of herself. A complete fool.

It's not the first time, she mused. And perhaps, in a way, excusable. All I could see was a very public picture revealing my very private feelings. Then that silly little article . . . Then remembering Gail's spouting off about romantic press and Colin's image. Cassidy caught herself before she scowled. Well, I won't have to listen to her much longer. I'd better start picking up the pieces. It's time to start thinking about tomorrow. A new job, she concluded dismally. A new start, she corrected. New experiences, new people. Empty nights.

"Fortunately, I finished the face yesterday," Colin commented. "Your expression's altered a dozen times in the last ten minutes. Amazing what a range you have."

"I'm sorry. I was . . ." She searched for a word and settled on an inanity. "Thinking."

"Yes, I could see." His eyes caught hers. "Unhappy thoughts."

"No, I was working out a scene."

"Mmm," Colin commented noncommittally then stepped back from the easel. "Not a particularly joyful one."

"No. They can't all be." She swallowed. "It's finished, isn't it?"

"Yes. Quite finished." Cassidy let out a quiet sigh as she watched his critical study. "Come, have a look," he invited. He held out his hand, but his eyes remained on the canvas.

It surprised her that she was afraid. Colin glanced up at her and lifted a brow.

"Come on, then."

Her fingers tightened around the nosegay, but she walked toward him. Obediently she slipped her hand into his extended one. She turned and looked.

Cassidy had tried to imagine it a hundred times, but it was nothing like what she'd thought. The background was dark and shadowy, playing on shading and depth. In its midst, she stood highlighted in the oyster-white dress. Her nosegay was a surprising splash of color calling attention to the frailty of her hands. Pride was in the stance, in the tilt of her head. Her hair was thick and gloriously tumbled, offsetting the quiet innocence of the dress. It was hair that invited passion.

There was a delicacy in the bones of her face she had been unaware of, a fragility competing with the strength of the features. She had been right in thinking he would see her as she had never seen herself.

Her lips were parted, unsmiling but waiting to smile. The smile would be to welcome a lover. The knowledge was in her expression, along with the anticipation of something yet to come. The eyes told everything. They were the eyes of a woman consumed by love . . . the eyes of innocence waiting to be surrendered. No one could look at it and remain unaware that the woman in the painting had loved the man who painted it.

"So silent, Cass?" Colin murmured and slipped an arm around her shoulders.

"I can't find the word," she whispered then drew a trembling breath. "Nothing's adequate, and anything less would sound platitudinous." She leaned against him a moment. "Colin." Cassidy tried to forget for a moment that the eyes in the painting were naked with love. She tried to see the whole and not the revelation of her emotions. Secrets, he had said. Dreams.

Colin kissed her neck above the silk of the dress then released her. "Rarely, an artist steps back from his work and is astonished that his hands have created something extraordinary." She could hear the excitement in his voice, a wonder she had not expected him to be capable of feeling. "This is the finest thing I've ever done." He turned to her then. "I'm grateful to you, Cassidy. You're the soul of it."

Unable to bear his words, Cassidy turned away. She had to cling to some rags of pride. Desperately she kept her voice calm. "I've always felt the artist is the soul of a painting." Cassidy dropped the nosegay on the worktable then continued to wander around the room. The silk whispered over her legs. "It's your—your imagination, your talent. How much of me is really in that painting?"

There was silence for a long moment, but Cassidy didn't turn back to him. "Don't you know?" Cassidy moistened her lips and struggled to keep her tone light as she turned around.

"My face," she agreed; then, gesturing down the dress, she added, "My body. The rest is yours, Colin, I can't take credit for it. You set the mood, you drew out of me what you already saw. You had the vision. It was a wish you asked me to be, and that's what you've made. It's your illusion." Saying the words caused her more pain than she had believed possible. Still, she felt they had to be said.

"Is that how you see it?" Colin's look was speculative, but she sensed the anger just beneath the surface. "You stood, and I pulled the strings."

"You're the artist, Colin." She shrugged and answered lightly. "I'm just an unemployed writer."

After a long, silent study, he crossed to her. There was a steady calculation about the way his hands took her shoulders. She had felt that seeking, probing look before and stiffened her defenses against it. His fingers tightened on her skin. "Has the woman in that portrait anything to do with you?" He asked the question slowly.

Cassidy swallowed the knot in her throat. "Why, of course, Colin, I've just told you—"

He shook her so quickly, the words slid back down her throat. She saw the fury on his face, the vivid temper she knew could turn violent. "Do you think it was only your face I wanted? Just the shell? Is there nothing that's inside you in that painting?"

"Must you have everything?" she demanded in

despair and anger. "Must you have it all?" Her voice thickened with emotion. "You've drained me, Colin. That's drained me." She flung a hand toward the canvas. "I've given you everything. How much more do you want?"

She pushed him away as a tidal wave of anguish engulfed her. "You never looked at me, thought of me, unless it was because of that painting." She pushed her hair back with both hands, pressing her fingers against her temples. "I won't give you anymore. I can't, there isn't any. It's all there!" She gestured again, and her voice shook. "Thank God it's over."

With a quick jerk, she was out of his hold and running from the studio.

C assidy spent the next two weeks in the apartment of vacationing friends. Leaving a brief note for Jeff, she packed up her typewriter and buried herself in work. She unplugged the phone, bolted the door and shut herself in. For two weeks she tried to forget there was a world outside the people and places of her imagination. She lost herself in her characters in an attempt to forget Cassidy St. John. If she didn't exist, she couldn't feel pain. At the end of the interlude, she'd shed five pounds, produced a hundred pages of fresh copy and nearly balanced her nerves.

As she returned, hauling her typewriter back up the steps to her apartment, she heard Jeff's guitar playing through his door. For a moment she hesitated, thinking to stop and tell him she was back, but she passed into her own apartment. She wasn't ready to answer questions. She considered calling Colin at The Gallery to apologize, then decided against that as well. It was best that their break had been complete. If they parted on good terms, he might be tempted to get in touch with her from time to time. Cassidy knew she could never bear the casual friendliness.

She packed up the dress she had worn on her flight from the studio. Her fingers lingered on the material as she placed it back in the dress box. So much had happened since she had first put it on. Quickly she smoothed the tissue over it and closed the lid. That part of her life was over. Turning, she went to the phone to call The Gallery. The clerk who answered referred her immediately to Gail.

"Why, hello, Cassidy. Where did you run off to?"

"I have the dress from the portrait and the key to the studio," Cassidy told her. "I'd like someone to come pick them up."

"I see." There was a brief hesitation before Gail continued. "I'm afraid we're just terribly busy right now, dear. I know Colin particularly wanted that dress. Be sweet and drop it by? You can just let yourself into the studio and leave everything there. Colin's away, and we're just swamped."

"I'd rather not—"

"Thank you, darling. I must run." The phone clicked. With a quick oath of annoyance, Cassidy hung up.

Colin's away, she thought as she picked up the dress box. Now's the time to finish it completely.

A short time later Cassidy pushed open the back door of Colin's studio. The familiar scents reached out and brought him vividly to her mind. Resolutely she pushed him away. Now is not the time, she told herself and walked briskly to his worktable to set down the dress and key.

For a moment she stood in the room's center and looked about her. She had spent hours there, days. Every detail was already etched with clarity on her memory.

Yet she wanted to see it all again. A part of her was afraid she would forget something, something small and insignificant and vital. It surprised her that the portrait still stood on the easel. Forgetting her promise to leave quickly, Cassidy walked over to study it one last time.

How could he look at that, she wondered as she gazed into her own eyes, and believe the things I said? I can only be grateful that he did. I can only be grateful he believed what I said rather than what he saw. Reaching out a hand, she touched the painted violets.

When the door of the studio opened, Cassidy jerked her hand from the painting and whirled. Her heart flew to her throat.

"Cassidy?" Vince strolled into the room with a wide smile. "What a surprise." In seconds, her hands were enveloped by his.

"Hello." Her voice was a trifle unsteady, but she managed to smile at him.

He heard the breathlessness in her voice and saw there was little color in her face. "Did you know Colin has been looking for you?"

"No." She felt a moment's panic and glanced at the door. "No, I didn't. I've been away, I've been working. I just . . ." She drew her hands away and clasped them together as she heard herself ramble. "I just brought back the dress I wore for the portrait."

Vince's dark eyes became shrewd. "Were you hiding, madonna?"

"No." Cassidy turned and walked to a window. "No, of course not, I was working." She saw the sparrow, busily feeding three babies with gaping mouths. "I didn't realize you were going to be in America this long." Say anything, she told herself, but don't think until you're out of here.

"I have stayed a bit longer in order to convince Colin to sell me a painting he was reluctant to part with."

Cassidy gripped the windowsill tightly. *You knew he would sell it.* You knew from the beginning all that would be left would be dollars and cents. Did you expect him to keep it and think of you? Shaking her head, she made a quiet sound of despair.

"Cassidy." Vince's hand pressed lightly on her shoulder.

"I shouldn't have come here," she whispered, shaking her head again. "I should've known better." She started to flee, but he tightened his grip and turned her to face him. As he studied her, he lifted a hand to brush her cheek. "Please . . ." She closed her eyes. "Please don't be kind to me. I'm not as strong as I thought I was."

"And you love him very much."

Cassidy's eyes flew open. "No, it's only that I—"

"Madonna." Vince stopped her with a finger to her lips. There was a wealth of understanding in his eyes. "I've seen the portrait. It speaks louder than your words."

Lowering her head, Cassidy pressed the heel of her hand between her brows. "I don't want to . . . I'm trying so very hard not to. I have to go," she said quickly.

"Cassidy." Vince held her shoulders. His voice was gentle. "You must see him . . . speak to him."

"I can't." She placed her hands on his chest, shaking her head in desperation. "Please, don't tell him. Please, just take the portrait and let it be over." Her voice broke, and when she found herself cradled against Vince's chest she made no protest. "I always knew it was going to be over." She closed her eyes on the tears, but allowed herself to be held until the need to release them faded. He stroked her hair and kept silent until he felt her breathing steady. Gently he kissed the top of her head then tilted her face to his.

"Cassidy, Colin is my friend—"

"Interesting." Cassidy's eyes darted to the doorway . . . and to Colin. "I'd thought so myself." His voice was quiet. "It appears I've been mistaken about more than one person recently." Even before he crossed the room, Cassidy felt the danger. "Gail told me I'd find you up here," he said when he stood directly in front of them. "With my *friend*."

"Colin . . ." Vince began, only to be cut off with a fierce look.

"Take your hands off her, and keep out of this. When I've finished, you can pick up where you left off."

Hearing the fury in his words, Cassidy nudged out of Vince's hold. "Please," she murmured, not wanting to cause any trouble between them. "Leave us alone for a moment." When Vince's hand stayed on her arm, she turned her eyes to him. "Please," she repeated.

Reluctantly Vince dropped his hand. "Very well, *cara*." He turned briefly to Colin. "I've never known you to be mistaken about anyone, my friend." He walked across the room then closed the door quietly behind him. Cassidy waited an extra moment before she spoke.

"I came to return the dress and the key." She moistened her lips when he only stared down at her. "Gail told me you were away."

"How convenient the studio was available for you and Vince."

"Colin, don't."

"Setting yourself up as a duchess?" he asked coldly. "I should warn you, Vince is known for his generosity, but not his constancy." His eyes raked her face. "Still, a woman like you should do very well for herself in a week or two."

"That's beneath you, Colin." She turned and took a step away, but he grabbed a handful of her hair. With a small sound of surprise and pain, she stared up at him.

His eyes were shadowed and dark, as was his chin with at least a day's growth of beard. It occurred to her suddenly that he looked exhausted. Thinking back, she knew he had never shown fatigue after hours of painting. His fingers tightened in her hair.

"Colin." In defense, she lifted a hand to his.

"Such innocence," he said softly. "Such innocence. You're a clever woman, Cassidy." His hands came to her shoulders, quickly, ruthlessly. She stared up at him in silence, tasting fear. "It's one thing to lie with words, but another to lie with a look, to lie with the eyes day after day. That takes a special kind of cheat."

"No." She shook her head as his words brought back the tears she had stemmed. "No, Colin, please." She wanted to tell him she had never lied to him, but she couldn't. She had lied the very last time they had been together. She could only shake her head and helplessly let the tears come.

"What is it you want from me?" he demanded. His voice became more infuriated as tears slipped down her cheeks. The sun fell through the skylight and set them glinting. "Do you want me to forget that I looked at you day after day and saw something that was never there?"

"I gave you what you wanted." Tears became sobs and she struggled against him. "Please, let me go now. I gave you what you wanted. It's finished."

"You gave me a shell, a mask. Isn't that what you told me?" He pulled her closer, forcing her head back until she looked at him. "The rest was my imagination.

Finished, Cass? How can something be finished when it never was?" His hand went back to her hair as she tried to lower her head. "You said that I'd drained you. Have you any idea what these past weeks have done to me?" He shook her, and her sobs grew wilder.

"You were right when you told me that painting was nothing more than your face and body. There's no warmth in you. I created the woman in that painting."

"Please, Colin. Enough." She pressed her hands over her ears to shut out his words.

"Do you cringe from the truth, Cassidy?" He tore her hands away, forcing her face back to his again. "Only you and I will know the painting's a lie, that the woman there doesn't exist. We served each other's needs after all, didn't we?" He pushed her aside with a whispered oath. "Get out."

Freed, Cassidy ran blindly for escape.

CHAPTER 10

It was late afternoon when Cassidy approached her apartment building. She had walked for a long time after her tears had dried. The city had been jammed with people, and she had sought the crowd while remaining separate. The pain had become numbed with fatigue. She was two blocks from home when the rain started, but she didn't increase her pace. It was cool and soft.

Inside her building she began an automatic search for her mailbox key. Her movements were mechanical, but she forced herself to perform the routine task. She would not crawl into a hole of despair. She would function. She would survive. These things she had promised herself during the long afternoon walk.

With the key at last in the lock, Cassidy lifted the cover on the narrow slot and pulled out her mail. She riffled through the advertisements and bills automatically as she started for the stairs. Her feet came to an abrupt halt as she spotted the return address on one of the envelopes. *New York*.

For several minutes she merely studied it, turning

it over then back again. Walking back to her mailbox, she pushed the rest of her mail back inside then leaned against the wall. A rejection slip? she reflected, nibbling her bottom lip. Then where was the manuscript? She turned the envelope over again and swallowed.

"Oh, the devil with it," she muttered and ripped it open. She read the letter twice in absolute silence. "Oh, why now?" she asked and hated herself for weeping again. "I'm not ready for it now." She forced back the tears and shook her head. "No, it's the perfect time," she corrected then made herself read the letter again. There couldn't be a better time.

She stuffed the letter into her pocket and ran back into the rain. In ten minutes she was banging on Jeff's door.

Guitar in hand, he pulled open the door. "Cassidy, you're back! Where've you been? We were ready to call out the marines." Stopping, he took his eyes from the top of her head to her feet. "Hey . . . you're drenched."

"I am not drenched," Cassidy corrected as she dripped on the hall floor. She hoisted up a bottle of champagne. "I'm much too extraordinary to be drenched. I've been accepted into the annals of literature. I shall be copywritten and printed and posted in your public library."

"You sold your book!" Jeff let out a whoop and hugged her. His guitar pressed into her back.

Laughing, Cassidy pulled away. "Is that any way to express such a momentous occurrence? Peasant." She pushed back her sopping hair with her free hand. "However, I'm a superior person, and will share my bottle of champagne with you in my parlor. No dinner jacket required." Turning, she walked to her own door, pushed it open then gestured. Grinning, Jeff set down his guitar and followed her.

"Here," he said after he had closed the door and taken the bottle from her. "I'll open it, you go get a towel and dry off or else you'll die of pneumonia before the first copy hits the stands."

When she came back from the bathroom wrapped in a terry-cloth robe and rubbing a towel over her hair, Jeff was just releasing the cork. Champagne squirted out in a jet.

"It's good for the carpet," he claimed and poured. "I could only find jelly glasses."

"My crystal's been smashed," Cassidy told him as she picked up her glass. "To a very wise man," she said solemnly.

"Who?" Jeff raised his glass.

"My publisher," she announced, then grinned and drank. "An excellent year," she mused, gazing critically into the glass. The wine fizzed gently.

"What year is it?" Jeff lifted the bottle curiously.

"This one." Cassidy laughed and drank again. "I only buy new champagne."

They drank again then Jeff leaned over and kissed her. "Congratulations, babe." He pulled the damp towel from her shoulders. "How does it feel?"

"I don't know." She threw her head back and closed her eyes. "I feel like someone else." Quickly she filled her glass again. She knew she had to keep moving, had to keep talking. She couldn't think seriously about what she had won that day or she would remember what she had lost. "I should've bought two bottles," she said, spinning a circle. "This is definitely a two-bottle occasion." She drank, feeling the wine rise to her head. "The last time I had champagne . . ." Cassidy stopped, remembering, then shook her head. Jeff eyed her in puzzlement. "No, no." She gestured with her hand as if to wipe the thought away. "I had champagne at Barbara

Seabright's wedding in Sausalito. One of the ushers propositioned me in the cloakroom."

Jeff laughed and took another sip. A knock sounded. Cassidy called out, "Come in, there's enough for—" Her words were cut off as Colin opened the door.

Cassidy's color drained slowly. Her eyes darkened. Jeff looked quickly from one to the other, then set down his glass.

"Well, I gotta be going. Thanks for the champagne, babe. We'll talk later."

"No, Jeff," Cassidy began. "You don't have to—"

"I've got a gig," he announced, lifting her restraining hand from his arm. She saw him exchange one long look with Colin before he slipped through the door.

"Cass." Colin stepped forward.

"Colin, please go." Shutting her eyes, she pressed her fingers between her brows. There was a pressure in her chest and behind her lids. Don't cry. Don't cry, she ordered herself.

"I know I haven't any right to be here." There was a low harshness in his tone. "I know I haven't the right to ask you to listen to me. I'm asking anyway."

"There isn't anything to say." Cassidy forced herself to stand straight and face him. "I don't want you here," she said flatly.

He flinched. "I understand, Cassidy, but I feel you have a right to an apology . . . an explanation."

Her hands were clenched, and slowly she spread her fingers and stared down at them. "I appreciate the offer, Colin, but it isn't necessary. Now—" she lifted her eyes to his "—if that's all . . ."

"Oh, Cass, for pity's sake, show more mercy than I did. At least let me apologize before you shut me out of your life."

Unable to respond, Cassidy merely stared at him. He

stooped to pick up the bottle of champagne. "I seem to have interrupted a celebration." He set the bottle back and looked at her. "Yours?"

"Yes." Cassidy swallowed and tried to speak lightly. "Yes, mine. My manuscript was accepted for publication. I had a letter today."

"Cass." He moved toward her, lifting a hand to touch her cheek.

Cassidy stiffened and took a quick step back. Catching the look that crossed his face, she knew she had hurt him. Colin slowly dropped his hand.

"I'm sorry," Cassidy began.

"Don't be." His voice had a quiet, final quality. "I can hardly expect you to welcome my touch. I hurt you." He paused, looking down at his hand a moment before bringing his gaze back to her face. His eyes searched hers. "Because I know you as well as I know myself, I'm aware of how badly I hurt you. I have to live with that. I haven't the right to ask you to forgive me, but I'll ask you to hear me out."

"All right, Colin, I'm listening," Cassidy said wearily. She drew a deep breath and tried to speak calmly. "Why don't you sit down."

He shook his head and, turning, moved back to the window and looked out, resting his hands in the sill. "The rain's stopped and there's fog. I still remember how you looked that night, standing in the fog looking up at the sky. I thought you were a mirage." He murmured the last sentence, as if to himself. "I had an image in my mind of a woman. My own idea of perfection, a balance of qualities. When I saw you, I knew I had found her. I had to paint you."

For a moment he lapsed into silence, brooding out at the gloom. "After we'd started, I found everything in you I'd ever looked for—goodness, spirit, intelligence, strength, passion. The longer I painted you, the more you fascinated me. I told you once you bewitched me; I almost believe it. I've never known a woman I've wanted more than I've wanted you."

He turned then and faced her. The play of the light threw his features into shadows. "Each time I touched you, I wanted more. I didn't make love to you that night on the houseboat because I wouldn't have you think of yourself as just one of my lovers. I couldn't take advantage of your being in love with me."

At his words, Cassidy's eyes closed. She made a soft sound of despair.

"Please, don't turn away. Let me finish. The day the painting was finished, you denied everything. You said the things I'd seen had been in my own imagination. You were so cool and dispassionate. You very nearly destroyed me. . . . I had no idea anyone had such power over me," he continued softly. "It was a revelation, and it hurt a great deal. I wanted more from you, I needed more, but you told me you had nothing left. I was angry when you ran away, and I let you go. When I came here later, you were gone.

"I've been out of my mind for over two weeks, not knowing where you were or when—worse, *if*—you were coming back. Your friend next door had your cryptic little note and nothing else."

"You saw Jeff?" she asked.

"Cassidy, don't you understand? You disappeared. The last time I saw you, you were running away from me, and then you were gone. I didn't know where you were, or how to find you, if something had happened to you. I've been going slowly mad."

She took a step toward him. "Colin, I'm sorry. I had no idea you'd be concerned. . . ."

"Concerned?" he repeated. "I was frantic! Two

weeks, Cassidy. Two weeks without a word. Do you know what a helpless feeling it is to simply have to wait? Not to know. I've haunted Fisherman's Wharf, been everywhere in the city. Where in heaven's name were you?" he demanded furiously then held up a hand before she could answer. She watched him take a deep breath before turning away from her. "I'm sorry. I haven't had much sleep lately, and I'm not completely in control."

His movements became restless again. He stopped and lifted Cassidy's discarded glass of champagne. Thoughtfully, he studied the etchings on the side. "An interesting concept in a wineglass," he murmured. Turning back, he toasted her. "To you, Cass. To only you." He drank then set down the empty glass.

Cassidy dropped her eyes. "Colin, I am sorry you were worried. I was working, and—"

"Don't." The word stopped her, and her eyes shot back to his. "Don't explain to me," he said in more controlled tones. "Just listen. When I walked into the studio today and saw you with Vince, something snapped. I can give you excuses—pressure, exhaustion, madness, take your pick. None of them make up for the things I said to you." His eyes were eloquent on hers. "I despise myself for making you cry. I hated the things I said to you even as I said them. Finding you there, with Vince, after looking for you everywhere for days . . ." He stopped, shaking his head, then moved back to the window.

"Gail arranged the timing very well," he said. "She knew what I'd been through the past two weeks and knows me well enough to predict how I'd react finding you alone with Vince. She sent him up to the studio on a fictitious errand before I got back to The Gallery. She told me the two of you were meeting up there. She made the suggestion, but I grabbed on to it with both hands." He rubbed his fingers over the back of his neck as if to release some tension.

"We'd been occasional lovers up until about a year ago when things got a bit complicated. I should have remembered whom I was dealing with, but I wasn't thinking too clearly. Gail's decided to take a long—perhaps permanent—sabbatical on the East Coast." He paused a moment then turned to study her. "I'd like to think you could understand why I behaved so abominably."

In the silence Cassidy could just hear Jeff's guitar through the thin walls of the apartment. "Colin." Her eyes searched his face then softened. "You look so tired."

His expression altered, and for a moment she thought he would cross to her. He stood still, however, keeping the distance between them. "I don't know when I fell in love with you. Perhaps it was that first night in the fog. Perhaps it was when you first wore that dress. Perhaps it was years before I met you. I suppose it doesn't matter when."

Cassidy stared at him, robbed of speech. "I'm not an easy man, Cassidy, you told me that once."

"Yes," she managed. "I remember."

"I'm selfish and given to temper and black moods. I have little patience except with my work. I can promise to hurt you, to infuriate you, to be unreasonable and impatient, but no one will love you more. No one." He paused, but still she could only stare at him, transfixed. "I'm asking you to forget what makes sense and be my wife and my lover and mother my children. I'm asking that you share your life with me, taking me as I am." He paused again, and his voice softened. "I love you, Cass. This time, my destiny's in your hands."

She watched him as he spoke, heard the cadence of his native land grow stronger in his speech. Still he made no move toward her, but stood across the room with shadows playing over his face. Cassidy remembered how he had looked when she had flinched away from his touch.

Slowly she walked to him. Reaching up, she circled his neck with her arms then buried her face against his shoulder. "Hold me." His arms came gently around her as his cheek lowered to the top of her head. "Hold me, Sullivan," she ordered again, pressing hard against him. She turned her head until her mouth found his.

His arms drew tight around her, and she murmured in pleasure at their strength. "I love you," she whispered as their lips parted then clung again. "I've needed to tell you for so long."

"You told me every time you looked at me." Colin buried his face in her hair. "I refused to believe I'd fallen in love with you, that it could have happened so quickly, so effortlessly. The painting was nearly finished when I admitted to myself I'd never be able to live without you."

His voice lowered, and he drew her closer. "I've been crazy these last two weeks, staring at your portrait and not knowing where you were or if I'd ever see you again."

"Now you have me," she murmured, making no objection when his hands slipped under the terry cloth to roam her skin. "And Vince will have the portrait."

"No, I told you once some things can't be sold. The portrait has too much of both of us in it." He shook his head, breathing in the rain-fresh fragrance of her hair. "Not even for Vince."

"But I thought . . ." She realized that she had only assumed Vince had been speaking of her portrait. There was a new wealth of happiness in the knowledge that Colin had not intended to sell what was to her a revelation of their love.

"What did you think?"

"No, it's nothing." She pressed her lips against his neck. "I love you." Her mouth roamed slowly up his jawline, savoring what she knew now was hers.

"Cass." She felt his heart thud desperately against hers as his fingers tightened in her hair. "Do you know what you do to me?"

"Show me," she whispered against his ear.

With a groan, Colin kissed her again. She could taste his need for her and wondered at the strength of it. Her answer was to offer everything.

"We'll get married quickly," Colin murmured then took her lips again, urgently. Inside her robe, his hands ran in one long stroke down her sides, then roamed to her back to bring her closer. "Very quickly."

"Yes." Cassidy closed her eyes in contentment as his cheek rested against hers. "I already have the perfect dress." She sighed and nestled against him. "What will you title the painting, Colin?"

"I've already titled it." He smiled into her eyes. *"Sullivan's Woman."*

THE BRAND NEW NOVEL
from the *New York Times* bestselling author

NORA ROBERTS

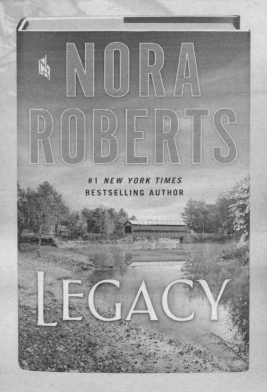

A tale of family tragedy, healing love,
and unnerving suspense.